boys, bears,
AND A SERIOUS PAIR OF
hiking boots

boys, bears,
AND A SERIOUS PAIR OF
hiking boots

ABBY McDONALD

CANDLEWICK PRESS

NEW HANOVER COUNTY PUBLIC LIBRARY
201 Chestnut Street
Wilmington, NC 28401

This is a work of fiction. Names, characters, places,
and incidents are either products of the author's
imagination or, if real, are used fictitiously.

Copyright © 2010 by Abigail McDonald

All rights reserved. No part of this book may be reproduced,
transmitted, or stored in an information retrieval system
in any form or by any means, graphic, electronic, or
mechanical, including photocopying, taping, and recording,
without prior written permission from the publisher.

First edition 2010

Library of Congress Cataloging-in-Publication Data
McDonald, Abby.
Boys, bears, and a serious pair of hiking boots / Abby McDonald.
— 1st ed.
p. cm.
Summary: Seventeen-year-old Jenna, an ardent vegetarian
and environmentalist, is thrilled to be spending the summer
communing with nature in rural Canada, until she discovers
that not all of the rugged residents there share her beliefs.
ISBN 978-0-7636-4382-9
[1. Self-perception—Fiction. 2. Wilderness areas—Fiction.
3. Environmental protection—Fiction. 4. Social action—Fiction.
5. Canada—Fiction.] I. Title.
PZ7.M4784174Bo 2010
[Fic]—dc22   2009026015

09 10 11 12 13 14 MVP 10 9 8 7 6 5 4 3 2 1

Printed in York, PA, U.S.A.

This book was typeset in Sabon.

Candlewick Press
99 Dover Street
Somerville, Massachusetts 02144

visit us at www.candlewick.com

CHAPTER ONE

"Re-use! Re-duce! Re-cycle!"

"Don't get mad; get green!"

"Save a planet, save a tree, in the end it'll save you and me!"

The chants filter through the open windows at the end of final period, drifting on the warm breeze. Ms. Lockhart pauses, walking over to check out the noise, while the rest of the class cranks their necks around and strains to get a better look.

I just cram my books into my bag and wait, poised on the edge of my seat.

The second the final bell rings, I spring into action: racing to my locker, I grab some last-minute supplies and dash out of the building. I can see the Green Teens already, marching in a circle on a plot of land at the end of the field, past the graffitied bleachers and batting cages.

The school board is proposing to sell it off to developers; already there are tire tracks cut into the muddy ground and the beginnings of a construction site taking shape. But not for long.

"You didn't wait!" I arrive, breathless, at the edge of the grass. I pause for a moment to kick off my ballet flats—not exactly off-road shoes—and yank on a pair of flower-print plastic boots.

"I know, I know," Olivia apologizes, skidding down the dirt bank. Her own matching boots are already filthy from the mud. She grabs a couple of my bags and eagerly rifles through them. "Did you bring the banners? And sign-up sheets?"

"Check and check!" I pull a Greenpeace shirt over my regular tank top. "And cookies, too."

"Perfect!" She grins. She's braided blue yarn through her hair for the occasion, the same shade as the paint on the signs we were up half the night making. "Then we're all set."

We take our places in the middle of the group, unfurling a ten-foot-long banner and joining in the chant. After six major demonstrations, and our weekly Saturday morning session handing out flyers at the Fairview Mall, Olivia and I are protest experts. We need to be. With the old Green Teen leadership graduating, it's up to us to keep the spirit of environmentalism alive and well at North Ridge High.

"Louder, everyone! We need them to hear us all the way to the parking lot!" Olivia yells through the megaphone we, ahem, "borrowed" from the AV room. Volume and visibility—those are the keys to a good protest, I've learned. And plenty of snacks. One time we tried an all-day sit-in outside City Hall to demand better recycling services, but I forgot to bring provisions; the group lasted exactly two hours before the aroma wafting from a nearby pretzel van became too much to bear. Needless to say, we still have to trek out to Maplewood with our paper and plastics, and I haven't forgotten the Fig Newtons since.

Sure enough, after a few minutes a curious crowd starts to gather, drawn by the shouting and—yes—the lure of those cookies. A group from my study hall looks around with interest, and a handful of cheerleaders even stop to ask what's going on.

"Never underestimate the power of free food." I grin, giving Olivia a high-five with my free hand. "What do you say, time for phase two?"

"Do it." She nods.

Passing my corner of the banner over to an eager freshman recruit, I retrieve the stack of clipboards and begin circulating with sign-up sheets.

"What is it this time?" A guy from my econ class is loitering suspiciously near the crowd. His collar is popped, and he's spent the last semester idly kicking the back of my seat, but every signature counts. "Saving the whales?"

"That was last week." I keep smiling at him: my infallible "you know you want to help me out" grin. "Right now we're trying to stop them from building on the field."

"Are they going to put up a mini-mall?" He looks hopeful. "Man, a Pizza Hut would be awesome. Or a Chili's!"

"No," I answer, thankful. I'm all for a challenge, but convincing a thousand teenagers to pick the joys of nature over double pepperoni with extra cheese? That might be out of my league. I move closer, pen outstretched. "But do you really want to have this field paved over? Bit by bit, we're losing all the natural habitats and green space in the area, and we won't be able to get them back. What about the local ecosystem, and wildlife, and—?"

"Whoa." He backs off, looking alarmed. "Relax, Jenna!"

It's obvious I'm not going to win this one with logic and sense, so I decide to try a new tactic. "It's OK—you don't have to sign now," I coo. "I mean, we've got two whole weeks of classes before summer vacation. We can talk through all the issues together, in tons more detail. I could even ask Mrs. Paluski to pair us up!" I beam as though I'm just thrilled by the thought of describing every detail of our cause. "I'm sure I'll convince you. Eventually."

He practically snatches the pen out of my hand to sign.

"Aw, thanks." I grin, taking back the clipboard to check my progress. Fifty-six down, just another thousand to go. . . .

The crowd around us has swelled to about a hundred students by the time I see Principal Turner huffing his way across the field. I intercept him at the edge of the grass with my best innocent look. "Anything I can help you with?"

"Jenna Levison." He eyes the dirt and puddles suspiciously. "To what do we owe this particular show of—"

"Community spirit?" I finish hopefully. "Environmental awareness?"

"Disruption and disobedience." He folds his arms and glares at me. As if they can sense the battle to come, the crowd behind me turns to watch, while the rest of the Green Teens pause their chanting.

I gulp.

No matter how many angry officials I face, I still feel like I'm doing something wrong (OK—something *really* wrong). But I can't back down. Backing down won't save the field from construction, and it certainly won't make the rest of the Green Teens believe in their new leaders. It's my job to deal with authority now. Preferably without winding up in perpetual detention.

"Is this about the demonstration last week?" Deciding that distraction is the best form of defense, I try to steer him away from the melee. "Because the *Star-Ledger* said it was a great example of youth engagement. They even invited us to a dinner for community leaders."

"Congratulations." His response is dry. "So, what is it this time? I'm assuming there is a point to all this." Turner surveys the motley crew with a weary expression.

"You're selling off the back field!" Olivia appears beside me, her voice ringing with accusation. What she lacks in height, she more than makes up for in volume. "They're going to rip it up and build condos!"

"And?" Principal Turner is unconcerned. "Those proposals were announced months ago."

"Yes, but we've discovered the plans will endanger a rare species," she announces proudly. "One that will have its habitat destroyed by the greedy, profit-driven decision-making of the school board. Not to mention the generations who will be robbed of a prime natural environment for the sake of—"

"Yes, yes." Turner waves at her to stop. He pinches his sinuses for a moment, as if he's got a headache coming on. "Endangered species?"

"Knieskern's beaked-rush," I confirm, hoping I got the pronunciation right.

Turner brightens. "You're getting worked up over a type of grass?"

"Just because it's not something glamorous like a bald eagle doesn't mean it's not important!" Olivia protests, hands on her hips.

"I agree." Then, if his agreement wasn't worrying enough, Turner begins to smirk. "Knieskern's beaked-rush certainly needs protecting." He gives us a smug smile. "Although since it's a wetland species, I don't think we're in danger of breaking any laws here on dry land, do you?"

Busted.

"But the ground is pretty damp," Olivia argues in vain. "Miss Kirk won't let us practice cross-country back here because of that time Meghan skidded and sprained her ankle."

"It wouldn't take much to commission an independent wildlife assessment," I add, trying to be the voice of reason. "Maybe delay the sale by a couple of months and—"

"Enough!" Turner suddenly explodes. "I want you and your . . . fellow agitators packed up and gone. Do you hear me?"

We both take a step backward. His face is turning a strange shade of pink.

"You may have complete disregard for my authority, young ladies, but perhaps some of your, your *comrades* care about their college applications!"

I hear fearful murmurs behind me, but despite my faint lurch of panic, I don't surrender. The school has been waving around that "college application" trump card for years now, but every single one of the Green Teen seniors got accepted into their first-choice college. It's an empty threat. At least, I hope it is.

Luckily, I have one last card to play, too. "You know, why don't I give that nice woman at KPXW a call?" I turn to Olivia theatrically. "The one we met at that last council meeting?"

"You mean Linda, in the news department?" Olivia catches on, answering with an exaggerated frown.

"That's right. She did say to call if we were doing any more protests." I glance back at Principal Turner. "I bet they'd have a crew out here in no time to see what all the fuss is about."

"Great idea." Olivia pulls out her cell phone. "I think I've got her number here. . . ."

"That won't be necessary!" Turner suddenly has a change of heart. "Why don't we, uh, all calm down?"

"We are calm," I answer sweetly. "We're just trying to protect the environment."

"And that's very admirable." His bald spot is shiny with sweat, and I can just see him picturing the local evening news: "Evil Principal Kills Defenseless Wildlife!" He pauses. "Didn't you say something about an independent assessment . . . ?"

"To study the natural impact of construction," I finish, handing him a flyer. "See? The federal hotline number is right there."

We wait. Olivia clutches my hand, and we both cross our fingers. Behind us, the crowd grows restless.

Finally, Turner gives a long, mournful sigh. "Very well. I'm sure we can delay the final approval for a while." He looks around, defeated.

"Omigod!" Olivia shrieks, clutching me with joy. "We did it! We did it!"

The Green Teens begin to cheer, and I feel a wave of pride sweep through me. Victory!

We're enveloped by shouts and high-fives as the group celebrates, but I remember to turn back. "Thank you!" I tell Turner. "Really, I mean it. Thank you!"

He almost rolls his eyes, turning to go, but before he can even take a step, Olivia grabs a sign and lunges forward.

"Don't mess with the Green Teens!" she yells, just inches from his face. Turner jerks back in shock, and the ground underfoot must be wetter than he expected, because he lands heavily on one foot and starts to slip. I gasp, but there's nothing I can do. His foot slides forward, his body tips back, and before any of us can move, he skids ass-backward into a huge puddle of noxious liquid.

Squelch.

"See?" Olivia sniggers. I grab her arm to shut her up, but she just can't help laughing triumphantly. "Wetlands. We told you so!"

CHAPTER TWO

Principal Turner's newfound love of the environment doesn't extend to the mud all over his wrinkled mall-store suit. His lecture on respect and authority lasts forever, and if that isn't dull enough, he has us stay late to slosh gray paint over parking lot graffiti as penance. By the time I pull into our driveway and unpack the panniers on my bike, it's almost dinnertime.

"Hey, Mom. Sorry I'm late." I haul an armful of cloth bags into the gleaming kitchen, spilling lentil and soy-bean packages all over the counter. The day I announced I was going to eat only fair-trade, free-range, vegetarian produce was the day my mom suggested I buy my own groceries. I don't mind. It saves me from accidentally eating food from some corporation that exploits migrant workers or injects their produce with growth hormones.

"Hi, sweetie." Mom has the phone trapped against her shoulder as she whisks dressing in a glass jug. Her blond hair is sculpted into a perfect bob, and she's wearing neat gray pants and a creamy silk blouse. "Remind me to switch cable companies." She sighs, leaning over to land a quick kiss on my forehead as I pass. "They've had me on hold forever." She tastes the dressing and pauses, adding another sprinkle of pepper. "Good day?"

"Good enough." I shoot her a nervous glance, not sure if news of our protest has made it through the PTA gossip tree yet. But it looks like I'm free and clear, because she just suggests, "You should go wash up before dinner. I made your favorite, that tofu-nut bake, and your father should be down in a minute."

"Dad's home for dinner?" I drift into the dining room. As usual, the table is set perfectly with napkins and silverware, a tall vase of fresh lilies in the middle. But unusually, there are three settings. I pause. "What's the occasion?"

"No occasion, just a nice meal together." She gives me a distracted smile and then grips the phone suddenly. "Hello? Finally! I want to talk to someone about our billing. . . ."

I charge upstairs and quickly change out of my mud-and-paint-splattered clothes. I should really keep another set in my locker, along with all the other Green Teen essentials: markers, highlighted copy of the Constitution, wire cutters . . .

My phone vibrates with a text from Olivia just as I'm struggling into a dinner-appropriate skirt.

Well? U grounded, or can we party?

So far, so good! I tap out in reply, and scrub a way-ward splash of mud off my arm. My parents still have . . . reservations about this environmental "phase," as they like to call it. They're happy to take the good parts, like when we got awards for community involvement. They were thrilled to go shake hands with the mayor and listen to what role models we are. But the rest? I can't even convince Dad to carpool to work. Olivia is so much luckier: her parents were big hippie activists when they were younger, so they completely understand that a few detentions are worth it when it comes to making a difference.

Awesome! Pick u up @ 8.

I hurtle back downstairs and slide into my seat just as Mom brings out the food: tofu for me and a juicy pot roast for them. I waver for a moment, entranced by the delicious meaty aroma. No, I remind myself, dragging my gaze away, back to the nutritious meal in front of me. You don't need meat to have a good time. See: Tofu. Yum.

"Anything new at school, Jenna?" Dad asks, passing me the rolls. He loosens his tie, looking tired. He's been working so much recently; our conversations are usually just zombie-like mumbling in the morning over breakfast.

"Nothing much . . ." I bite down on a slice of cucumber. "Oh, wait, I found a great summer internship to apply for. It's with Earth Now — that nonprofit I told you about? It'll just be basic reception stuff, answering phones, sorting mail, but they have a really great program of seminars on conservation and environmental entrepreneurship I could attend."

Mom frowns. "Honey, I don't think—"

"I'll still be able to keep my weekend job at Dr. Endelstein's office," I add quickly, in case they object. "The hours are flexible, and it'll look really good on college applications." There, the masterstroke. Surely they can't argue with that.

There's silence. My parents give each other a meaningful look, and then Mom puts down her fork.

"Jenna, there's something we need to talk about."

Oh, crap. They know about the protest; I can just tell.

Slouching lower in my seat, I brace myself for the worst: disappointment, concern, and yet more pleas for me to give it up and accept the wanton destruction of the planet. But instead, Dad clears his throat.

"We're thinking of trying something different this summer."

"Like what?" I blink, still expecting the patented "Don't jeopardize your future" lecture, maybe even with a side of "You'll regret this when you wind up in community college/ on the streets/languishing in jail unable to floss."

"The company is sending me overseas for a few months, to liaise with their European offices."

"That's . . . great?" I'm still confused.

"So I decided we should go stay with Grandma," Mom finishes. She plasters a bright smile on her face, reaching for her glass of wine. "You know she's been having problems since that hip replacement, and I've even found a job teaching a summer session at one of the prep schools nearby."

I pause, slowly taking it in. "Did you say, 'we'?" I send

a silent plea to the universe that I misheard her, that it was just a slip of the tongue, but to my horror, she nods.

No. Freaking. Way.

"What about my internship, and the Green Teens?" I protest, realizing too late that they won't care.

Dad pats my hand sympathetically. "I know you have plans, but you can do those things in the fall."

"I can't, not for the internship!" I stare at them in dismay. Don't they realize that the Green Teens have a whole summer of events planned? Thinking quickly, I try to come up with a solution. "I can stay here, with Olivia!"

Mom shakes her head. "It's far too long to impose on any of your friends."

"Dad?" I turn, imploring him, but he's no use.

"It's already settled, I'm afraid. We've found a family to sublet the house, so it's a done deal." My horror must be showing, because he tries to comfort me. "Think of it as an adventure! I know it's not ideal, but you'll get to explore a new city and make friends. It's only for a couple of months."

A couple of months? I slouch back, defeated. But as the news sinks in, I realize that something's not right—and I don't just mean the destruction of my summer plans. Mom's smile is fixed too brightly, and Dad is gulping back his second glass of wine.

And then I remember what happened before.

"Are you . . . ?" I start, nervous, but the words stick in my throat.

Mom looks up. "What's that, honey?"

I pause, all my earlier courage deserting me. Facing down Principal Turner is nothing compared to real, harsh questions like this. "Nothing," I say quietly, and push the tofu around my plate for another five minutes while they chatter about all the wholesome activities I'll be able to do in Orlando. Now I know what people mean when they talk about the elephant in the room. Only to me, it feels like a full circus, complete with acrobats, performing seals, and a marching band trumpeting, "Your parents are splitting up!"

But I don't say a word.

I tell myself that I'm over-reacting, getting paranoid or something. I mean, Grandma *has* been having problems with her hip, and Dad *did* say something about a new client overseas. But no matter how much I try to ignore the hollow feeling in the pit of my stomach, I can't. Because of last time.

It was during my freshman year. Dad was gone a month—a business trip, they swore—but I caught Mom crying twice, crumpled alone in the laundry room when she thought I was upstairs. And then he came back, and she started going to the hair salon every week, and wearing those outfits, and cooking meals from scratch to serve in the perfect dining room. Nobody ever said a thing about it, and I still can't find the words to ask.

"Can I be excused?" I finally abandon my food, appetite gone. "Olivia's picking me up soon."

"Are you going out?" Mom pauses.

I nod, already out of my seat. "Miriam Park is having a girls' night in," I lie, naming a girl from my lit class who drives around in a gas-guzzling SUV and wears heels to class. Heels! Mom, of course, loves her.

Just as I hoped, her face relaxes. "Oh, that sounds like fun."

"I'll be back by eleven thirty!"

CHAPTER THREE

I grab my purse and head out to the front of the house
to wait, balancing back and forth along the edge of the
sidewalk like I used to when I was a kid. We live at the
end of a quiet cul-de-sac, with neat front lawns and new-
grown trees spaced twenty feet apart, looking as thin and
pathetic as they did when we first moved in. I long for
grass that isn't mowed down to an inch high, and wildlife
beyond a few birds and a stray fox. Olivia's parents were
going to take us on vacation, camping out in a national
park so we could actually enjoy the nature we're working
so hard to save, but I guess that's out now.

I sigh, kicking a pebble along the curb as I think of the
summer that awaits me instead. Grandma's development
in Florida is paved in sand-colored tile, with bright fake

turquoise pools sunk into the ground and lone palm trees potted at the edge of every pathway. There are panic buttons in all the pastel rooms and motorized golf carts whirring down the streets, bussing the residents to early-bird dinners and bridge at the community hall.

I don't think I've ever laid eyes on another teenager there.

By the time Olivia's third-hand blue Honda rattles into view, I'm past gloomy and into wallowing.

"Go to Disneyworld, learn to play bocci, and completely lose my mind," I tell her, wrenching open the door. I collapse into the passenger seat.

"What?" She stalls, then lurches back into gear as we make a messy three-point turn. Well, five-point.

"Things I can do in Orlando." I sigh. "My mom is dragging me down with her. For the whole summer."

"Orlando!" Her dismay is gratifying. "But—"

"I know."

"And—"

"Yup." We fall silent in joint horror as I rummage in the glove compartment for a new CD. The Polaroid Kids: they know about loneliness and pain.

"What am I going to do without you?" she wails, making an illegal left turn. "We were going to picket the Chamber of Commerce about fair trade! And hang out by my pool! And sneak into all the graduation parties!"

"I guess you'll have to do all that with Cash now." I slump lower.

"We've been dating like, three weeks," she protests, but I catch her blush all the same.

"You really liiiike him." I use a singsong voice, happy to change the subject. "You wanna kiiisss him. You're gonna *do it* with him."

"Jenna!"

Cash (as in the late great country singer, not the capitalist tool of ownership) is the handsome dreadlocked boy who came to her rescue last month. We were handing out leaflets at the mall when this burly middle-aged man started arguing with Livvy—towering over her and ranting about natural progress and human achievement through landfill sites and pollution. Just when things were getting kind of scary, Cash stepped in, making the man back off and Livvy practically swoon at his feet. He's a senior at a school across town and the founding member of their Earth Activism group. In other words, he's perfect.

"Come on, you're lucky," I say, with only a (completely reasonable) hint of jealousy. "The most eligible guy down in Orlando is probably, like, fifty."

"I don't know," she pretends to muse. "I can see you with a silver fox."

"Ewww!" Now it's my turn to blush. "Livvy!"

She laughs, reaching over with one hand to grab her purse and rummage for the bag of jelly beans she always carries. "No, but seriously, we'll find someone for you tonight. I bet Cash has tons of cute friends, ready to quote Thoreau at you and gaze dreamily into your eyes—"

"Right before I leave the state." I take a handful of candies and divide them up by color on my palm.

"Hey, this way you can have a crazy, reckless fling!" Livvy is still flushed by thoughts of Cash.

"I'll settle for a normal, boring date," I tell her wryly. She makes a face as we stop at a traffic light.

"That only works if you actually let them ask you out. Or, you know, say yes!"

I eat another jelly bean and change the subject. It's not that simple—as any teenage girl would agree. Finding a guy who's cute, smart, and actually likes me is hard enough, even without the basic requirement that he be into environmentalism, too. I mean, the last guy to ask me out was Jaz Simpson, and he spends all weekend at monster-truck rallies!

By the time we pull up outside Cash's house, on the edge of town, our list of ways I can avoid the summer in Florida is still empty, but I refuse to wallow anymore. "Let's face it: I'm doomed," I declare brightly, climbing out of the car and surveying the tangle of teenagers milling around in the front yard. Groups are sprawled on blankets on the ground, and some kind of punk music blasts out from the house every time the door opens. "So let's just have as much fun as possible before I go, OK?"

"Deal!" Olivia agrees.

The party turns out to be pretty fun. Even when Olivia abandons me to go hang out with Cash, I don't mind. That's what's so great about the Green Teen project and eco stuff in general: even though I don't know any of the kids here, we've got some common ground to talk about, so I don't feel like an outsider. Just like guys on the football team can talk about plays and practice all the time, and the indie kids always have music as their fallback topic, I have environmentalism. Soon I'm relaxing with a group in the living room, chatting about our favorite books, and — sure enough — Thoreau.

Suddenly, Olivia comes tearing into the room. "Jenna!" She grabs my arm, bouncing up and down with delight. "I've got it!"

"What? Wait, calm down." I laugh. She's so excited, you'd think her parents just bought her a hybrid.

"Your summer!" she squeals. "I totally have the answer." Without even pausing for breath, she launches into a complicated story. ". . . and Cash was talking about his plans for next year, because you know how he's taking time off before college, and he said that his friend Kris said that his cousin was doing, like, a volunteer road trip across the country working at farms and co-ops and stuff, and that he — Cash, not Kris's cousin — might do the same, either here or up in Canada. Canada! You see?" She beams at me expectantly. "I really am a genius."

"Ummm . . ." I don't see. At all.

"Canada!" she exclaims again, this time with more of a "Duh!" expression. "Didn't you say your godmother Susie moved up there?"

I gasp. "Susie!"

"Uh-huh!"

Susie, aka my mom's wild roommate from college, who's spent the last twenty-odd years dealing blackjack in Vegas/dancing burlesque in Atlantic City/traversing the world with nothing but a clutch purse and three packages of Oreos. Until six months ago, when she met a hunky woodsman up in British Columbia and decided to get married and settle down to live in domestic wilderness harmony.

I stare at Olivia, wide-eyed, as a light appears on the horizon, a choir of angels sound, and the grim specter of becoming Hunter Creek Retirement Community's reigning bridge champion melts blissfully away.

In other words, I'm saved.

CHAPTER FOUR

"And the mountains are a kind of purple-gray. There's still snow at the top of some." I press my forehead against the cool glass, gazing in awe at the towering scenery. It's only two weeks later, and I'm squished at the back of a Greyhound bus winding its way through the Rocky Mountains. My parents meant business when it came to our summer plans: just two days after school let out, Mom packed her car full of suitcases and hit the road to Florida, while Dad took a cab to the airport — both of them swearing that this was nothing but a summer change. I still don't know if I believe them, but when the flight reached cruising altitude and I settled in with my pretzels and seatback movie, I made myself a promise. This time, I'm not going to dwell on all the scary possibilities I can't control. Thoughts of my parents, and the dreaded D-word, banished to the very back of my mind—and they're going to stay there for the rest of summer.

"Man, you're so lucky." At the other end of the crackling phone line, I hear Olivia give a wistful sigh. "How are you feeling?"

"Kind of tired," I admit. "The flight was six hours, and then I got straight on this bus. . . ."

"The wilderness isn't exactly convenient," Olivia agrees.

"But I'm excited, too," I add, blinking at the vast landscape of rock and forest, individual landmarks lost in a blur of peaks and ridges. It feels surreal to hear her voice all the way out here, as if I'm suspended in this weird place between our familiar banter and the foreign surroundings, clouded and misty. I snuggle deeper into the folds of my sweatshirt. "I still can't believe we pulled this off. I'm going to owe you forever."

"Uh, yeah, you are." Olivia laughs. "But couldn't you have packed me in that massive suitcase of yours? I nearly died from smog inhalation getting into the city for my interview today."

"Wait, what interview?"

"OK, so I didn't want to say anything, in case it didn't come through," she confides gleefully, "but Cash has found the most amazing thing. There's this collective in upstate New York, where they run, like, seminars on sustainability and earth issues and all kinds of things, and it turns out they hire camp counselors and staff workers! If it works out, we'll spend the whole summer, and go to all the sessions and things—for free."

"That's awesome!" I have to admit, I've felt kind of bad, abandoning her to summer in Fairview alone. "But, wait." I pause, then drop my voice so the other passengers can't hear. "Does that mean you'll be up there with Cash? Like, living together?"

She laughs, "Jenna! Not like *that*. We'd be staying in the staff dorms, single-sex. Do you think my parents would ever agree otherwise?"

"Maybe not." For all their Bohemian stories, Livvy's parents are overprotective when it comes to boys. "Anyway, that's so great! We're both going to have the best time this summer."

"I know!"

Four hours later, I'm still not bored by the amazing scenery slipping past outside; but I am seriously over this bus ride. My legs ache, my butt's gone numb, and Henri (the French backpacker beside me), is fast asleep, a thin ribbon of drool stretching to his shoulder. Every few minutes he mumbles and snorts, slumping closer toward me.

I break and call Olivia again. My parents upgraded me to an international plan before I left, and while this may not be an emergency, as such . . . "So tell me more about this camp place."

"It's amazing," she replies immediately, as if we never hung up. "I've only seen brochures so far, but it's set up like a retreat, with yoga in the mornings and—"

"Wait—I think they're calling my stop," I interrupt, hearing a yell from the front of the bus.

"Stillwater!" the driver calls again.

"That's me!" I cry. "Livvy, I'll call you back when I'm settled, OK?"

"Say hi to Susie for me!"

Clutching my backpack, iPod, and magazines, I maneuver over Henri—still drooling happily—and trip down the steps. My overstuffed suitcase is already sitting on the ground in front of me, bulging as if the seams will give way any second now, but before I can ask a single thing, the doors hiss closed and the bus moves slowly back toward the highway, leaving me on the edge of a dusty asphalt road.

Alone.

I look around, confused. The road is empty, with nothing but a simple signpost marking the stop. Thick trees stretch up in every direction, edged at the top of the valley by rock, but there's no building or bus station to be seen. And definitely no Susie.

I try to call, but she isn't picking up her cell. I shiver for a moment, feeling very small in the midst of this huge vista. Back home, there's always a man-made horizon: billboards or high-rise condos or a plane soaring overhead. I've always found it annoying, but now, I half-wish there was at least a gas station to make me feel less alone. This hard strip of highway is the only hint of human life in the whole valley.

Then I take a deep breath of mountain air—crisp and cool as if it's been through a dozen purifiers—and remind myself that *alone* is a good thing. It's just me and nature, the way I've always wanted. I'm Thoreau, out by Walden Pond; I'm Eustace Conway, traversing the Appalachian Mountains. I'm . . .

Hungry. And in need of a bathroom.

I look around, hoping a vehicle will materialize on the dusty road, but the asphalt is empty. It curves gently back to the highway in one direction, disappearing into dense trees the other way. Wait. I blink at the thick wall of foliage blocking my view. What if I'm being completely stupid, and Stillwater is really just around the bend?

My bladder likes this line of thought; it likes it a lot. Besides, what's my alternative: standing here, waiting for dark? I gulp, imagining the things that could be lurking in the forest, just waiting for night to fall.

Hoisting my backpack onto my shoulders, I set off along the road.

Sadly, Stillwater is not hidden just around the next bend. Or the next one. And by the time a cold drizzle begins to fall, it's clear that my wheeled suitcase really wasn't designed as an all-terrain vehicle. Finally, after bouncing bravely over rocks and cracks and stray tree branches, it gives up. Sending a wheel spinning into the undergrowth, it flips over to die right there on the side of the road. I let out a damp whimper. I'm wet and tired, and right now all I want is a hot shower, a large meal and—oh, Lord—a restroom.

Finally, I hear the sound of an engine in the distance, like a choir of polluting angels. Struggling to take off my backpack, I turn just in time to see a mud-splattered white pickup truck speeding toward me from the highway, heading into town. My heart leaps. I know that hitchhiking is way up there on the list of Risky Behaviors That Will Get a Teenage Girl Killed (or Worse), but I think wandering the forest alone trumps it. I step out into the road so they're sure to see me, wave my arms, and practically jump up and down to catch the driver's attention.

The truck speeds past.

As I'm left in its muddy wake, I realize that the media has been lying to me all these years: small towns aren't full of welcoming, down-home folks brimming over with family values and kindness; they're all selfish, heartless people who'll leave a young girl stranded by the edge of the road to die with—

Another truck!

This one is coming from town and makes an awkward U-turn in the road before spluttering to a stop next to me. The window rolls down, revealing a blast of angry emo music and the sullen face of a teenage girl. She's maybe my age, with pale skin almost hidden behind a sheet of lank black hair—the kind dyed with cheap drugstore stuff so that it sucks all light and joy into its vortex of blackness. (I know these things. Livvy has a history of bad DIY dye jobs, and many a night I've had to run over with peroxide and plastic gloves to undo whatever "interesting" color combinations she whimsically decided to try.)

"I'm Fiona." The girl sighs. There's a pause. "Well?" She gestures at the passenger side impatiently and I finally recognize her name.

The stepdaughter!

"Fiona, hi!" Despite her scowl, as of this minute, she's my favorite person on the entire planet. I haul my bags into the truck bed and collapse gratefully next to her in the front. "I'm so glad to see you—you have no idea."

"Uh-huh," she mumbles.

"I thought I sent Susie the right bus schedule, but maybe it was out of date or something. I was just starting to worry—"

Fiona leans over and turns the stereo back up, drowning my voice with drums and a booming guitar riff.

Okaaay.

I sit in silence as we drive for another few minutes until soon, I can see the faint outline of houses through the forest. My excitement returns. "Have you lived in town long?" I can't help but ask over the wailing death cries. "Is there much to do around here?"

Susie didn't tell me much about Stillwater itself. The town doesn't merit a web page or Wikipedia entry, but the brief mentions of it on tourism sites talked about the "wild, rugged wilderness." They didn't, however, say if there was a coffee shop or access to tofu.

Fiona rolls her eyes. "See for yourself."

I look back out the window. We're turning onto what has been optimistically named Main Street: a wide, tree-lined stretch of buildings with a small church marking one end and the dirty pumps of a local gas station at the other. There's a single traffic light stranded uselessly midway down the empty street, and a Canadian flag ripples slowly from the top of the steeple, a flash of red against the gray mountains above.

"This is . . . it?" I ask, my heart sinking. I was expecting small-town, but this is *small*. I count a handful of abandoned storefronts, along with a grocery store, a tavern-type place, and a disheveled building claiming to be a bookstore/map center. It's a long way from the shiny, air-conditioned climes of the stores back home, complete with the organic deli and cute tearoom.

"Great!" I try to sound upbeat. "It's so . . . cute."

Fiona gives me another look before pulling over at the side of the street. "Wait here," she orders, then hops down and dashes through the rain over to Johnson's Home & Hardware. Racks of garden tools are spilling onto the front porch, and there's a faded hand-painted sign advertising fishing bait and tackle.

I manage to follow her orders and wait for approximately three minutes before climbing out of the truck.

"Ummm, Fiona?" I find her leaning against the front counter, seemingly not doing anything at all. "Is there a restroom anywhere I could use?"

She smirks at me before turning to face the empty store. "Ethan!" she bellows. "Jenna really needs to pee!"

I cringe, bracing myself to meet the weathered old owner (because hardware store guys have got to be old and weathered). "Sure," the answering yell comes from the decorating aisle. "Just go right on back." There's a pause, and then from behind a stack of paint cans emerges a boy. An incredibly hot teenage boy.

"Bathroom's up the stairs on the left." He grins, teeth flashing white against his tanned skin.

"Umm, thanks," I manage, staring at the dark hair, dark eyes, and the obvious muscles beneath the faded blue T-shirt.

"No problem. When you've got to go, you've got to go."

Then, as if I'm not sufficiently mortified, a second boy appears. This one has dirty blond hair and broader shoulders than the first, but I can see from their jawline and slightly uneven noses that they're related. He thrusts a pack of toilet paper at me, his lips curling at the edges as if he's amused by my embarrassment.

"Better take this. I think we're out."

Fiona sniggers.

"Umm, thanks . . ." I look down at the pack. Charmin Ultra Soft. "OK, I'm going to . . ." I gesture uselessly behind me. The blond boy snorts with laughter as I back away, then turn to flee up the stairs.

I locate the tiny bathroom and barricade myself in, my face burning with embarrassment. I know I'm supposed to be a mature young adult, cool with my bodily functions and fluids and everything else that comes along with it, but God—that has to be the worst first impression in the history of mortifying first impressions.

And I'm stuck with it.

CHAPTER FIVE

When I've gathered enough courage, I reemerge and mumble good-bye to the boys before following Fiona back to the truck. She drives past Main Street, deeper into the forest. Now that the stereo is off, I can't help but notice the silence here. No traffic noise, no airplanes, nothing— just a heavy kind of quiet I can almost touch. The rain has stopped, leaving the air fresh and crisp, and with water droplets shimmering off the trees it looks like—

"No. Way." I gasp, staring out of the truck in complete shock.

For a moment, Fiona gives me a look as if we're actually in this together. "They've been renovating for three months," she says, stressing every word to convey the horror of constant construction. "We only got running water back last week. You're lucky." With that, she tugs the keys out of the ignition and disappears toward the house.

Except that calling it a "house" is being generous. A huge old clapboard Victorian looms up in front of me, but half the roof is missing, plastic sheeting is flapping in the place of at least two walls, and as I edge nervously toward the scaffolding, I can see a vast black hole in the middle of the main entryway.

"Hello?" I call into the void, careful not to trip. "Is anyone here?"

Susie warned me they'd be doing some work, but somehow, I pictured elegant faded wallpaper and a few broken tiles, not this . . . disaster zone.

"Jenna!" I hear Susie's cry from somewhere inside. "Don't move—I'll be right there."

Eyeing the dust and broken floorboards around me, I take her word as law and stay frozen to the spot until she appears at the far end of the hallway.

"Jenna!" she cries again, advancing to smother me in a huge hug. I wrap my arms around her tightly, both of us squealing like small children. We're almost the same height, but she still manages to envelop me in warmth and motherly kisses. "God, how long has it been? Since that Christmas, right? And look at you now, so tall and grown-up!"

She holds me at arm's length to study me, and I happily study her right back. Gone are the straight, glossy hair and the patent-leather boots I last saw tap-tapping their way down Manhattan streets. In their place are haphazard blond curls caught back in a bright green scarf, a paint-splattered man's shirt and jeans, and a pair of scuffed sneakers.

She catches my stare and laughs. "Don't worry—all this just means I know my way around a kitchen now. Come on, you must be starving—Fiona said the bus was delayed for hours."

I don't correct her, letting her pull me through the house to a room with four solid walls and the smell of cheesy goodness wafting in the air. I must look starving, because Susie doesn't say another word before settling me in a chair and presenting me with a bowl brimming over with pasta. "You're still a vegetarian, right?"

I nod, mouth already full.

"Adam will bring your bags in when he gets back—don't worry. As you can see, we're kind of rough around the edges right now." Susie's expression becomes kind of apprehensive. "Which means you'll be doubling up in Fiona's room for now. Just until we get another bedroom finished," she adds quickly.

I nod again, admittedly with less enthusiasm.

"I'm so glad you're here." Susie beams at me again. "I've missed you, kid!"

I swallow. "Me too—missed you, I mean. And I want to say thanks for this, letting me stay. I won't be any trouble, I promise," I swear. Given the choice between Grandma's luxury condo and this construction site, I'd still choose Stillwater.

Susie looks amused. "You, trouble? Kid, you were always the one keeping me in check. Don't tell me you've decided to become a rebellious teen?"

At that moment, Fiona slouches into the room and slumps at the table. She looks expectantly at Susie, who—to my surprise—goes over to the stove and serves up a plate of food, then deposits it in front of Fiona as if she's a queen. I blink. Fiona doesn't even murmur any thanks; she just picks up a well-thumbed book and begins to read, ignoring us both as she picks at her food. I squint to make out the title. *The Bell Jar.*

Cheerful.

"So, this place is pretty large." I turn back to Susie, who's pouring out a cup of coffee. Unless Fiona has a brood of (God, hopefully more upbeat) siblings, it seems kind of strange for them to be rattling around in such a huge house.

"Didn't I say? We're opening up a B and B," Susie explains, obviously excited. "Stillwater's first!"

"Wow." I blink, trying to imagine the place as habitable, let alone a tourist spot. "That's a big project."

"Uh-huh." She takes a sip from her mug. "But this will all be fixed up soon, and it's such a perfect spot. . . ." Susie gives a contented sigh, as if she's not sitting in the middle of sawdust and safety hazards. Then again, she did spend three months living in a shack in Ecuador, volunteering with drug-addicted children, so maybe this house—and Fiona—doesn't seem like such a challenge to her.

"Anyway, we can talk about that all summer! Right now, I want to hear everything about your life," Susie insists, so I begin to chat about school, and Olivia, and all the Green Teen work until Susie interrupts me for a moment to turn to the other side of the table.

"Fiona, honey—it's time to put the book away. We have a guest."

"I thought she was part of the family." Fiona doesn't look up, but her tone says plenty. "Isn't that what you've been saying all week?"

"Yes, but you still need to put the book away." Susie's voice is pleasant. "Now."

"Dad lets me."

"I let you do what?" A tall, broad-built man walks into the room, hoists off his tool belt, and puts it on a counter with a clatter. He's blond, with a fuzzy beard and wispy hair framing his tanned face. As he leans over to kiss Susie's forehead, I catch the soft look that comes into her eyes and begin to understand why she was so quick to leave the luxuries of running water and move all the way out here.

"She says I have to stop reading." Fiona pouts. "Do you want me to be completely illiterate?"

Adam laughs good-naturedly. "If it means we get a nice family dinner, then sure, pumpkin."

Pumpkin? I nearly choke.

"Fine!" Fiona scrapes back her chair. "I wasn't hungry anyway." She makes for the stairs, but Adam stops her.

"Are you going out this evening?"

Fiona sighs. "Maybe."

"Then why don't you take Jenna along, introduce her to everyone? You'd like that, right?" He turns to me expectantly.

I'm torn. It's obvious that Fiona doesn't want me trailing after her, but I can't wait to meet the other kids in town—and make a better first impression than back at the hardware store. "Sure, that could be fun. If it's OK with you, Fiona," I add quickly.

She rolls her eyes. "Whatever. I'm going now, so you need to hurry up."

"The lake is just down that path." Susie follows us out to the front yard and points across the road, to where a faint trail disappears into the forest. The trees are thick and wet from the rain, blocking out the dusk light. I shiver.

"And it's safe out here?"

Susie laughs, handing Fiona a flashlight. "Of course it is. Just don't go off alone; that's the only rule. And be back by ten."

"Dad said eleven." Fiona challenges her. I bite my lip. Adam said ten as well.

"Fine." Susie sighs. "Eleven. Since it's your first night, Jenna." She smiles at me, and I feel a spark of guilt. Or maybe that's just a mosquito bite. "Have fun, girls!"

Fiona doesn't bother with good-byes; she just pulls up the hood of her black sweatshirt and charges into the forest. "Thanks, Susie," I call out, hurrying to keep up. "See you later!"

Within moments, I've almost lost sight of Fiona's figure in the trees. "Wait up," I pant, trying not to trip on a tree root. I'm wearing my favorite red Converses, but they're still no match for the rocky path worn into the ground, littered with tree branches and chunks of dirt.

Fiona pauses and turns back, hands on hips. "What's wrong now?"

"Nothing." I force myself to smile at her. "I just thought we could take it slower, maybe talk." I plan on making friends with this girl if it kills me.

Fiona sighs, but slows her pace a fraction. "Talk about what?"

"I don't know." I squint at the dim trail ahead and think of things we might have in common. Something tells me she's not into Green Teen stuff. "How are you liking that book from dinner, the one by . . . ?" My mind goes blank, just for a couple of seconds, but it's enough for Fiona to finish my sentence with a withering glare.

"Sylvia Plath. You know who that is, right?"

"Yes." I try not to sound defensive. "She wrote poetry, too. Didn't she kill herself in the end?"

"Yup. The unappreciative literary world drove her to her death."

Lovely. "So." I try another, less depressing topic. "Have you got any plans for the summer?"

"I wish." Fiona kicks a tree stump. With her clumpy Doc Martens, I think the tree loses that battle. "Dana is in Calgary, Nina's traveling with her folks. Everybody's gone and I'm stuck at home with Dad and Susie." Her voice twists on the last word.

"The stepfamily thing can be tough." I offer a tiny bit of sympathy. "Getting used to someone new must be hard."

"What do you know?" she shoots back, scowling. "Are your parents divorced?"

I swallow. The million-dollar question is out there, drifting between us like a third person, but I can't bring myself to think about it—or confide in this bratty, unforgiving girl.

"Fine," I acknowledge. "So maybe I don't know exactly what you're going through. But I know Susie, and she's great."

"Great?" Fiona does that snorting thing again. "She's a complete bitch, interfering in everything. Did you see her at dinner? Nagging me like she even has a right. She's ruined everything. Dad and me were just fine before she came along."

I'm tempted to jump to Susie's defense, but something tells me that wouldn't help with this "making friends" project of mine. I bite back a reply and keep trailing after her through the trees. I can see daylight ahead, where the dense forest seems to end, but just before we emerge out of the trees, Fiona turns back to me one last time.

"And you can forget about being BFFs or a good influence or whatever it is that bitch has planned. I don't want you here, either." With that, she pushes back a final branch and strides away.

CHAPTER SIX

I pause for a moment, still hidden among the trees. I'm on the edge of a small clearing beside the lake; worn patches of grass and wildflowers stretching to a thin, stony beach and tall pine trees looming up above. It's absolutely stunning, but for once, nature is the last thing on my mind. Farther up the shore, I can see a handful of kids, hanging out in what seems to be a picnic area. They all look pretty young—boys tossing around a baseball, and a couple of girls sitting on a bench, bent over a magazine—but Fiona slouches past them without a word, toward a fire pit, where the older guys from the hardware store are sprawled on the ground.

This is the big Stillwater social scene?

My stomach flutters with nerves. Of all the things I worried about, making friends wasn't on the list; you don't spend every weekend at the mall trying to convince shoppers to reuse and recycle without getting pretty comfortable talking to strangers. But now, seeing just how small this town really is, I can't help but panic. Suppose I can't get over that embarrassing first impression? Am I doomed to spend the rest of the summer alone, with nothing but Fiona's bitchy comments for company?

Taking a deep breath, I brace myself and walk over toward the group. Fiona has settled alone on the edge of the water with her book, so I'm left to make my own introductions.

"Hi, guys," I venture brightly, arriving at their little circle. My voice sounds almost too perky in the shadows, but I add a wide smile and carry on. "Ethan, right? And umm . . ." I trail off, waiting for them to introduce themselves. They don't. "I'm Jenna," I say, finally.

After a beat, Ethan speaks. "Hey, Jenna." He holds his hand up in a semi-almost-wave. He's wearing a faded T-shirt and a pair of cargo pants, and his brown hair is curling gently over the collar of his shirt as if it desperately needs a trim. "How are you doing?"

"Good. Tired, but I've been traveling all day. Well, since yesterday," I correct myself, trying not to feel self-conscious as everyone blatantly gives me a once-over. Even the younger boys have stopped their ball game to check me out, and while I'm dressed pretty casually like them, in a tank top and jeans, I can't help but feel like the outsider I guess I am.

"Cool. Well, you know my charming brother, Grady." Ethan nods to where Grady's carving at a block of wood with a ferocious-looking pocketknife. "And that's Reeve."

The last boy looks up briefly from arranging firewood. His hair is short and dark, almost black in the fading light, and there's a calm kind of aura around him—quiet and methodical next to Grady's restless hacking. He gives me a brief smile and what could almost qualify as a nod before turning back to his task.

So, they do things casual out here. Low-key. I can deal with that.

"Great to meet you. I mean, again," I add, looking at Grady. "Because, you know, we met before, in the store. . . ." I stop myself before I can babble (or rhyme) any more. I forget that's what I used to be like, plunged into an unfamiliar crowd, but apparently, my vocal chords have some kind of muscle memory: instant awkwardness.

Grady nods, smirking. "You're the girl who needed to pee."

Oh, God, I knew it.

Despite the overwhelming desire to turn and flee all the way back to New Jersey, I force myself to perch on a log, (realizing only when my butt hits the wood that it's wet from the rain). Ignoring the squelch, I ask brightly, "So what are you guys up to?"

"Just hanging out," Ethan replies. He leans back on his elbows, watching me.

"Cool." I keep that big smile on my face. It turns out that the kids of Stillwater, British Columbia, are by far my toughest audience. Shifting around to get comfy, I try to think of something interesting to say.

Finally, Grady looks over. "Where are you from, anyway?"

"New Jersey," I answer quickly. "Well, a suburb out in—"

"And you're what, a sophomore?"

"Going to be a senior." Do I really look fifteen?

"Same as us," Ethan pipes up. "Reeve's just graduated."

"Really?" I turn to him. Again, I can't help noticing that he has the kind of taut body that half our football team would kill for. "So, are you going to college, or . . . ?" I trail off, wondering if I've made a mistake. They drum it into us so often at school, it's easy to forget that not everyone goes to college, especially not out in these small towns.

"Maybe." Reeve speaks at last. He's stacked the wood and is carefully building a fire now, laying branches in a crisscross pattern and pushing twigs and dead leaves into the gaps. As I look closer, I see cuts and bruises all over his knees.

"What happened?" I point at his legs. "Are you OK?"

He looks down at the scars proudly. "This is nothing. Last time I went bouldering, I took half my elbow off."

"Bouldering?"

"You know, climbing. Rocks."

"Oh. Right." I pause. "Isn't there safety gear you can use—padding and stuff?"

Reeve grins, clearly amused by the idea. "Not if you want to do it right. The gear restricts your moves," he explains. "It's better just to take the knocks."

"Oh," I repeat faintly. Because blood and gore is better.

"So, what do you do for fun?" Reeve gives me a vaguely encouraging smile. He strikes some matches in quick succession and touches them to the kindling until the fire slowly crackles to life.

"Normal stuff, I guess." Then I remember that normal in this town means hurling themselves up a cliff face and playing with knives. "You know, music, movies . . ."

"What bands are you into?" Ethan asks, rummaging in a bag. He pulls out a can of soda and then offers it to me. I lean across and take it, pleased.

"All kinds, mainly indie stuff, some rock. I like the new Jared Jameson album," I offer, hoping they're not all secret death-metal fans.

Luckily, Ethan nods in recognition, "Yeah, I've been meaning to check that out."

Emboldened, I continue. "And I do a lot of environmental stuff too. I'm part of this group in school — we campaign for different eco causes, organize rallies and protests and things."

Reeve looks over. "You mean like conservation?"

"Sure, and fund-raising, letter-writing: anything to raise awareness." I smile, rueful. "You guys probably take it for granted, living right out here in the middle of nature, but a lot of people don't even know about the threat of global warming, or the damage that's being done to the environment because of logging, and . . ." I stop, remembering my non-babble policy. It's easy for me to get carried away with this stuff, but I've got the whole summer; I don't need to hit them with my full Green Teen platform just yet.

"Global warming, huh?" Reeves studies me. I can't

quite tell his expression in the dim light, but something in his voice sounds tense. "Why not fight AIDS or third-world poverty or something that really hurts people?"

I pause, thrown. "Global warming does hurt us. Flooding, droughts . . . It's already started, and it's going to get worse if we don't act."

"And you're going to stop it?" I can hear the smirk in his voice.

I fold my arms. "I'm going to try."

"With what, a school recycling campaign?" he shoots back.

"Dude," Ethan interrupts, "the wood's too wet. We need more." He gives Reeve a warning look.

"Fine," Reeve answers in a clipped voice. He begins to stack a fresh batch around the flames, poking angrily at the fire with a long gnarled branch. I look around, confused. What did I say that was so bad?

"So, you think you can take the five-nine up by Macaw Ridge?" Ethan turns to his brother, obviously changing the subject. They launch into coversation about rock grades and climbing routes, while Reeve slouches on the other side of the fire, studiously ignoring me. Fiona is still buried in her book, so I have nothing left to do but sit—watching the bright flames and wondering what I did wrong.

CHAPTER SEVEN

Another hour creeps past, painfully slowly. I get bitten by about twenty mosquitoes, scrape my elbow on the log, and learn more than a Jersey girl ever needs to know about fly-fishing equipment, but that weird tension from before hasn't gone anywhere. In fact, it feels worse. All my attempts to ask questions or make a friendly comment are cut off by the boys' in-jokes and banter, until I just sit back, defeated.

An unexpected wave of loneliness rolls through me. Casual and low-key is one thing, but now the boys aren't even trying to be friendly—aside from Ethan, who manages to throw a halfhearted smile in my direction every now and then. My dreams of a fun-filled summer are rapidly deflating: now I think I'll be lucky to even have a single conversation.

When the lake is just an inky shadow in the dark, I finally crack. "Fiona, do you want to get going?"

"What time is it?" She's deigned to join us by the fire, but she's still reading—with the help of a pocket flashlight.

I check the glowing display on my cell phone. "Ten thirty."

"No," she says stubbornly. "I'm waiting until eleven."

"Just to spite Susie?" I can't believe how petty she's being. "Just sit out on the porch. She'll never know the difference."

"Nope." Fiona turns another page and nibbles at an Oreo. Yes, she brought snacks. No, she hasn't offered me any.

I sit, resigning myself to another half hour feeling out of place, until Ethan speaks up.

"I could walk you back," he offers, pulling on a green sweatshirt. "I'm pretty much ready to go."

"Would you?" I look at him with relief. Jet lag is hitting hard, and even the foldout bed in Fiona's room seems like luxury to me.

"Sure." He unfolds himself and gets up, brushing dirt from his jeans. "Grady?"

"I'll stick around a while more." After some dedicated carving, Grady's chunk of wood now resembles a smooth pebble. He looks up at us, hair gleaming a dark gold in the firelight. "Tell Mom I'll be back soon."

"Hang on." Reeve is just a silhouette across the fire as he slings a battered nylon bag across his shoulders and pulls on his sneakers. "I need to borrow your belay device for tomorrow."

"Oh, right." Ethan hangs back to wait for him.

I pause on the edge of the clearing, uneasy. Maybe this isn't the best idea. They seem harmless enough, but disappearing into the forest with two strange boys . . . ? Surely that would feature on the Risky Behaviors That Will Get a Teenage Girl Killed (or Worse) list.

I don't have time to change my mind, because Reeve strides past me, asking, "You ready?" in an impatient voice — as if I was the one holding us up — and then they charge into the trees, leaving me to stumble on behind in the dark.

"Guys?" I call after the bobbing light. "Ethan, can you wait a — oww!" My ankle gives way on the edge of a sharp slope, and I twist over on it, falling heavily to the muddy ground.

The pain isn't terrible, but part of me feels like giving up and just sitting there. I can see the rest of my trip stretching out in front of me, lonely and full of bugs and boys who'll barely even speak to me, let alone —

Wait. Where are they?

I pull myself to my feet. "Ethan?" My voice catches in my throat. I can't see their flashlight anymore or hear anything but the haunting rustle of the trees and my own beating heart. "Reeve? Guys, where are you?"

It's completely dark now, heavy like a blanket around me. I can't make out anything but the ominous black shapes all around. My stomach lurches with fear, but I try not to panic. Cautiously, I edge forward. If I just keep walking in a straight line, won't that get me back to the road eventually? Then maybe I can call Susie to come pick me up, and—

Something grabs me from behind.

I scream.

"Arrrghhh!" I lurch away from my unknown assailant. In an instant, I think of all the terrible things that could be lurking in the dark. "HELP ME!" I scream, propelling myself forward into the trees. I make it half a dozen steps, and then I hear laughter.

Laughter!

A flashlight switches on and I turn to see the half-lit shadows of Ethan and Reeve behind me, falling over themselves with glee.

"Man, where'd you learn to scream like that?" Reeve's whole body is shaking. He grins, a smile that could slay teenage girls the world over, but right now, I'm not even remotely impressed. "My ears are still ringing!"

"Aren't you city girls supposed to be tough?" Ethan gasps for air, clinging to a tree branch to keep himself upright.

I gape at them in disbelief. In an instant, my fear turns to anger.

"What the hell are you DOING?" I yell, surprised at my own force. I shove Reeve, hard. He stumbles backward. "Do you think that was funny? DO YOU?"

"Whoa, calm down." Ethan pulls me back. "It was only a joke."

"A joke?" I cry, shaking. "What kind of morons ARE you? Or is that what passes for funny out here?"

Reeve is still grinning. "Aw, get over it. We didn't mean any harm."

"No harm?" I force myself to take a deep breath and calm down. It's all OK, I tell myself. Everything's OK. When my heartbeat finally slows, I look at them, amazed. "Do you have any idea how scared I was? That's not funny, guys. It's not!"

Ethan begins to look contrite. "Hey, I'm sorry—we didn't mean it."

Reeve agrees. "It's not like we would have left you here for real."

"How should I know?" I shoot back. "I just met you. You could be . . . anything!" I shiver, realizing again how vulnerable I am out here.

"Yeah, well, we're not like that." Reeve's tone gets sharper, as if I'm the one who's offended him.

I hug myself tightly, trying not to snap. "Look, can we just get out of here, please?"

Reeve makes an exaggerated gesture, like he's bowing to me. "As you wish."

Perfect. I'm recovering from a minor heart attack and the guy wants to stand around quoting *The Princess Bride*. I glare at him and then follow Ethan—and the warm glow of their flashlight—back out of the forest. I stumble a couple of times, on tree roots and stray rocks, but even though Reeve reaches out to help me, I snatch away. I don't need any of his kind of help.

"I can take it from here," I say in a clipped voice, the minute we're through the trees.

Ethan looks unsure, hair falling in his eyes. "I don't know. . . . We're not supposed to let you girls go off alone."

Now he's worried about my personal safety? "See that light over there?" I point. "That's Susie's. I'll be fine—if you can both hold off on attacking me again."

"It was a joke!" Reeve says again, getting exasperated. "You don't have to get so wound up about it."

"Wound up?" I can't believe this guy. "You're the one playing dangerous pranks!"

"Whatever." He turns to walk toward his truck, yelling behind him, "Ethan—you coming?"

"Uh, sure." Ethan looks at me almost apologetically. "See you around, Jenna. Sorry," he adds quietly before jogging after Reeve. They climb into a mud-splattered white pickup truck—the same mud-splattered pickup truck that left me wet and cold on the side of the road earlier this evening. Reeve starts the engine and makes a swift U-turn, pulling past me with a rattle of tires in the dirt and a blast of some macho rock song.

And I limp miserably back to the house.

CHAPTER EIGHT

"COLDCOLDCOLD!"

Stumbling backward as a jet of ice-cold water hits my skin, I scramble for the faucet. It's too late. By the time I manage to shut the water off, I'm so frozen that even my goosebumps have goosebumps.

I hear someone running up the stairs, and a few moments later, there's a knock. "Sorry!" Susie apologizes through the bathroom door. "I forgot to tell you about the water — it runs cold for the first five minutes!"

"No problem!" I manage to answer, even though my teeth are literally chattering. "I'm OK! It's . . . refreshing!"

Susie laughs. "We should get it fixed up in another couple of weeks. In the meantime, how about I make you some breakfast?"

"Uhhmmmm." I manage a faintly upbeat response.

"Blueberry pancakes coming right up!"

She retreats, leaving me to wrap myself in three different towels and collapse, shivering, while I wait for my body temperature to return to normal. And then I wait some more. In fact, I linger as long as possible in the small, blue-tiled bathroom, until I realize that for all her Bohemian leanings, Susie probably prefers clothing at the breakfast table, and that means getting back to my suitcase. Which is in Fiona's bedroom.

Bracing myself, I cross the hallway, remembering to tap lightly on the door in case she's changing or something. I've never shared before, but I'm guessing that a good roomie always knocks. There's silence, so I creep in, blinking to adjust to the dark shrouding the room. Even though it's after nine a.m., thick, purple drapes are still blocking out all sunlight. Mixed with the navy paint on every wall and an array of bleak emo posters, the effect is pretty depressing.

"Umm, Fiona?" After reaching around blindly in the dark for five minutes, I finally have to speak up. "Would you mind if I opened the drapes a little? I need to get dressed and I can't really—"

A mumble emerges from her motionless form. I take that as a yes.

"Thanks!" I whisper. With light, soon comes the locating of clean underwear, and in no time at all, I'm dressed and armed with sandals and my notebook. "Susie's making pancakes," I offer. Fiona pulls her comforter up over her head. "OK, well, see you later!"

I let myself out quietly. It's my first morning in

Stillwater, the sun is shining, and the sweet buttery smell of deliciousness is wafting from the kitchen, but still, I feel a pang in my chest—and my ankle. I miss home. I miss Olivia. I didn't think being away would be a breeze, but I didn't expect homesickness to set in so soon.

I wonder what my parents are doing, in their separate corners of the world. Dad's already texted me, a brief line about jet lag and meatballs, but I can't help wondering if—

No.

Carefully putting all thoughts of the future out of my head, I maneuver my way down the stairs and past that gaping pit in the hallway. The sun is streaming in fierce strips through the window frames, and I can hear Susie singing along with a pop song on the radio down the hall. Something about the calm domesticity of the scene helps ease the tight sadness I have bubbling in my chest.

I'm not powerless, I remind myself, clinging to my number-one mantra. I got here, didn't I? To this sprawling wilderness, to what *I* wanted my summer to be. All I have to do now is learn the intricacies of Susie's plumbing system, read a few of Fiona's dystopian novels, and find some way of getting along with the Stillwater boys.

And, as Principal Turner would agree, I'm nothing if not persistent.

After a stack of pancakes drenched in genuine Canadian maple syrup (one of the bonuses of being north of the border, although the other—bacon—I sadly had to refuse), I put together a tote bag of beach supplies and prepare to head out to the lake for a swim in that glorious sparkling water. But for some reason, my feet won't take me farther than the front yard.

"Everything OK, Jenna?" Adam finds me sitting on the porch. He's unloading planks of wood from the back of the truck but pauses to check on me, scratching absently at his beard.

I pretend to fuss with my ankle—still kind of swollen after my fall. "Oh, yeah. I'm good." I nod vigorously, shooting another look across the dirt road at the dense trees. In daylight, they look innocent enough, but I feel a chill across the back of my neck when I remember last night and how scared I was in the dark.

Adam follows my gaze. "It can take a while to get used to it out here. Susie couldn't sleep properly for weeks when she first arrived—all the noise we get from the forest at night."

"I'm fine," I repeat, embarrassed. "But . . . I think I'll just hang out here today. Settle in," I add quickly.

"Good plan." He nods gently. "Maybe you can drag Fiona out of her room sometime before noon."

I doubt it, but nod. "Sure, maybe. Well . . . thanks."

"Uh, anytime." He blinks and then seems to collect himself. "I better . . ." He grips the plank of wood again. I nod, and he hoists another armload onto his shoulder and disappears into the house.

I let out a breath. The awkwardness between us will fade, I'm sure, but right now, it's still weird to be around him; he's like some distant relative I'm supposed to be comfortable with, despite the fact that he's a complete stranger.

A complete stranger who thinks I'm a scared kid, afraid of the forest.

I take one last look across the street at the trees, green and dappled with sunlight.

Maybe tomorrow.

I spend the morning in the backyard instead, stretched out in the hot sun and working on some letters. I have a big blue binder of the names of all my important congressmen and state government officials, and whenever I get some free time, I work my way through the list with letters about Green Teen issues and the environment. I used to shoot e-mails over, copying everyone to the message, but then I realized they just filter them into a "crazy activist" file and forget about them. A handwritten note, on the other hand, seems to have way more impact.

"Jenna!" Susie calls when I'm contemplating another layer of sunscreen.

"Out here!" I yell back.

"Oh, hey." She emerges from the house, covered in sawdust. "Your mom called, but she was in a rush, so I said you'd call her later."

"Everything OK?"

"Well, she did say she was about to go shopping with Milicent. . . ." We share a grimace. Grandma is nothing if not demanding company. Susie pauses to brush dust off her arms. "Now that I've found you, can you do me a favor?"

"Sure." I sit up slowly and wait for the sun-daze to subside.

"I need a bunch of stuff from the store, but I'm waiting on a delivery." Susie holds up a list, her expression hopeful. "Can you run out for me? It won't take a minute."

"No problem," I agree immediately. I need to get these letters in the mail, and after all, I owe Susie. If it weren't for her, I'd be trailing around every housewares department in the Orlando metro area right about now. "Is there a bike I can use?"

"Uh, I think you'll need the truck for this one—unless you can fit five cans of paint in your backpack!" She hands me the scrap of paper just as the phone begins to ring. She jogs back toward the house. "You should find everything at the hardware store!"

I'm losing an epic battle when my cell rings. With one eye on the road, I reach over for my purse. "Olivia? I take back everything I ever said about your driving."

She laughs, faint and crackling from bad reception. "What do you mean?"

"Tell me how the hell to drive stick!" I hear a grinding sound from the engine and try to pump the clutch again. A bicycle doesn't have these kind of problems—oh, no, just five gears and two pedals—and no cloud of exhaust fumes either.

"How's it going out there? Have you been mauled by wild bears yet? How's Susie?" Livvy peppers me with questions. I check the road, but it's clear in both directions, so I don't bother to pull over. Switching the phone to my other hand, I turn the radio down.

"It's going . . . OK." I realize how hesitant I must

sound, so quickly continue. "Susie's great, she's really settled up here, and Adam seems decent enough."

"And the step-kid?"

"Umm, don't ask." I yank the truck into third gear with a lurch. It's lucky there's no one around to see my bad driving, just an empty stretch of asphalt lined thickly with trees. I don't think I've ever seen such a quiet road— I'm so used to dense traffic and four-lane highways.

"You'll have to send me photos," she insists. "I want to see all the mountains and everything."

"I will, but . . ." I pause. "I didn't realize, but it might be kind of hard to keep the Green Teen stuff going up here."

"You're in the middle of nature!"

"I know!" The irony isn't lost on me. "But everyone drives around in these hulking great pickup trucks, and the AC is running all the time . . ."

"Maybe it could be like a project," she suggests. "Give the town an eco-makeover while you're there. I know how you love a challenge."

I laugh. "Do not!"

"Umm, you so do. Besides, what else are you going to do? You can't work up there, right?"

"Nope, I'm on a tourist visa." I sigh, thinking of my college account. My parents are giving me a guilt allowance, but I was planning on saving all my summer earnings. "Maybe I should," I muse. "They could be environmentally friendly by the time I leave! Anyway, what's up with you?"

"We got the job!" Olivia exclaims.

"At the collective? That's awesome! Why didn't you

say something to begin with?" I cheer. "What will you be doing?"

"Cleaning, cooking, basic stuff. But I've got a list of the workshops they offer, and they all sound so amazing." She sighs happily. "Plus, I get all that time away from my parents—with Cash!"

"Uh, yeah, how are they taking that?"

She giggles. "I haven't told them about him yet—that he's going to be there, I mean."

"So what did you say?"

"You'd be proud of me, it was like, Jenna-worthy levels of planning! First, I left some of the camp leaflets lying around, so they could see . . ."

I settle back in the driver's seat and listen to Olivia's familiar chatter, watching carefully for the turn-off to Main Street. Apparently there's only one, but I'm sure I'll miss it all the same.

"So then I just had to have Cash's friend pose as one of the other counselors and—"

"Omigod!" I scream, slamming on the brakes. The truck shudders to a stop. I sit there, seat belt painfully tight against my chest and my breath coming fast.

"Jenna? Jenna? Are you OK?" Olivia cries.

When I recover the phone from the side of my seat, Livvy is having a minor meltdown. I swallow, staring at the street ahead in disbelief. "I . . . I'm OK. I think."

"What the hell happened?"

"A moose." I whisper, in case it hears me.

"What?"

"There's a moose. In the road." I blink, but the thing

in front of me doesn't disappear; it just swishes its tail and sniffs the asphalt. It's utterly surreal, seeing something up close that's only ever been on my TV or in a magazine.

"That's amazing! What does it look like?" Livvy gasps. "Are you sure it's not a deer?"

"It's too ugly to be a deer." I study the animal, calling on my extensive knowledge of holiday cards. "Maybe it's mutant goat." I shake my head. "What does it matter what it is? It's big and horned and it's right in the middle of the road!"

"Is it moving?"

"No. It's just standing there." The beast turns and looks at me with big eyes from under a set of twisted antlers. By instinct, I duck down, hiding behind the dashboard. "Now it's staring at me! Should I get out?"

"Calm down!" Livvy laughs.

"Helpful, thanks!" I hiss. "But I don't have much experience dealing with wild, rampaging beasts!"

"You should probably stay where you are."

I take my hand off the car door. "You're right—it can't get me in here. Can it?" I hit the all-locks button. "What do I do?"

"Just drive around it." She still sounds amused.

"I can't," I bite back. "It's right in the middle of the road. And anyway, what if it charges at me?" I slowly peer up over the steering wheel. It's still there, standing idly just ten feet from the truck.

"I doubt it will. But you could try scaring it out of your way," Livvy suggests.

"With what?" My purse contains many things, but

weaponry doesn't really figure on my list. "I can't really walk over with my iPod and play it the last Katy Perry single!"

She giggles. "Then use the horn."

"What if that just makes it mad?"

"You've got to do something," Livvy points out. "Or are you going to sit there all day?"

"You're right." I brace myself. "I'm trying the horn." Gingerly, I hit the steering wheel. The sound bellows out on the quiet road.

"Well?"

I peer up again. "Nothing. It's not moving." I try again, but the moose just swishes its tail at me. "Maybe it's deaf."

Livvy laughs. "So what's your next plan?"

"I don't know. Wait! I think it's moving!" Slowly, the thing looks from side to side and takes a tentative step forward. "That's right," I tell it. "Keep going; go frolic in the forest with all your moosey pals."

It takes another step.

"Come on, just a little farther . . ." I hold my breath, willing it to go.

"Is it working?"

"Almost . . . almost . . . gone!" I shout in triumph as the creature plods slowly into the woods. I exhale a long breath of relief.

"Man, Cash isn't going to believe this." Livvy sighs. "Your second day, and you get to see a moose."

I shudder. "Next thing, I'll be torn apart by wolves."

"There are wolves?"

"Uh-huh." I ignore her enthusiasm.

"That's so awesome. Oh, hey, I've got to go pack. I leave tomorrow, but I'll call as soon as I'm settled in!"

"Miss you," I tell her with a pang.

"Bye, hon."

CHAPTER NINE

Having triumphed over stick shift *and* a disgruntled moose, I barely give a thought to the Stillwater boys as I browse the dusty hardware-store aisles. It's not until I arrive at the front counter to find Grady slouched over the cluttered desk that I remember my not-so-warm welcome.

"Hi," I say, smiling brightly. "Can you help me out?"

Grady doesn't even look up from his car magazine. A blue baseball cap is pulled low over his eyes, emblazoned with some kind of sports insignia of an evil-looking whale. "I'm busy."

I blink. The store is empty, nothing but faded linoleum and stands of old fishing bait. "Umm, I was wondering if you carried energy-saving bulbs, because —"

He leaves.

Seriously. Just picks up his magazine and ambles past me out of the store. I stare after him in disbelief.

His brother, Ethan, emerges from the back room. He's wearing a blue plaid shirt with the sleeves rolled up, his arms full of bug spray. He dumps the cans on the counter, sending some of them clattering onto the floor. "Don't mind him."

"What . . . ? I mean . . ." I look around, mystified. "What did I even do?"

"Besides have a major freak-out last night?" Ethan shoots me a knowing look, hair falling in his eyes. "I don't know, maybe call us all dumb-ass hicks with no sense of humor . . ."

"I did not! And he wasn't even there!"

He gives a lazy shrug. "Doesn't matter anyway. Grady gets like that all the time. What did you need?"

I pass over the list. "I didn't say those things," I insist again, worried. "I wouldn't."

"Yeah, but you'd think them." Ethan seems unconcerned. "We've got these up front, I think." He ambles toward the other end of the store. "All this stuff's for Susie, right?"

"Yup." Suddenly, I realize that his tone is actually friendly. I hurry after him.

"She's in here all the time these days." He drags a ladder over. "Practically keeps us in business."

"I was wondering about that." I pause, looking out of the smudged windows at the quiet expanse of street. "It's summer, but . . . where is everyone?"

"Last night wasn't enough excitement for you?"

I narrow my eyes, but he seems to be just teasing.

"It used to be busy. Well, busier," he corrects himself,

climbing up to pass the first paint can down. "But the mill closed down a couple of years ago; that pretty much sucked most of the trade out of town. We settled down again, but then that luxury resort out on Blue Ridge opened last year, and everything just dropped off. They'll come off the highway for gas on their way out, but that's about all."

"Luxury resort," I repeat. My heart sinks. I don't like the sound of that. Susie could make her B and B as charming as possible, but it would still be a big old house on a dusty back road.

"Spa, gourmet cooking, the works." Ethan climbs down. "This is all we've got. I could put an order in for more, but your best bet is probably just to drive down to Kamloops and stock up." He names a town I remember passing through on the bus—hours away.

"Thanks." I look back at the list. "Say, you don't have any green brands, do you?"

He shakes his head. "Only the colors you see right there. Maybe I saw some beige out back . . ."

I smile. "No, I meant, nontoxic, biodegradeable . . ." I trail off. "Never mind." A trip to the city it is. "Does Susie know about this?" I ask, following him to the cash register. "About the serious lack of visitors, I mean."

He looks awkward. "Yeah, but she thinks she can turn it around. Single-handedly make Stillwater a vacation spot, that kind of thing."

"Sounds like Susie," I agree.

"We all hope she's right," he adds quickly, ringing up some paint rollers. "But, well, you should see the Blue Ridge place. Even their website looks like a million bucks."

"You have Internet?" I perk up. Susie hasn't hooked us up yet, and I'm already feeling twinges of withdrawal.

He laughs. "We're not completely backward out here."

I blush.

"Come take a look." He circles the counter and pulls out a huge old laptop hanging together with duct tape and sheer willpower. "I'm saving for a MacBook," he explains, ruefully waiting for it to power up. "And a better car. And college . . ."

"Tell me about it."

"See?" Ethan clicks away and then swivels the cracked screen toward me.

" 'Blue Ridge,' " I read aloud, " 'the luxurious side to nature.' " The web page shows the same sprawling valley that Stillwater inhabits, but glistening through the steam from a hot tub, high in the mountains. A monogrammed towel rests thick and fluffy beside a glass of champagne; a slice of chocolate cake sits on a gleaming white plate. Yup, I'd buy into that, if only I had a spare . . . "Five hundred dollars! A night?"

Ethan laughs darkly. "And that's just the starting rate. If you want, you can get helicoptered in and have gold particles massaged into your face."

"Right, gold particles. For when silver is just passé."

He closes the laptop. "So, you see why we can't really compete? *Stillwater — the muddy side to nature.* Doesn't have the same ring to it."

"Nope." I giggle. "Shame. I mean, not everyone wants to eat French cuisine and wrap themselves with kelp — some people actually like all that outdoor adventure stuff.

You have activities and things like that here in town, right?"

"Sure." He nods. "Grady and me run mountain-biking trips, when there are any people around. And we have a bunch of kayaks and fishing equipment. But it's hardly a full-service alpine adventure center. With valets."

"True." I want to linger a while more and chat with Ethan, but Grady slouches back in and takes up residence behind the counter again. He gives me an impatient look.

"Got everything?"

I look down at the collection of heavy bags at my feet. "Yes." I ignore his tone. "Thanks, Ethan."

Thanks for the only five minutes of friendly conversation I've had since arriving in this town.

I can't help but worry as I drive back to the house — keeping a careful eye out for stray moose this time. My godmother is notorious for leaping into new and exciting projects without paying much attention to details, but what happens when the B and B opens its freshly painted doors to find . . . no guests?

I find Susie in one of the downstairs rooms, wearing her paint-stained overalls and a bright pink scarf in her hair.

"Find everything?" she asks, scraping uselessly at the wallpaper with a blunt knife edge.

"Almost." I put down the first box and rummage around for a shiny new tool. "This should make things easier."

"Oh, thanks!" She sets to work with the scraper and right away, a whole strip of hideous 1970s orange-print paper peels clean off the wall. "Want to try? It's fun. Like peeling off dead skin when you get a sunburn, you know?"

"Sure." I take another tool and set to work on the other wall. She's right: the process is strangely satisfying. "So, the B and B . . ." I rip a long piece away. "Do you think it'll be a hit?"

"For sure!" Susie beams, wiping a damp curl of hair out of her eyes. "The setting is perfect, and this house has so much potential." She gathers a great heap of wallpaper and piles it into a black garbage bag. I look around. There are three more bags over by the door, and industrial cleaning containers scattered across the floor.

"Have you thought about the environmental impact of all this construction?" I ask, taking a break from the stripper. "Because there's always a risk you could disrupt the wildlife with all the noise, and—" I stop, struck by a sudden genius idea. "Ooh! You could make the whole place eco-friendly! With solar panels, and composting in the yard, and only earth-friendly, salvaged material." I look over, eager. "I read about these new homes out near Long Island that are totally self-sufficient—they only use what energy they get from the sun, and the whole development is built out of—"

"Whoa, Jenna!" Susie stops me, laughing.

"Sorry." I pause sheepishly. "I can get carried away. But what do you think of the idea?" I look at her expectantly. "It could be a real selling point for the place. Eco-tourism is supposed to be getting really big—people going out to stay in rain-forest huts and stuff. You could be the Canadian version!"

"I think we've got enough on our hands just getting this place habitable in time." Susie goes back to work.

"But it could be a real draw. I mean, that Blue Ridge place is selling luxury, so this would be a whole different angle." I can already think of half a dozen ways to make the B and B an eco-paradise. It's just what Olivia was talking about: my perfect summer project!

"Jenna . . ."

"And it wouldn't even be much work! I mean, much extra. You're in such early stages here, you could easily switch to new plans." I beam happily. Helping out would be the perfect way to repay Susie for having me stay, plus it would totally make up for the carbon damage of my flight and all this driving.

But Susie doesn't seem so enthusiastic. "It's a nice idea, sweetie." She gives me an indulgent smile, the same one my parents use when I come home from yet another protest. "But it's really not possible right now."

"Why not?" I don't wait for a reply. "I know it messes up your schedule, but it'll all be worth it later. And—"

"Jenna." She stops me again, her smile slipping. "I appreciate your . . . enthusiasm. But making things eco-friendly isn't a priority, I'm afraid. I know how much all this means to you," she adds. "But honestly, we'll be lucky to finish on budget as it is."

"That's the great thing about setting up as self-sufficient!" I argue. "You save tons in heating and electricity costs down the line."

"Jenna." Susie says my name again, but this time there's an irritated edge to her voice that stops me short. "I don't think you understand. I'm losing sleep over the mortgage and construction costs right now. We barely have hot water, the roof still leaks, and I can't start advertising for guests because we don't have a single finished room!" She looks at me, clearly exasperated. "Spending a fortune on solar panels or whatever is the last thing I need!"

There's silence. I feel the fierce flush of blood rushing to my cheeks.

"Sorry," I answer in a small voice. "I . . . I didn't think."

"I know, sweetie." Susie manages a tired smile. "You're just trying to help. I appreciate that." She starts pulling away at the wallpaper again, and I go back to my task, my skin still tingling with embarrassment.

I've never been one of the rich kids in school, flashing around designer clothes and new iPhones, but suddenly I feel like the worst kind of princess. Going on about expensive plans when they're already in debt! I scrape harder at the walls, trying to put all my discomfort into the work, but all I can hear is my own voice babbling away with those expensive ideas.

"Want some lemonade?" Susie asks after a moment, her voice bright. She's humming along to the radio again, as if the whole scene is forgotten.

"I'll go!" I duck back through to the kitchen, glad of an excuse to get away. As I gather ice and glasses and pour Susie's homemade lemonade, I feel a tremor of unease. I never thought twice about the cost of my organic food and fair-trade herbal teas back at home. Whatever the price, I figured it was worth it to be environmentally friendly. But that was in New Jersey, surrounded by BMWs, McMansions, and sweet sixteen blowouts. Here in Stillwater, I wonder if all my talk of sustainable eco-friendliness is making me sound like a good Green Teen activist — or just a spoiled brat.

CHAPTER TEN

Even though Susie doesn't say another word about our conversation, I find myself trying extra-hard to be sensitive and helpful over the next few days: pitching in with chores and trying not to say another word about Green Teen projects. Even when I see Fiona tossing empty soda cans in with the regular trash, I just bite my lip—and sneak back later to pick them out and put them in a separate recycling bag. Not that it helps melt her cold, cold heart. Nope, eco-speak or no eco-speak, Fiona is as icy with me as when I first arrived.

"Hey, Fi, do you want—?" I come to a stop on the front porch. She's curled up with a book as usual, wearing an oversize hoodie and a scowl, but Ethan and Grady are there too, loitering in the shade. "Hi, guys! I didn't know you were here." I pause, feeling awkward. "Umm, I was just going to break out the Ben & Jerry's? You want some?"

"No, thanks." Ethan gives me a vaguely friendly grin, his sunglasses pushed up on the top of his head. Grady ignores me, slouched in one of the wicker rocking chairs. Like his brother, he's wearing cut-off jeans and a T-shirt, with one of his baseball hats pulled low.

"Well . . . cool." I linger in the doorway, painfully aware of my sweaty tank top and the baggy shorts I borrowed from Susie to paint in. "So what's up?"

"Uh, we were actually trying to get Fiona to help out with something." Again, it's Ethan who speaks. He leans against the porch rail and shoots Fiona a hopeful look. She snorts.

"And I'm trying to get them to leave me alone."

Ethan must be used to her sunny disposition, because he just rolls his eyes good-naturedly. "I kind of got the idea the other day, after we were talking," he explains to me while Grady squishes ants with the toe of his sneaker. "All that stuff about outdoor adventures, and Stillwater being the muddy side to nature, you know? I figured there are people out there who are into that kind of thing; we just have to get them into town." Ethan's expression is enthusiastic. "So we're going to make a website about Stillwater. Not the boring stuff, like the town council or whatever, but all the different activities you can do around here. We could take pictures, and shoot video . . ."

"That's a great idea!" I exclaim.

He shoots Grady and Fiona a satisfied look. "Glad *someone* thinks so."

"Whatever." Fiona flips another page, looking up briefly to frown at him. "Why are you even asking me to help?"

"Because we could have a section for the B and B too. I mean, like advertising for guests, helping them plan their trip."

"And?" She's unimpressed.

Ethan sighs. "And, I figured you'd want in. Don't you want to help out your dad?"

Apparently not. Fiona glares at him. "None of this was his idea—it was all Susie's. So what if it fails? Maybe then she'd go back to wherever she came from." She brightens at the thought.

"They're married." I speak up, unable to keep the disbelief from my voice.

"Yes. And nearly fifty percent of all marriages end in divorce." She sounds pleased. "So the odds are pretty much even they won't last."

"C'mon, Fi." Grady finally pitches in, bored with killing innocent bugs. He shifts restlessly, drumming his hands on his knees as if he can't wait to be moving again. "We've got the kayaks all set to go, and Susie's lending the video camera."

"You'd just have to paddle around and look like you're having fun." Ethan takes up the case. "OK, so maybe not even fun," he corrects himself. "I could edit around that. But I need someone to be the face of it—to do all the activities and show how great it is around here."

"And be part of false advertising? No thanks." Fiona pauses, glancing up with a sly smile. "Why doesn't *she* do it?"

The boys look over.

"Uh, that's OK," Ethan says quickly. "We can manage by ourselves; it's no problem."

"But I could help." My voice comes out plaintive. "I mean, if you need someone." I backtrack, forcing a casual shrug. "It could be fun."

"I don't know. . . ." Ethan looks at me, his blue eyes dubious. "You ever kayaked before?"

"Well, no," I admit. "But I'm a fast learner!"

Not convinced, he turns to his brother for input. Grady puts his hands up and smirks. "Dude, this is your thing. Just tell me where to be and when." He gets up and begins to saunter down the front steps. Ethan wavers.

"I guess . . ."

"It could be a good angle," I add, trying to convince him. The prospect of freezing water doesn't exactly fill me with joy, but I've been rattling around in this house for days now with no one but Fiona for teenage company. "You know, the newcomer, testing out everything. And I've taken some website design classes, so I could even help out with that side of it too, and—" I stop myself before I go too far.

Olivia is right: I love a project. Whenever the Green Teens come up with a plan, I usually wind up running the whole thing. I can see right away it would be easy for me to jump in here and take over, but after what happened with Susie and the eco-idea . . . I keep my lips shut and remind myself to keep to the backseat.

"Why not?" Ethan finally relaxes. He shrugs, as if to say, What the hell? "I, uh, guess that would be cool."

"Awesome!" I beam. "When do you want me?"

Which is how, two hours later, I wind up on the rocky banks of a river in the mountains above town. Strapping myself into a bright orange life vest and helmet, I survey the rushing, ice-cold water with no small amount of trepidation. "Are you sure about this?"

"One hundred percent." Ethan gives me a supportive grin, waving the video camera. We cocooned it in a bunch of plastic bags to make it splash-resistant, and I just pray that it's enough. "Now could you look less, you know, terrified? This is supposed to make people want to come out here, not be some public safety warning."

I plaster a smile over my nerves, approaching the shallows and the small kayak that's supposed to deliver me safely downstream. Trees overhang the banks on each side, shading us with green and cool, but out in the middle of the river, the sun reflects brightly on the clear water.

Ethan carefully clambers into a double vessel behind Grady and settles in with the camera. Reeve is already way out ahead in his own small kayak, grinning at my clumsy reluctance, so I say a silent prayer and climb in, using the double-ended paddle to push myself off the riverbed and into open water.

"Why don't you guys get life jackets?" I call over.

They're sitting there in regular clothing while I'm buried under a scratchy inflatable vest that's already making me way too hot.

Grady snorts. "Only total beginners need them." He starts to paddle with the current, and left alone, I have no choice but to follow—one tentative stroke at a time.

After fumbling around for a few moments, I actually manage to point the boat in the right direction, but that's where my natural aptitude ends. It feels completely weird to have my feet trapped together in front of me, and as I plunge the paddle uselessly in the water, I find myself lurching dangerously from side to side.

Oh, God.

"What was that?" Ethan calls back. He's pointing the camera at me, and I realize that my pitiful performance is getting captured on film.

"Nothing!" I try to smile brightly as I splash in a slow circle. This may be an epic fail, but I still need to look as if I'm having fun.

"Try and feel the balance," Ethan calls helpfully. "Maybe only paddle one stroke on each side."

People do this voluntarily? For *fun*?

I try again, this time keeping my body rigid and using the paddle as balance: making one stroke on my left side, then quickly switching over before I lean too far. To my surprise, it seems to work—better than before, anyway. I get the kayak facing downriver and actually manage to move forward with the current. My mortal fear of tipping over, however, doesn't seem to ease.

Within a minute or two, I catch up with Ethan and Grady.

"See? Not so bad," Ethan says from behind the camera. I keep my eyes fixed in front of me. The water is still and calm for now, but every tip and roll of the kayak sends a new panic right through me. "Relax!" he calls, laughing.

"Seriously," Grady agrees, stretching lazily as if he's sitting on a couch. "This is nothing."

Nothing to them, maybe, but I've been raised with chlorinated pools and bobbing lane dividers, not a surging flow of Rocky Mountain water. Still, this is for Susie. I gather my courage and follow them around the first bend.

By the time we break for a rest about an hour downstream, my arms are aching and I've got serious pins and needles in my calves, but at least I've yet to flip over into the icy water.

"Try keeping your knees elevated," Reeve suggests, watching me jump up and down on the shore. "I usually put a rolled-up sweatshirt under my legs."

"Oh, thanks." I'm surprised by the friendly tone. His attitude today has seemed pretty chilly, but maybe I'm reading him wrong. "Want a cookie?" I offer him the bag I stashed along with juice and an apple. He takes one and puts it in his mouth whole, then turns away from me, stripping off his T-shirt.

I try not to stare.

It's not that I haven't had exposure to naked teen-boy torsos. My (only) ex, Mike, was part of the whole Christian youth scene, but that just meant our pants stayed on.

For three months. But watching Reeve gulp down water like something out of a photo shoot, I realize that there's a big difference between Mike's pale, kind of skinny, naked chest, and Reeve's body, which is tanned and taut, with compact sinewy muscles and shoulder blades that ripple as he moves . . .

I eat another cookie.

"Want to see what I've got so far?" Ethan collapses beside me, sprawling out in the sun.

"Absolutely!" I say, too loud, happy for any kind of distraction. Ethan shows me the small viewfinder screen and lets the footage run.

"Oh, this stuff is great!" There are beautiful shots of the scenery: water lapping gently against the shore, birds flying overhead, even some fish darting around in the shallows. And then there's me. "Noooo," I moan quietly. I look like a giant orange safety hazard, bundled up in all my protective gear. And as for that grimace of fear . . .

"It's not so bad," Ethan insists with a lazy grin. "We can cut all the flailing, and the splashing. There are moments where you actually look like you're having a good time. See, here"—for a brief second, I smile on-screen— "and here."

"It's a start," I agree reluctantly. "And all the nature stuff is exactly what will sell this place. Maybe soon, we can actually get some tourists in town!"

When we get on the water again, I'm happy to put the flailing, inept version of myself behind me. Instead, I'm paddling like a pro now, gliding effortlessly along the river as I enjoy the warm sunshine. Without all that panic clouding my mind, I can see that this is actually kind of relaxing, nothing but the breeze, calm water, and the beautiful—

Suddenly, the water isn't quite so calm. It's getting choppier, the current speeding me downstream. "Umm, guys—what's happening?" I try back-paddling, but I can't slow down.

Reeve turns back with a devious grin. "Now we get to the fun part!"

Fun? I gulp, swerving around a rock in my path. The relaxing trip has suddenly turned into a white-knuckle ride. My whole body tenses up, and I squint through the splashes, trying to follow the boys' path between rocks and shallow sections.

"Can we"—I feel the kayak scrape against something as I hurtle faster down the river—"maybe slow down just a—?"

"See you on the other side!" Reeve calls, and then disappears around a bend. Literally disappears: when I make it after him, he's gone, and there's only a mass of foam and choppy water where he once—

"Agggghhhhhhhhhhhhhhhhhhh!"

The river drops away and suddenly I'm falling, nothing but air and emptiness beneath me for what seems like an eternity until I hit, a slap against the water that jolts right through me. Water drenches my face and I'm fighting for my balance, but there's no time to steady myself—even to breathe—before the kayak is caught in the current and plunges on through the waves. To the next fall.

Oh, God.

My whimper is lost in the sound of pounding water as I shoot off another ledge and plummet again. It can't be far, no more than four feet or so, but those milliseconds I spend in the air seem to last forever. Then I'm crashing to the river again, choking on a faceful of water and clinging to my paddle for dear life. I hear a whoop of glee as Ethan and Grady land behind me.

These people are insane.

We hurtle through two more drops before the river evens out again, and by then, I'm soaked through and at serious risk of a nervous breakdown. The minute we're all on a calm stretch of water, I catch up to Reeve.

"Fun, right?" His blue eyes are flashing with excitement.

"Fun?" I splutter through a mouthful of river water. "What the hell was that? You could have warned me!"

"Come on, it's cool." He expertly swoops between two dangerous-looking outcroppings of rock. I say a quick prayer and lurch after him. "And if you want some warning, then fine—we've got another three stretches coming up."

I can't believe this guy.

"No." The first time I say it, it's too quiet for even me to hear, so I yell it again, louder over the sound of the falls ahead. "No!"

There's no sign anyone's even heard me: both other kayaks plunge ahead around the bend, leaving me frantically back-paddling alone in the middle of the river. Three more falls? I don't want to go even another stroke in this tiny plastic hell-vessel, let alone another few miles. But my feeble swipes are nothing compared to the current. As soon as I tire, it sweeps me on again, toward the inevitable rapids.

I have absolutely no control over what's happening. There's nothing left for me to do but take a breath, close my eyes, and brace myself for the worst.

CHAPTER ELEVEN

"Show me that part again, when she flips over!"

"Wait, wait—here it is! And then . . . smash! Man, that beaver dam didn't stand a chance."

Grady still hasn't stopped laughing by the time we arrive back in Stillwater. The boys have merrily passed that camcorder around for the last half-hour, snorting with amusement as they replay my crash. What started as gentle teasing has worn down my patience until I can't wait to get away from them.

"I get it: I'm hilarious," I finally pipe up from the back. "Can you give it a rest now?"

Reeve ignores me. "Fast-forward to when she trips on that rock again. Yup, right there!" I hear the sound of my startled cry as I catch my foot and tumble back into the river with a huge splash.

I sink deeper into the wet upholstery, gazing miserably out the window as we turn toward Susic's. Bad enough to capsize like that, but I took out a protected habitat in the process, crashing through the web of sticks and branches like it was a barrier at the edge of a racetrack. And they've got it all on film.

"Watch your step," Ethan teases as we pull up by the yard. "Don't want you tripping again."

I glare at him and slip down from the truck. My hair is plastered wet against my head, and I'm soaked through all the way to my underwear. I just want a hot shower and some dry clothes. Oh, yes, and my dignity back. "Can I have the camera now?"

"I don't know. . . ." Reeve dangles it out the open window, just out of reach. I try to take it, but he pulls it back into the truck, grinning playfully the whole time.

"You wanted me to edit the film!" I protest, reaching for it again. "What are we, like, in fifth grade?"

"What's the magic word?" Ethan calls over. His grin is friendly, but my patience snaps.

"Now!" I finally grab the damn camera and wrench it out of Reeve's hands. I only said yes to this doomed outing to try and make friends with them, but they've been so busy ripping into me, they've barely paused for breath!

"She's stressed," Reeve says to the others as if I'm not even here.

Grady nods. "Probably just mad she messed up her hair. It is pretty messed up."

"Not as bad as that poor beaver's dam, though."

"Mmmmhhhn!" I stifle a sound of frustration and

start toward the house, my shoes squelching with every step. They keep laughing.

After that splashing failure, I don't hear from the guys again, so I decide to take a break from making friends with the Stillwater teens. Instead, I become Susie's demolition apprentice, write fifteen more letters to my congressmen and women, and rack up significant cell-phone charges texting Olivia — now settling into her collective in upstate New York. For one whole week, I manage to live the kind of helpful, constructive, creative, and productive summer routine that would have most parents flipping cartwheels and cheering with joy.

By the end of it, I'm lonely as hell.

"So which is it today, Jenna? You want the big hammer for the wall or the small one for the frames?" Susie greets me in the morning in her paint-splattered overalls, brandishing our tools of destruction.

"The small one," I decide, tying my hair back in one of her printed scarves. "I think I pulled something swinging at the cinder block yesterday."

"It's all in the shoulder action," she agrees. The toaster pops, we each take a Pop-Tart, wrap it in a paper towel, and face today's task like the well-oiled construction machine that we are.

"You guys are pathetic," Fiona informs us, slouching through the kitchen. She grabs a box of cereal and then finds a milk carton in the fridge, not even pausing before she takes a swig.

"Umm, germs!" I protest.

She rolls her eyes. "Susie can buy more." Breakfast in hand (and bitchy comment of the day dispensed) she retreats back to bed.

Susie smashes through the first chunk of wall. I jump back.

"Well, on the plus side, she did refer to you by name, rather than just 'she' or 'her.'" I look to see if Susie is going to show any frustration at all. Other than tearing the house apart, I mean.

Nope. She just sets her mouth in an even smile, as if her stepdaughter isn't the most aggravating child since Veruca Salt. "Why don't you add milk to that grocery list, before I forget?" She punctuates her suggestion with another loud crash.

"Okaay." I do as I'm told. Far from me to argue with a woman armed with a sledgehammer, even if I do think all that pent-up rage might be better expressed by, you know, actually *expressing* it.

"That reminds me—I was thinking you and Fiona could take the truck down to the city this weekend, maybe go shopping together?" Susie actually looks enthusiastic. "It's a two-hour drive each way, but you could make a day of it and catch a movie, pick up some decorating things. It could be fun."

Fun? With Fiona?

I pause, thinking of four hours in a confined space with her. "Maybe," I say, politely. "Sure. If she wants to."

"Great. You know, you've spent so much time helping me out, you haven't had much chance to hang out with her." Susie looks concerned, as if this is actually a bad thing. "If you girls want to go swimming, or get an ice cream or something, go right ahead. Don't worry about all this mess."

I look over carefully to check if she's joking, but no, there's nothing but a concerned mom-type expression on her face.

"I . . . don't think that's a problem," I say slowly. "We see each other plenty. I mean, we are sharing a room."

If by "sharing" you mean "begrudgingly allowing me a tiny corner and a single drawer."

"Sure, but you need some girl time!" Susie still looks sincere, but she is wielding that sledgehammer with a lot of enthusiasm. "To talk, bond, relax!"

Crash. Another section of wall falls away.

"Is . . . is everything OK?" I ask hesitantly, before a thunder of footsteps heralds Fiona's delightful return.

"What the hell are these?" she yells, waving some catalogs around.

Susie lowers the hammer. "They're for your room." She smiles—with what must be superhuman strength. "Since we're redecorating the whole house, I thought it would be nice for you to pick out some things."

I look back at Fiona. Surely she can't find a way to make that generous offer into a tantrum.

Oh, how little I know.

"You don't get to say how I have my room!" Fiona yells, furious. "It's my room. Mine!"

I carefully withdraw behind a counter.

"And what's so wrong with the way I have it right now, huh? Just because it's not stupid and bland and chintzy like how you want the rest of this house!" She hurls the magazines down. I catch a glimpse of the covers: Crate & Barrel, IKEA, Anthropologie? Man, I should be so lucky as to have a vintage-inspired quilt forced on me.

"This isn't just your house!" Fiona sure has a set of lungs on her. "It's mine, too, and I don't want you touching any of my stuff!" Finally, she turns and storms out.

Susie looks forlorn.

"I think it's a great offer," I say, moving closer to comfort her, but she just looks at me with a big fake grin.

"Hey, I just remembered . . . I need to do some stuff in the yard! You've got plenty of other things to do, right?"

I nod. "Are you sure you don't want . . . ?"

"No! I'm fine!" She swallows back what I'm pretty sure are tears. "See you later!"

I have no choice but to let her hurry into the backyard and disappear behind the old workshop. If she were a friend my own age, I wouldn't wait a moment before sitting her down and forcing her to talk about what's wrong, but she's not. I forget it sometimes, when she acts like we're just pals, but she's a grown-up, and right now, the twenty-odd years between us are like a gaping chasm. With a sigh, I exchange my hammer for a bag and my binder, and change my ugly work shoes for some sneakers.

After all, we need more milk.

I'm wandering Main Street with a raspberry Popsicle, enjoying the gorgeous mountain panorama and clear blue sky when I hear a faint call. Adam is over by the gas station, his arms full of boxes, and he's not alone. Reeve and

Grady are chatting with him, slouching in their summer uniform of cut-offs and Ts. I quickly cross the street.

"Hi!" I arrive with a smile. It's been days since my little kayaking mishap, so hopefully the guys will have forgotten—

"Demolition girl, hey." Grady smirks at me, idly spinning his cap on one finger.

No such luck.

"Hey, yourself," I answer casually, as if their constant teasing isn't already getting old. Adam is a few paces away, talking on his cell, so I'm left to face them alone. "So . . . what's up?"

"Nothing much." Reeve shrugs. He shades his eyes with one hand against the sun and gives me a lazy smile, but his eyes linger so long that I have to wipe my face to check for Popsicle stains. Nope, all clear.

"How'd that video turn out?" Grady finally asks. "*Extreme* enough for you?"

"It looked great," I reply, determined to stay upbeat.

"Cool." He smirks in that dismissive way of his. There's a long silence. My smile starts to slip.

"So, when's the next project?" Adam finally returns, looking back and forth between us. "Another adventure for the website? You know, that could turn out to be a really great advertising tool."

Grady doesn't seem to care. He shrugs. "I don't know; that's Ethan's thing. Maybe this weekend?"

"That sounds like fun." Adam is oblivious to the weird tension. He smiles broadly at us. "A good way for you to get out and see the mountains, right, Jenna?"

"Yup. Just let me know what you're planning!" I say brightly. "I'm up for whatever."

They exchange a look.

"Sure," Reeve agrees slowly. "Maybe."

"Don't call us, we'll call you," Grady quips. It seems good-natured, so I force a laugh.

I decide not to linger. "I, umm, have to get some errands done."

"See you back at the house." Adam gives me a reassuring smile. Reeve nods a farewell, but that's all: the boys just turn back to themselves and keep talking.

I walk away quickly, my flip-flops slapping against the asphalt.

I know it's only because I'm new in town and that these things take time, but suddenly, I'm just so tired of trying. Trying to be friendly, trying to be fun—I have to be constantly on my guard, laughing off their stupid jokes and acting like I don't care.

But I do.

I duck into the nearest store, blinking at the dim light. I'm in the map center, I realize quickly. The main room is set up with a couple of tables in the middle; maps and tourist posters pinned to the walls, yellowed and fading. More maps are curled in boxes on the floor, and there are stacks of big books on mountain terrain and forestry boundaries. I circle the dusty table, wondering when it'll be safe to go outside again. There's only so long I can hide out in a room full of old papers, but then I see an entrance to a second, back room.

Jackpot.

Shelves of dusty paperback books cover every wall, from old sci-fi to crime to my personal escapist favorite, bodice-ripper romance novels. Since I arrived, I've had nothing but Fiona's dense fantasy novels to browse (filled with characters named things like Faa and Gdun on a grand quest to protect the city Liinck from the evil Magushun tribe), so with a satisfied sigh, I pluck an armful of possibilities from the sagging shelves and settle in the corner chair to decide which feisty-yet-historically-accurate heroine is going to transport me away from my worries.

"Were you looking for anything in particular?"

The voice startles me. I shoot up in my seat, knocking into a stack of books balanced on a shelf beside me. I make a grab for them, but the pile tumbles to the floor.

"Crap! I'm sorry."

"Don't worry." The owner of the voice waves away my concern. A sturdy woman in her fifties or sixties, she has long gray hair in a thick braid and is wearing a white shirt, khaki pants, and a pair of worn hiking boots. "I have too many of them anyway; they just sit around gathering dust."

I scrabble on the floor to retrieve the books. They seem to be old nature manuals: how to navigate cross-country with nothing but a needle and a magnet, that kind of thing.

"You're Susie's kid, eh?" She stares at me with sharp blue eyes. "Heard all about you."

"Her goddaughter," I explain, unnerved. The woman's

accent is thicker, more Canadian than any I've heard so far. With the boys and Fiona, you would just figure them for Americans, but there's no mistaking this voice—especially with that *eh*. "I'm just, ummm, staying for the summer."

"Hmm . . ." The woman narrows her eyes at me thoughtfully. I shift, uncomfortable, and reach for my stash of romance novels.

"I just wanted to take these . . ."

She nods and strides back through to the main room. I follow, piling the books on the front desk while I root around in my pockets for change.

"*A Breathless Seduction, Her Wild Ways* . . ." The woman reads out the titles as she notes them down, her lips curling with amusement. I feel a twinge of embarrassment, especially when the covers—full of heaving bosoms and bare-chested men—are laid out carefully on the desk. "And *The Modern Mountain Man's Survival Guide.*" She adds a battered green hardback.

"Oh, no—that must have gotten mixed in by mistake." There are no heaving bosoms on this cover, just a torn dust jacket with a black-and-white photo of a rugged young man looking out over a valley, a dead animal of some kind slung over his shoulder.

The woman smiles at me for the first time. "Ah, take it. You look like you could use some pointers."

I open my mouth to protest, but close it, wordless. So I'm not ready to hike cross-country or skin a live rabbit, but those aren't exactly on my agenda this summer.

"Thanks," I say instead, counting out the grand total of three dollars in foreign coins and taking my books. "I'll, umm, see you around."

"I'm sure you will." She gives me another grin, this time with a hint of mischief. "And tell me when you're done with those kids' stories—I've got the real stuff in a box upstairs!"

My mouth drops open again, this time in shock. Blushing furiously, I clutch the books and hurry out of the store. The bell clatters loudly behind me as I emerge back on the street.

The real stuff . . . ?

Nope—not even going to go there!

CHAPTER TWELVE

"So there's really nothing happening with all those hot boys?" Olivia asks, disappointed, after finally exhausting her news about camp, Cash, and conservationism. It sounds like she's found utopia over at that retreat of hers: they're up early every morning for classes and nature walks, and she hasn't even complained about kitchen duty yet.

"Nope." I switch my cell phone to my other ear and stretch out my arm. Dedicated gossiping takes its toll on a girl's muscles. "I haven't seen them in a couple of days. They're probably avoiding me. . . ."

"Ugh, that's so lame."

"Mmm-hmmm." I reach for my bag of jelly beans. It's corny, I know, but with our old ritual, I can almost forget there's a whole continent between us.

"Still, at least you've got nature," she offers. "I can totally imagine you taking long walks and reading out by that lake. I bet you're in heaven!"

"Right," I agree slowly. The truth is, I haven't ventured into the forest since my first night in town, but it sounds pretty pathetic to admit it.

"I love the grounds here." She sighs happily. "The staff cabins are pretty basic, but we're right by the woods, and there's even this river that runs through the edge of the property."

"Lots of dark corners to sneak off to, huh?"

She giggles in confirmation. "It almost makes up for the chemical toilets. We don't even get running water between ten and five."

"Eww."

"I know!"

My talk with Olivia makes one thing clear: seventeen is far too old to be scared of going into the woods. So, armed with my trusty Converse sneakers and a beach bag packed with water, snacks, and all kinds of sunbathing essentials, I brace myself and set off toward the lake. Alone.

I shouldn't have waited so long. It's amazing how different it is in broad daylight. Last time, the trees loomed dark and ominous above me, but now they're green and lush, with sunshine falling through the branches and dappling the ground. Instead of stumbling after a thin flashlight beam, I can amble along what turns out to be a clear pathway, which winds gently through the undergrowth before emerging at that gorgeous clearing.

I let out a contented sigh as I dump my bag down on a patch of grass, then quickly strip down to my bikini. The lake sparkles in the midday sun, and there's nothing but the faint sound of birdsong and the gentle lap of water to be heard. Now this is perfection!

After a brisk—but invigorating—swim, I collapse on my scratchy plaid blanket. I still can't get over how beautiful the scene is: a smattering of fluffy clouds in the sky and hot sun on my bare skin. Dropping one arm over my eyes, I lie back and finally relax. The stress of packing and travel and trying to make nice with the Stillwater kids all drifts away, until—

"Oh. Hi." The voice comes from behind me. I sit up, yawning, to find Reeve a few feet away. I can't help but notice he's already shirtless, wearing cargo shorts with a towel slung over his shoulder.

"Hi," I say cautiously. Right away, I'm aware of how little I'm wearing as well. I finally filled out this year, getting fleshy in places that before were only bones and skin, and I'm still not used to it. I reach for my tank top.

"Don't mind me," I add once I don't feel so naked. "The water's great."

He nods, dropping his towel on the ground beside me. Then he strips off the shorts, revealing some black-patterned board shorts underneath, and heads for the water without another word.

There goes my relaxing afternoon.

He swims for a while, making it all the way over to the small island in the middle of the lake, while I shift around, suddenly restless. If I leave now, it'll be obvious it's because of him, but I can't doze back to sleep either. Finally, I give up trying to sunbathe and reach for my notebook instead.

I'm halfway through a list of Green Teen plans for the new school year when I hear Reeve come out of the water. I ignore him, forcing myself to keep my eyes down, even when he walks back over and takes his towel. I'm not usually so self-conscious, but these Stillwater boys make me feel off-balance, like I don't know what they're thinking.

"What are you working on?" Reeve stands over me, dripping on my pages.

"Just some lists." I close my notebook firmly. "Stuff to do back home."

I figure he'll leave now that he's done with his swim, but instead, he flops down on the ground a few feet away from me, facing the water. I study him surreptitiously from under my sunglasses. His hair is gleaming black in the sun, wet through, and I notice the shadow of a birthmark on the back of one shoulder, like a smudged map.

There's a long silence.

"How did your climbing trip go?" I ask eventually, deciding to be friendly. He looks over, puzzled. "With Ethan? You were talking about bouldering? Last week."

"Right, that." He nods slowly. "It was cool."

More silence.

I roll over onto my stomach and begin to play with the pebbles scattered on the thin grass. I'm beginning to notice the differences between the guys now. Grady is abrupt and always restless: he would have left by now or still be out in the water. Reeve is sitting almost perfectly still, but instead of the relaxed vibe Ethan always gives off—like he could care less about anything going on—Reeve seems like he's holding back all this energy.

I don't know what he's waiting for. Maybe he's just hanging around to be polite, like me, but the silence drags on even longer this time, until I'm tempted to run back into the freezing lake to get away from this awkwardness. Instead, I rummage through my bag for a granola bar and find that nature manual I picked up by accident. *The Modern Mountain Man's Survival Guide.*

The pages are old and yellowed in places, with dark rings from someone's coffee mug, but I flick through, curious. It reads like any other manual, with tips for building shelter and tracking animals and other things I hope I'll never have to try, but the author's crotchety style sucks me in. *Jeremiah B. Coombes,* it says on the back cover, under another photo of him—this time, brandishing a hunting knife. I can just imagine what he's like now, old and grumpy, banging on a nearby surface with his cane as he lectures his unfortunate grandkids about the importance of a good hatchet.

I flip the page.

Stay away from a creature's home turf. Whether it's a cave, nest, or plain ol' hole in the ground, that place means everything to an animal, and it'll fight tooth 'n' nail to keep you away. Track it away from the habitat and take the upper hand on unfamiliar ground.

That sounds about right. I remember Fiona's outrage that Susie would even think about redecorating her gloomy pit of a bedroom. Her reaction seemed over the top, but according to Jeremiah here, it was just a primal instinct to protect her habitat. Fiona and the black bear: just a species or so apart.

I read on, amused.

People spend their lives trying to cut a path through the wilderness, and all they get is a sore arm and a blunt blade. The trick is to follow the trail already laid in the woods. Nature ain't ever going to change for you—you've got to make your plans around what you can't control. It's raining, so are you going to stand there cursing the clouds or get on out of the storm?

Get out of the storm, obviously, unless you want to get struck by lightning. I shoot a sidelong glance at Reeve. He's looking more relaxed now, propped up on his elbows, his eyes closed as he tilts his face up to the sun. I wonder what Olivia would say to this situation. I can almost hear her now, urging me to flirt and crack jokes, or whatever it is girls do around cute boys. Then again, she hasn't had the pleasure of being drenched, ditched, and dismissed by the aforementioned cute boys. . . .

A breeze kicks up suddenly, scattering some of my papers from their folder. Reeve reaches them before me.

"'Green Teen target list,'" he reads, holding the page

out. A smile slowly curls on his lips. "Wow, you really are serious about this environment stuff."

"So what?" I snatch it back.

Reeve lifts his eyebrows. "Nothing . . . It's just, you're on vacation." He regards me with amusement, like he's caught me with a stack of textbooks. "It's kind of weird to be working like that when there's no extra credit or anything. Don't you have other stuff to do—fun stuff?"

"Maybe I enjoy this," I reply lightly, refusing to rise to the bait. "Saving the planet seems like a good use of my time, I figure." Reeve studies me for a second, his expression unreadable.

"Is that what you think you're doing?" His tone has changed; it's got that edge to it again. "So what are your plans for Stillwater, huh? Going to swoop in and save us from using plastic bags, or something?"

I push my sunglasses up and look at him, puzzled. "You don't have to make it sound like that. Small things matter, OK? Maybe not on their own, but if people change how they think, and start paying attention—"

He cuts me off with a look. "You really figure you know best, don't you?"

"I'm just trying to do something good in the world," I protest. I'm used to people disagreeing with me, but I wouldn't have expected it from someone like Reeve, who goes hurling himself down rivers every weekend.

"Good?" He repeats the word slowly, his voice tight. "Sure. Because places getting shut down, people losing their jobs—it's all just great if it's helping the *environment*."

"I don't know what—" I blink, but then it dawns on me, what Ethan said in the store. I swallow.

"Is this about the mill?" I ask, hesitant. He shrugs, as if it's no big deal, but I can tell from the flicker of his jaw that I'm onto something. "It closed, right?" I ask, watching him. "What happened?"

"What do you think?" He's back to acting calm again, sitting there plucking grass out of the ground, one blade after another. "Your people got new codes passed, protecting all of this"—he nods out at the valley—"and they shut it down."

"Oh." I'm not sure what to say. I can't believe he'd prefer that this gorgeous landscape be destroyed, but then I think of Main Street, with the boarded-up storefronts and the emptiness around town. "I'm, ummm, sorry."

"For what?" He looks at me, blue eyes almost sad. "It's done. And I'm guessing if it were up to you, you'd make the same call."

I don't answer that.

Reeve gets to his feet, brushing dust off his legs.

"You don't have to go." I look up at him, feeling strangely guilty. "I mean—"

"I've got work to do." He shrugs. "Real work, I mean." He shoots a pointed look at my Green Teen binder, then pulls on his sneakers, slings his towel over his shoulder, and walks away.

When he's disappeared into the forest, I flop down again, unsettled. It's terrible how the mill closing affected everyone in town, but what am I supposed to say: that we should just let logging companies raze the wilderness to the ground? I take a gulp of water from my bottle—now lukewarm—and try to shake off my unease. He's wrong about the Green Teens. What we do matters.

Lying down, I let my arms fall wide onto the grass. It was back in freshman year when I first joined the group; friends from junior high had all scattered or thrown themselves into the sprawling new school with teams and clubs, but I just . . . drifted. I still can't pin it down exactly. It wasn't like I was bullied or excluded on purpose, but I was lost in a way I'd never felt before: unfamiliar faces rushing everywhere, hallways filled with kids who seemed so certain of their place in the world. I hovered on the edge of my old crowd and ate lunch at a table of strangers, alone. Some days, I could go from the school bus to classes to home again, barely even speaking a word to anyone but my teachers.

Even thinking of it now, the loneliness is something I can taste.

I tried to join in, of course. I tried out for field hockey and volunteered to build sets for the theater club, but I never really fit. I always felt like an intruder, laughing along at in-jokes I didn't understand and trailing after the real members like some pathetic puppy. And then I showed up at a Green Teen meeting one week, after I read their leaflet on global warming and student activism. It was a skeleton crew: barely six members sitting amid the debris of one of the art classrooms, and I lingered, unsure, in the doorway. But the leader, Miles, looked so happy to see a new recruit, he just beamed and swept me into the room.

"We're saved!" he declared, depositing me at a table

where another small, nervous-looking girl was painting a banner. "You can be in charge of posters."

That afternoon was the first time I felt like I belonged in that school, painting away with Olivia to the sound of unfamiliar indie music and the older kids' chatter. Only this time, I knew what they were talking about: conservation, clean-up programs, community outreach. I agreed with them; I could make a contribution.

I fit.

And now I'm on my own again. With a sigh, I turn back to Jeremiah B. Coombes and all his dog-eared survival tricks. Who knows? Maybe he can teach me something about handling three suspicious local boys and a resentful goth girl!

A hatchet and a good pair of boots—that's all you really need in the world.

—"Outfitting for Survival,"
The Modern Mountain Man's Survival Guide

CHAPTER THIRTEEN

"You should probably gas up before you hit the highway." Adam circles the beat-up station wagon for a final check. It's early(ish) morning, and I'm getting ready to head out on my first Canadian road trip. "I've put some bottled water in the back in case the radiator overheats again."

"Dad." Fiona sighs, snatching the keys. "I've driven down there before—alone," she adds, shooting me a look that makes it clear she'd rather be solo this time, too.

I don't mind.

After ten days, I'm getting immune to her drama-queen bitching. I don't know if it was the endless glaring or the five hundredth tormented sigh, but I've finally figured out that nothing I do or say will make Fiona like me—so I shouldn't even try. Instead, I've got a new plan.

The more I read through Jeremiah's grumpy advice about huntin', shootin', and fishin', the more I realized that maybe I don't have to be out in the wilderness to put his know-how to good use. If that section about animals and their habitats applies to Fiona just as well as a grizzly bear, then I'm betting the rest of it can be applied just as, umm, imaginatively. So, I'm going to do what Jerry (as I like to think of him) would demand and make sure I'm equipped for action. His version means scary hunting knives, plastic sheeting, and thermal underwear, but I get the idea. It's no use trying to bond with the Stillwater boys over all their adventure activities when I'm trailing along in my flip-flops: I need a serious pair of those clumpy, waterproof hiking boots.

"Here, Jenna, snacks for the road." Susie hands me a Tupperware container of sensible-looking carrot muffins. She's been beaming ear-to-ear ever since I suggested Fiona and I go into the city, and for some reason, I don't think it's because she's happy to get her out of the house. Susie wants us to be BFFs.

"We'll be fine," I reassure her, but she hugs me good-bye as if we're about to embark on an epic voyage cross-country. Fiona is already in the driver's seat, so I check my bag for essentials—iPod jack, earplugs, the wilderness manual—and climb into the car. I barely have time to slam my door and promise to call Susie at every major arrival/departure before Fiona guns the engine, leaving a cloud of dust in our wake.

"We should stop at the gas station, like your dad said," I suggest, shoveling tools and old candy wrappers into the backseat. "Pick up some more snacks. I'm going to need a ton of caffeine for my driving shifts."

"Who said you were driving?"

"What?" I laugh. "Come on, Fiona, it's like two hours each way!"

But evidently Fiona's a seasoned road hog, because she ignores me — driving the winding back road like it's a NASCAR track and pulling up by the gas pumps with a lurch. Never mind splitting driving duties out of fairness and equality; I'm going to need to take the wheel just to avoid whiplash.

"You can fill it up," she offers generously, handing me the credit card. "And get Doritos, the cheesy ones."

"Sure thing." I leap down and head into the air-conditioned building, making sure to pick up her junk food of choice before browsing the sodas. As my new guru says, when you find yourself stranded in a storm, it's best to take shelter and wait it out rather than make things worse by fighting it. Fiona is nothing if not a force of nature.

I've got an armful of Diet Cokes, Red Bulls, and Snapple when I bump into somebody by the register. "Sorry," I say, but since I'm hanging onto the bag of chips with my teeth, it comes out more as a mangled noise.

"Hey, no problem." The person laughs, helping me unload everything onto the counter until I can actually see who it is.

"Oh, hi, Ethan." My greeting comes out more hesitant than happy. I haven't seen him since that kayak disaster, so I brace myself for a crack about my fear of the dark/terrible balance/girly weakness, but he just nods at my haul of junk food.

"Hungry?" His sports sunglasses are propped on the

top of his head, pushing his dark fringe back up into messy spikes, and he's wearing a navy T-shirt with a small rip in the shoulder.

I smile, relieved. He's talking to me! "No, these are just supplies for the road—Fiona and I are driving down to the city."

"Good luck." He casually tosses a bag of chips from one hand to the other. "Last time I caught a ride with her, I managed about twenty minutes of that music, then I got out and walked. It was like, three miles."

I laugh. "I hid all her CDs during breakfast," I confide, "so it'll be my iPod or the radio."

"Nice move!" He pauses, looking around the empty store before turning back to me. "So . . . have you got room for one more?" Ethan's expression becomes hopeful. "I need to pick up some stuff. It's been ages since I made the trip."

"Umm, sure." I blink. "But we're heading out right now . . ."

"Give me two minutes?" I nod slowly. "Cool, I'll be right out." He abandons the chips and takes off, sprinting out of the building and disappearing across the street. I watch him go, wondering why he'd want to come along for—

"You getting those?" The gravelly voice of the old store clerk brings me back; she's already bagging my snacks.

"Oh, sorry." I pay quickly and walk back to the car, where Fiona is (surprise, surprise) waiting with a scowl, scuffing her Doc Martens in the dirt.

"Took you long enough." Today, she seems to be

making a bold new fashion statement, ditching the black and adding a green T-shirt to her usual dark jeans, with a baggy dirt-colored cardigan that looks like something a grandfather would wear. A color-blind grandfather.

"Here, Doritos." I toss her the bag. "And you'll have to wait some more. Ethan is coming, too."

"Great."

"I think so." I ignore her sarcasm. I'm still not sure why Ethan wants to spend hours locked up with us but it's something: a chance for me to try to get to know him away from the other guys.

Plus, he's another vote against Fiona should she manage to find a stray copy of *Misery Anthems, Volume 5* somewhere in the glove compartment. . . .

"I don't know — ever since he went solo, I haven't liked the music so much."

"Come on — it's way better than the Alarm stuff!"

"Yes, but he's such a skeeze — hitting on that girl from *5th Avenue*? I mean, she's fifteen!"

"Lucky guy."

"You would say that!"

"God, would you both just SHUT UP!" Fiona yells, sitting up from the backseat where she's been sprawled, ignoring us, for the last hundred miles. "I don't care about some washed-up rock star and those stupid reality-TV bimbos!"

I shoot Ethan a look. He's trying not to laugh.

"Relax." I glance in the rearview mirror. She's slumped back down, eyes closed in despair. "We're nearly there."

"Thank God."

I flip the radio to another station as the wide expanse of trees and mountains gives way to the strip-mall outskirts of the city. Fiona vetoed my iPod on principle, so we've been stuck with the best of the Canadian airwaves for the whole trip; in other words, country and butt rock. Ethan has been the only one happy, humming along with the manly relationship angst, while I grit my teeth and wonder how many times they can play Nickelback in a single hour.

Answer? Too many.

"What things do you need to get?" I ask him, drumming my fingers on the steering wheel as we begin to hit traffic. "Susie says there are a couple of malls, and then I thought I would wander downtown for a while, but it really depends on what you want." He doesn't answer, so I continue. "Music? Clothes? Books?"

Ethan looks embarrassed. "Uh, to be honest, I don't really need to buy anything."

"You don't?"

He shrugs, draping his arm out the open window. "I just wanted to get out of town for a while. It can get kind of . . . claustrophobic."

"Right, I can imagine," I agree. "Living in such a small town must be something else."

"I like it," he answers quickly, glancing over. "Don't get me wrong—I'm looking forward to college. I'm applying to UBC in Vancouver, and McGill out in Montreal— places with more than a thousand people. But for now, it's kind of nice. I know everyone; we've all grown up together . . ." He gives an awkward smile. "Must sound dumb to you."

"What? Why?"

"Well, you're from a big city."

"Is that what you think: that I'm some fancy city chick?" I laugh. "I've spent my whole life in the suburbs. I mean, sure, I can get into the city for trips and stuff, and my development is a lot bigger than Stillwater, but it's nothing great. Tracts and tracts of identical houses as far as you can see."

"Grass is greener, eh?"

I smile. "Except in this case, the grass really is greener here. And the trees, and rivers—"

"Pull in here to park." Fiona interrupts imperiously. I grit my teeth but follow her instructions, circling the lot and managing a tight display of parking that has Ethan applauding by the time I'm done.

"Thank you, thank you very much." I bow.

"Whatever." Fiona climbs out, slamming the door. "Don't even think about calling me before six." She takes off in the general direction of the mall, almost getting hit by a reversing van; the driver sounds the horn and leans out of his window, yelling at her. She ignores him.

"Wait, Fiona!" I scramble out of the car. "Where are you going? It's not even noon. Where should we meet?"

Turning back, she shrugs. "You think I'm spending another minute with you two? Call me tonight!" And with that, she all but jogs away.

"I guess it's just us then." Ethan joins me, hands bunched in his front pockets and a small nylon messenger bag slung across his body. He looks around, nonchalant at the idea of spending the afternoon together. "What's the plan?"

I regroup, pulling out my scribbled list. It's probably a good thing I won't have Fiona hanging around, making fun of my new task. "Well, there is something you can help me with. . . ."

"You want what?" Ethan says dubiously. Thirty minutes later, we've consumed half our weight in French fries in the yellow Formica food court. Now it's time for work.

"Hiking boots and a backpack," I confirm. "Sturdy shorts, waterproof socks—you get the idea."

We're standing in the middle of a vast outdoor activity store, surrounded on all sides by racks and rails full of functional, expensive clothing. By the looks of the array of labels on display, the collected scientific knowledge of the West has been directed at keeping hikers that little bit drier.

"Sure you don't just want to go to the Gap?" he asks, still faintly disbelieving.

"I need this stuff. My summer gear is more suited to, well, sunbathing," I admit, distracted by the video screen on the far wall—a pair of climbers dangling from a vertical rock face with their bare hands. I feel a lurch of vertigo just looking at them, so I quickly turn back to Ethan. "I want to be able to join in with all the activities you guys do," I explain. "I mean, can you see me out hiking in these?" I point down at my jeans for illustration. They're fitted, with frayed edges that are crying out to get caught on a stray tree root and send me tumbling over a cliff or something.

"OK, then we should probably go with the basics." Ethan seems to be warming to the task. He puts his hands on his hips and looks around like he's an explorer, set to conquer foreign lands. Which is exactly what I need. "Let's start at the feet and work our way up."

CHAPTER FOURTEEN

"Jenna! Phone!"

I drag my head up from my pillow and squint at my cell in disbelief. Seven a.m. People are alive at this hour? Alive, and calling me?

"Jenna!"

"Coming!" I manage to yell back. Fiona makes a groaning noise and pulls her covers up over her head. For once, I know how she feels. We stayed late in Kamloops for a movie and Chinese food, and by the time we got back, I was sleeping like a dead person in the backseat. If it hadn't been for Ethan gently shaking me awake, I'm guessing Fiona would have left me curled up out there all night.

I stumble out of her bedroom, skidding downstairs and only narrowly missing that gaping pit of doom in the hallway.

"Morning, sweetie." Susie hands me the phone with a sparkle in her eye.

"Hmmmhm," I yawn, eyes still half-shut. I don't even wait for a word before putting the phone to my ear. "Mom, there's something called a time difference, you remember that, right?"

"Uh, hi, Jenna."

It's not my mom. Unless she's had a sex change.

"Oh, hey, sorry." I'm paying attention now. "Who is this?"

"It's Ethan." He sounds suspiciously awake. "Is this a bad time, because I could call back later and—"

"No, no, it's fine!" Susie is still beaming at me, so I shoo her away and wander through to the kitchen. But I have to admit, I'm curious. "What's up?"

"Well, me and the guys were just going to head out riding, shooting some stuff for the next video. You want to come along?"

"A ride, like, horseback?"

He laughs. "No, mountain bikes. There are some cool trails up in the hills, and we've got some old spares lying around you could use. But don't worry if you can't make it—I just thought . . ."

"No! I mean, yes, I'd love to come!" I'm in shock: an actual invitation to join in? My tiredness gives way to excitement. "When did you want to meet?"

There's a pause. "Uh, we're actually leaving in ten minutes."

What?

"I'm sorry it's so last-minute," he continues. "I should

have mentioned something yesterday, but I didn't even think of it."

"That's OK," I answer faintly, trying to calculate how much time I'll need to shower, dress, and, you know, eat. "I can do that, no problem."

"You can? That's great. We'll pick you up in a while."

"Uh-huh." I hang up, just in time to hear the only working shower in the house start upstairs. "Fionaaaaaaa!"

I manage to make it out to the front porch ten seconds before the boys arrive. Thanks to my awesome roomie's timing, I haven't had time to shower or brush my teeth, but that's what deodorant and gum are for, right?

"Hey." Ethan bounds up the steps with the kind of enthusiasm it would take me three lattes to achieve. It's still cloudy out, and he's bundled up in a loose gray sweatshirt emblazoned with that sports logo I've seen Grady wear. I asked Adam about it, and he says it's for the Vancouver ice-hockey team. Ice hockey is *big* out here. "All set?"

"Sure!" Despite longing for the snug comfort of bed, I can't wait to get going. "I'm ready for action."

"And you're all outfitted, too." He takes in my clothing.

"Yeah, I was thinking about going for a skirt and halter," I joke. "But since I had these lying around . . ." I'm wearing my brand-new lightweight trail shoes: a sale bargain, along with the sturdy navy long-cut shorts I picked up.

"Cool. There are some great trails we've been exploring, away from the main road and with awesome slopes."

Ethan's voice is relaxed, but I still feel a tremor of nerves as I follow him out to the truck. It's even muddier than last time I saw it, complete with a clutch of mountain bikes strapped precariously in the flatbed, but it's what's inside that's worrying me. Or rather, who.

"Hi." I clamber awkwardly up into the main cab, squeezing against Grady. Ethan climbs in after me, until we're all crammed together on the passenger side while Reeve stretches out in the relative comfort of the driver's seat. I'm jammed between denim and faded T-shirts, so close I can smell the faint citrus smell of body wash and that manly deodorant scent.

I think of my own hasty hygiene routine this morning and wonder if maybe I should have fought harder for the bathroom.

"Hey." Grady grunts from under his baseball cap, and goes back to flipping through the radio dial. Reeve only nods in my general direction before starting the engine again and kicking us into gear. Casual, I get the message.

"Thanks for the invite," I begin, still feeling out of place as we follow the road farther up into the forest. "I've never really tried dirt bikes, but it sounds like fun."

"Yeah, well, this is just the kind of thing I need to get for the website," Ethan replies easily. On my other side, Grady finally lets the station stay on an indie rock song and sits back, his elbow digging into me. His hair is damp from the shower (oh, the shower!) and it drips slowly onto my bare shoulder.

"How's that going?" I try to shift the other way, but

that only presses me tighter against Ethan. "I brought the camera, like you said."

"Thanks. I've set up the basic page," he replies, "and uploaded the kayaking footage." At this, Grady makes a kind of snorting sound, but I try to ignore the memory of being upended into freezing cold water.

"Have you had many hits?" I ask, determined to keep the conversation going.

"Like, five?" He laughs. "But I'm not sending out the address until there's more up."

"True. I should take some photos of the B and B, but right now it would only scare them off!"

Ethan laughs, and I feel the vibrations against my side. "Yeah, what I've seen of the place isn't exactly luxurious."

"Never mind luxurious," I add. "It's still practically a health hazard." We suddenly speed around a bend, and I'm thrown against him.

"Ahem, don't mind us," Grady mutters on my other side, kind of sarcastic.

"Sorry," I apologize quickly, trying to disentangle myself.

"Don't worry—I can take it." Ethan looks amused. Grady makes another snorting sound. I look around, but nobody explains.

"Anyway, I'm really hoping this website project works," I eventually finish, deciding to ignore their in-jokes. Something's going way over my head, but I guess that's just what happens when you're new in town.

• • •

"Come on, give it a try!" Ethan cycles a slow loop around me later in the afternoon. After watching the boys hurl themselves down steep trails with no concern for the risk of breaking their necks and/or vital limbs, I decided to take on official filming duties — from the safety of a solid mound of dirt.

"I'm fine here!" I protest, still filming. Sunlight falls through the tree branches, dappling us with light, and I try to make the scene look as picturesque as possible — despite the mud streaking his face and the fresh bruises on his legs.

"You've got enough footage by now," he argues, speeding up. The tires slip against the dirt as he circles me on the incline, and I start to get dizzy just watching him. "Besides, isn't the whole point to show a newbie doing all this? Unless you get on the bike yourself, it's not the same."

"I don't know." I gulp. "I usually stick to flat terrain."

"Coming through!"

I jump back as Grady and Reeve come racing down the hill. They whoop past us, going at least twenty miles an hour, before disappearing into the thick undergrowth. "How can they even see where they're going?" I gape.

Ethan laughs. "You just hang on and hope for the best."

"I'm beginning to think that's a theme with you guys."

"You can start slowly," he points out. "You do have breaks."

I waver. Despite the sheer insanity, there is a small part of me that does want to try — to experience whatever it is that has the guys yelling with such triumphant abandon.

117

"OK," I say, suddenly brave. I edge down from my hill. "I'll do it."

"Awesome." Ethan is already dismounting. "I'll take that." Before I can back out, he's exchanging the video camera for gloves and kneepads. Fully protected, I walk slowly over to where "my" bike is resting against a tree.

"Brakes, pedals . . ." Ethan points out, joking. I fasten a helmet on and swing one leg over. "Seat height OK?"

I nod, not sure I'd know if it wasn't.

"Then you're all set."

I gather my courage, grip the handlebars, and push off, walking with my tiptoes for as long as possible before finally wobbling along. "Have fun!" he yells after me as—clutching the brakes for dear life—I slowly roll down the first hill.

OK, I tell myself: you can do this.

The ground is muddy, sending splashes of dirt onto my bare legs as I wheel through puddles, but it seems that as long as I keep the brakes on, my speed stays below heart-attack level. Swallowing back my fear, I keep my eyes peeled for obstacles and animals, swerving around the twisting trail like it's a minefield assault course. And to me, it is.

Again, I have to wonder about the Stillwater definition of *fun*.

"You going to let it go anytime soon?" Reeve swoops up the hill toward me, pedaling fast. He circles around, drawing level, and rolls along beside me. I don't answer, slowly clutching and releasing the brakes in a jerky motion to keep control. "The whole point is the speed!"

"I'd rather stay alive," I answer, carefully steering around a small hill just as he bounds right over it.

"I thought you were the fast one," he says cryptically, before skidding past me and around another bend.

I push on, my hands beginning to cramp with all this braking. Clutch, release; clutch, release. Then the ground begins to level out and I realize the major flaw in my "slow but steady" plan: heading down the hill at a snail's pace may have avoided mortal injury, but now I'm facing my first incline, and I don't have any kind of momentum to get me over it. I start to pedal, pushing myself up the slope with sheer thigh-work.

"I know," I tell my legs as they begin to ache in protest. "This isn't fair. I haven't prepared you for this. But I can't quit now—they'll never respect me if I don't finish the trail." And with Reeve and Grady's opinion of me hovering somewhere around zero, the only way to go—literally—is up.

"Oh, Lord, thank you." I reach the top of the hill with relief. The rest of the course stretches out in front of me, nothing but more steep slopes, hills, and bends winding their way across the woodland. If I keep going at this rate, I'll never finish. Or maybe . . .

What the hell.

I say a silent prayer and let go of the brakes, flying down the slope at twice my previous speed. Bouncing over twigs and rocks, I cling for dear life, but it works. The momentum carries me up the next hill and down again, even faster this time.

"Wheeeeeeeeeeeeeeeeeeeeee!" I can't help but cry out

as I hurtle along. It's like being on a roller coaster—only without the safety of a solid carriage and track. I brush past branches, ducking and swerving away from oncoming trees, and all the while, my heart is racing faster than these wheels.

So this is what they do it for—the rush, the adrenaline that's sparking in my veins.

I gasp for breath, flying along another stretch of trail until at last my bike begins to slow. Pulling to a halt on the top of a steep slope, I lift off my helmet and shake out my hair, glad of the cool air on my sweaty neck. An incredible glow is spreading all the way through me. I don't think I've ever felt this way: so brave, and exhilarated, and scared half to death all at the same time.

"Hey," Grady pulls up next to me, sweat marks showing through his red T-shirt and mud streaked across his face. "Can you tell my brother not to hog the camera? I want Reeve to get shots of me doing some jumps, OK?"

"Tell him yourself." I grin, stretching my arms. "You'll probably get back to him sooner."

"Yeah, but he's pissed at me for splashing mud near the precious equipment. And anyway, he'll listen to you."

"He will?" I repeat dubiously. "Why's that?"

Grady gives me a knowing look. "Because you're the one hooking up with him."

With that, he takes off down the hill.

Only a fool goes charging into a pack and expects anything more than a headache and an empty belly. Focus on lone animals instead, and pick them off when they stray from the herd.

—"Hunting Tactics,"
The Modern Mountain Man's Survival Guide

CHAPTER FIFTEEN

I want to kill Ethan. But I don't. Despite all my hurt and confusion, it's clear that blowing up at him would be my final strike. I don't want to wreck the friendly vibe I've finally got going with the guys, so I bite my lip and keep a lid on my anger for the rest of the day. I finish my ride, sit quietly, and even manage to smile at the right moments while he jokes around with Grady and Reeve, acting as if nothing's wrong.

But I still can't believe what he's done.

Even Olivia is no consolation. "Do you even know it's him talking?" she asks immediately. As soon as I get back to the house, I hit my speed dial. "It could just be the other guys jumping to conclusions, teasing him or whatever."

"Nope, it's him." I find an empty, half-finished bedroom upstairs and collapse. I have mud splattered all over my legs and an unfamiliar ache in my arms, but worse still is how hurt I feel. After our trip to the city, I thought we were friends. "They were making comments all day, kind of teasing him about it. I didn't realize at first, but now it makes complete sense. And he was going along with it!"

"Is it really so bad? I mean, maybe he's just got a crush on you. You did say he was cute," Livvy points out. I hear something in her voice.

"You OK?"

"What? Oh, yeah, I'm just kind of tired. We started a total sugar fast yesterday. Cash says it's really good for your system, but I'm crashing hard."

"Is that what you're supposed to do—cut it out entirely?" I frown. Olivia is like the candy queen. I don't think I've ever seen her without some chocolate or a sugary snack in her bag.

"I'll be fine," she promises. "It just shows how addicted I am! Alan—he's one of the group leaders here—he says that we need to pay as much attention to like, our own health, as we do the planet's."

"Umm, cool. And no, this isn't just a playground thing," I add. "I mean, the way Grady said 'hooking up,' he meant *hooking up,* and you don't go around trashing a girl's reputation if you like her. At least not if you ever want her to speak to you again." I remember how cool Ethan has been, the fun we had hanging out yesterday. "It doesn't make sense!"

"You need to talk to him, find out what he's been saying."

"I know." I sigh. "I just figured it would be best if I

cooled down first. Violence is not the answer—isn't that what they're always telling us?"

Talking to Ethan may be my plan, but he seems to have a different idea. I call twice that night, and again the next morning, but I just can't reach him. His mom, on the other hand, sounds delighted to "finally" speak to me.

"I'll let him know you called!" she coos. "I don't know where he's at right now, but I know he'll be sorry to have missed you."

"Umm, thanks," I answer slowly, leaving my cell number. "If he could just call . . ."

"Sure, sweetie. See you soon!"

"Did you and lover boy have a fight?" Fiona appears behind me in the hall, making me jump.

"Don't sneak around like that!" I exclaim, hanging up. "And no. Where did you hear that, anyway?"

"Come on." She smirks. "You guys were all over each other the other day."

"Were not!"

"I nearly barfed with all that flirting in the truck. And then the movie: 'Oh Ethan, let's see the action one,'" she mimics in a high voice. "'No, Jenna, not if you want to see the comedy.' Ugh." She shudders.

"So that's it—I hang out with a boy for what, a few hours, and then everyone acts like we're together?"

She gives me a smug grin. "If you wanted to get away with being a slut, you shouldn't have come to such a small town."

I storm away. It would be one thing if I *had* been

123

flirting—if I'd even had a crush on Ethan for them to pick up on—or if I'd spent more than one lousy afternoon alone with him, but God! At this rate, we'll be married by next week!

"Jenna?" Adam catches me as I barrel out the front door. He's working on the porch railing, and it seems like I never see him without that toolbox by his side. "Everything OK?"

"It will be," I snap, before catching myself. "Sorry, I'm just, kind of stressed." I try to take a few deep breaths. Adam is looking at me with quiet concern.

"Can I help at all?" He puts down the sandpaper, as if he wants to talk.

I shake my head, already backing down the porch steps. "Thanks, but I'm fine. I just need to talk to Ethan, that's all."

"Ethan, eh?" He scratches his beard. "I think he's out by Barlson's Creek."

I stop. "You mean he's not in town?"

He nods. "I ran into him about an hour ago—said he was going to get away and do some fishing. There are shallows about five miles out of town where the boys usually go; I'd say that was your best bet."

I pause. The chance to get Ethan alone is too good to pass up. "Is it easy to find?"

Adam chuckles. "Let me draw you a map."

Armed with scribbled directions, the truck, and a pair of waders, I find Ethan up above town where the river bends away from the road. Curving between boulders and driftwood, the water runs in a broad, shallow flow. I scramble down the banks and call across to where he's standing, knee-deep in the water.

"Hey!"

Ethan looks over and almost drops his fishing line. "Jenna? What are you doing here?"

"Well, I heard you were up here, so I thought I'd come learn something." I make sure to keep my tone even, hiding all traces of hurt and confusion.

"Uh, great." Ethan seems taken aback, but he begins wading toward the shore.

I wait, wondering about my next move. I spent the drive up imagining what it would be like to push his lying ass over into the ice-cold river, but now I'm not so sure. Ethan seems so nice, maybe he has a reason for saying the stuff he did.

Or maybe he's just an idiot.

He's reached dry land now and is busily sorting through his stash of equipment, finding me a spare rod and line. "I've got a folding chair, too, if you want to borrow it." He grins over at me, his face open and good-natured. "I'm guessing your legs hurt like hell after yesterday."

"Oh. Thanks." I study him, thrown. These aren't the actions of a lying scumbag. If I just charge ahead and start accusing him . . .

In an instant, I decide: maybe instead of confronting him head-on, I should play by the rules from my mountain man manual. Jeremiah says nothing about the intricacies of teen mating rituals, but he does have a whole section on understanding your prey. To really get inside an animal's head, you have to spend hours quietly observing it: tracking its routines, habits, behavior—everything.

Realizing that he's waiting for me, I walk over and take the unfamiliar equipment.

"Fly-fishing, huh?" I survey the clear, rushing river. "Where do I start?"

Once Ethan's shown me how to spool my line on the long rod and flick it out into the water, I set up beside him in the middle of the river. To my surprise, my anger soon drifts away. The water is rushing past me in a soothing flow, the sun warms my bare shoulders, and the tranquil calm of the breeze rustles at the overhanging branches. It's like the ultimate Zen paradise. I can definitely see why Ethan is always so laid back.

"What was that?" Ethan looks over, after we've been standing in companiable silence for about twenty minutes.

"Hmmm?"

"You sighed."

"I did? Oh, I was just relaxing. It's so peaceful out here." There's not a single man-made sound anywhere— nothing but water, wind, and occasional birdsong. It's as if we're the only people in the whole valley.

He nods, shifting his weight a little and testing the pull on his line. Like me, he's wearing thick rubber waders that reach halfway up his thighs, but he's stripped off his T-shirt and has nothing but his tackle bag strung across his chest. "I like to get away from it all and just chill up here. There isn't much to get away from in Stillwater, I know," he adds, "but sometimes I need a break. From my brother, especially."

Here's my chance. "What's Grady done?" I glance over, but Ethan just looks uncomfortable.

"Oh, nothing. Just guy stuff."

I decide to probe a little more. "Yeah, he was acting kind of weird yesterday, saying these things . . ." I keep one eye on Ethan.

His head whips toward me. "What kind of things?"

"Crazy things," I say meaningfully.

"Uh, yeah. Don't pay any attention to him," Ethan advises quickly. "Really, he just talks trash."

I break. So much for sly patience. "Trash, huh? You mean like saying we hooked up?"

"What?" Ethan looks as if he wants to bolt, so I flick my fishing rod over in his direction, tangling my hook in his line.

"You heard me—he's saying we were fooling around the other night." I can't help the plaintive note that comes into my voice. "And Reeve was in on it too, so don't even think about denying it. Why would you do that?" My voice rises accusingly. "You know nothing happened. I haven't even been in town two weeks, and already everyone thinks I'm some kind of slut!"

Ethan stands there wordlessly as I wait for the magic explanation that will make this all OK.

"I'm sorry," he finally says, in a quiet voice.

My mouth drops open. "So you did say something!"

"Not exactly!" He begins to edge away toward the

shore, but my cable picks up the slack and pulls taut against his rod. Ethan tries to untangle the lines, avoiding my gaze.

"Why would you do that? I thought we were friends, and then you turn around and—"

"They blew it out of proportion, OK?" He looks flustered. "I didn't mean for it to happen."

"So why didn't you set them straight?" I try to understand. "Just say, 'Hey, guys, nothing happened.'" I tug harder on my line, keeping it tangled in his. "Or how about warning me instead? I was completely ambushed—even Fiona's got the wrong idea. And your mother!"

"My mom?" Ethan tugs back. "What did you say to her?"

"Me? Nothing! But from the way she sounded on the phone, she thinks I'm your girlfriend. She tried to invite me to dinner!"

"Oh, man." Ethan is looking so miserable now, I almost feel sorry for him. Almost.

"You didn't have to pretend like that." I yank at my rod again. "I mean, were you trying to score points with the other guys, or what? It's not like you're some kind of loser who can't get a girl, or gay, or—"

At those last words, Ethan freezes.

I gasp.

"No. Way," I say slowly. He tries to cover and shrug it off, but a small vein is bulging in his forehead and his eyes dart back to me nervously. These would be the instinctive reactions Jerry said to keep a lookout for.

"You're gay?" I exclaim, my mind racing to figure this

out. "But what . . . ?" I make a move toward him, lowering my fishing rod, but the change in tension sends him reeling back, unsteady. "Ethaa—"

My warning cry is no use: he falls backward, still holding the line, which yanks me right after him.

With a splash, we both tumble into the river.

CHAPTER SIXTEEN

"This is getting to be a habit," Ethan says ruefully, shaking water out of his hair. We've managed to haul ourselves to shore. Now we're sitting side-by-side on the riverbank, drip-drying in the afternoon sun.

"You mean spreading rumors about girls to hide the fact you're gay?"

"No, I meant you and rivers—and how you always seem to end up in them." He tries to laugh, but it just comes out awkward and flat.

"Oh." I'm not sure how to react, and it's clear Ethan doesn't either. We both sit, staring at the water and avoiding each other's eyes. I scrunch parts of my tank top up in my hands and watch the trickle of water pool on the ground.

"You can take that off, if you want," he suggests, before adding, "It's not like I'm going to look."

"How do I know this isn't just some devious plan to see me topless?" I finally glance over at him. Despite my joke, Ethan looks truly miserable, his whole face shadowed with tension. I sigh. "I was just kidding."

"Uh-huh."

We sit in silence for a moment.

"So . . ." I say quietly, still watching the river. "Gay?"

"Yup."

"Right." I pause, wondering what to say. The way he answers is so matter-of-fact, it doesn't seem like he needs a big supportive speech about acceptance and being yourself. "So, I'm guessing this means you're not out."

He shakes his head. "No. Nobody knows."

"Even Grady?"

Ethan sighs. "Especially Grady."

"Oh."

There's another silence. I wonder what it must be like for him to hide something this major from his own brother. Suddenly, he grabs my hand, looking at me with wide, pleading eyes. "Please, Jenna, I know I messed up, but you can't tell anyone. I'm sorry about what they said, and—"

"Whoa, it's OK." I cut him off, uncomfortable with the desperation in his tone. "I won't say a thing!" I promise, squeezing his hand. "I swear."

He stares at me a second longer, as if he's not convinced, and then exhales slowly. "OK. I mean, thanks."

Another silence. I slowly let go.

Eventually, I have to ask. "So you did say we hooked up. To cover . . . all of this."

"I didn't say anything, not really." Ethan looks at me, apologetic. "I really am sorry. It's just, Reeve asked about us hanging out, and then he jumped to conclusions. And I let him. I shouldn't have," he adds hastily. "But I thought it was a good idea at the time, you know, to let them just assume . . ."

I flop backward onto the grass, tired out by all these revelations. "So now they think I'm the crazy, slutty city girl." I sigh, resigned.

"I'm sorry," Ethan says again. He lies down next to me, so that we're both staring at the clear sky. "It was a dumb idea."

"Really dumb." My top is still clinging to my skin, cold and damp. I think for a minute and then strip off my tank in one quick movement. "You said you wouldn't stare," I remind him, spreading out the fabric to dry. I cross my arms self-consciously over my worn polka-dot bra.

"Don't even worry."

I wait another minute before asking slowly, "So if you're cool with it, why don't you tell people? I mean, it's not exactly the Dark Ages around here—people seem decent."

He snorts. "Sure, when it comes to regular stuff. But Jenna, it's still a small town, and my parents . . . Let's just say they're big on their 'family values' stuff."

I feel another pang of sympathy. "That must be terrible."

"Not so much."

I sit up, surprised. "What?"

He shrugs, one arm slung over his eyes to keep out the

sun. "It's not a big deal. I'll come out when I move away to college, but for now, I don't mind." He catches my gasp of disbelief. "It's not all drama with this stuff, Jenna. I mean, not for me, anyway."

"But don't you feel like you're not being honest — that you have to hide part of yourself?" I can't believe he's being so nonchalant.

"But I'm not, not really. So I like guys? Big deal. It's not the sum total of my entire identity." He sits forward. "And if I came out here, then it would be. Everything would be different. Maybe I'd think about it if I, you know, wanted to date or whatever. But that hasn't happened yet." He tosses pebbles into the river, one by one.

"And nobody suspects anything?"

"You didn't." He turns and meets my eyes. "Seriously, it's not that big a deal. Sure, there's guy talk, and I play along with that, and sometimes I'll say something about liking some girl in school — someone with a boyfriend, who I couldn't date even if I wanted to — but aside from that . . . it doesn't come up. I just want to keep things normal, you know?"

I nod, dubious. It still doesn't sound right to me, to just shut off a whole side of his identity, but he seems to be content to keep it that way. And I would be too, if it weren't for one major flaw in the plan.

"I don't want to be your girlfriend. No offense," I add.

"None taken." He manages a half grin. "I can straighten it out, I guess." We both stop and smirk at his choice of words. He laughs. "You know what I mean."

"That would be OK? It wouldn't, you know, blow your cover?"

"No, it's cool. I'll just say I realized you weren't right for me."

"Or that I shot you down," I suggest. I'd prefer a version of the non-truth that made me look good, at least.

"Fine," he agrees, grinning. "I fell at your feet, proclaimed my love for you, but you refused."

"That's more like it." I smile, finally relaxing.

Ethan gets to his feet, surveying our pile of tangled equipment. "So, do you want to give it another try? I can't go home empty-handed."

"You mean the fishing? Sure." I put out my hands, and he helps pull me to my feet. "But I'm not catching anything, I promise."

It turns out I'm wrong. Barely ten minutes after we wade back into the river, my line begins to tug.

"Ethan!" I cry, taken by surprise. "What do I do?"

He splashes closer, applauding. "Reel it in, reel it in!"

"I don't want to!" I jiggle my rod, trying to dislodge whatever is caught on the line, but it just tugs harder. "I didn't want to actually catch anything!"

Ethan stares. "What do you mean?"

"I'm a vegetarian!" I explain, still trying my hardest to get rid of my catch. "I don't believe in killing animals."

He pauses. "Technically, a fish isn't—"

"Or fish!"

Ethan looks at me, bemused. "Then why did you—?"

"I left the cork on the hook! I didn't think anything would actually bite."

"Looks like something did." Shaking his head in amusement, Ethan takes the rod from me and begins reeling in the line. Sure enough, the cork is nowhere to be seen, and there's a fish flapping away on the hook: silvery gray scales sparkling in the sun. "It's a big one!" he says, admiring.

"I don't want a big one!" I wail. The fish is suspended over the water, gasping and thrashing around like it's in a huge amount of pain. At least, that's what it looks like to me. I watch it, guilty. "What do we do?"

Ethan looks uneasy. "Umm, this is when I smash its brains in with a rock."

"What?"

"It's too late to save it," he says hurriedly. "The hook's done too much damage. It'll just die in the water."

I let out a whimper. So much for rushing river and relaxing sun: I'm a murderer now. "You're sure we can't just let it go?"

"I'm sorry." He scrunches up his face. "But I'll make it quick!"

"OK," I say at last. "Do it."

I watch as Ethan grabs the fish off the line, wades over to the edge of the water, and presses it down on a boulder, still flapping around. He reaches for a smaller rock and raises it up. I cover my eyes as I hear a faint squelching noise. "Is it done?" I ask.

"Done."

I slowly lower my hands. The fish is lying there, a smear of silver gunk beside it on the rock. It's definitely dead.

"I'm a hypocrite," I murmur sadly. "I spend all this time telling people how killing animals is wrong . . ."

"Technically—"

"I know, it's a fish! But still . . ." I look at the lifeless body and sigh. "What do we do with it now?"

Ethan looks evasive again. "Umm, now we cook it over a nice open fire?"

I glare at him.

"What?" he protests. "I'm hungry; it's dead . . ."

"I've got snacks in the car," I inform him icily.

"C'mon . . ." Ethan puts his arm around me and steers me to shore. "It's dead now. Shouldn't we, you know, pay respect to it?"

"By eating the poor thing?"

He shrugs. "It's better than just letting it rot on the ground."

"You're serious!"

He sighs. "Jenna, this is what we do out here. We fish; we hunt; we eat stuff!"

"I don't agree with that," I tell him, stubborn.

"Fine." Ethan gives up. "You sit here and dry off. That just leaves more for me!"

He's serious. As I perch on a (non-fish-smeared) rock, letting my feet dangle in the cool water, Ethan busies himself. Taking out a hunting knife, he hacks off the fish's head, slices it open, and proceeds to scrape out all the slimy guts and tiny bones with swift motions.

"You've done this a lot, haven't you?" I say, watching curiously.

"My dad's been taking us out since I could walk." He grins. "I caught my first two-footer before I turned seven."

"That's . . . nice." The father-bonding part, not the fish killing, obviously.

"Hey, why don't you set up the fire, and I'll rustle us up a proper meal. It won't take long, now that I've got some decent bait." Ethan holds up a mess of fish entrails.

"Eww!"

He laughs, looking around. "There's a bunch of dry scrub over there. You do know how to make a fire, right?"

"Yes! Well, I'm pretty sure." I hop down. "It can't be that hard. . . ."

Ethan raises an eyebrow. "We'll see . . ."

My kindling skills pass the test, because soon we're settled around a small — but impressive — campfire. "Good job." Ethan applauds me, poking at the fish with a gnarled branch. He managed to quickly catch another and wrapped them in squares of newspaper, burying them deep in the embers. For all my promises to stick to the Doritos, I can't help but be intrigued by the singed packages.

"I cheated," I admit, pulling my sweatshirt hood up. Our clothes are dry now, and just in time — the afternoon has clouded over, and the temperature is dropping. "I just copied what I saw Reeve do on my first night."

"Hey, you got it going just fine." Ethan prods the fire. "OK, they're done."

"How can you tell?"

"Because now I'm really hungry." He grins. "So, what do you say? Going to honor Derek's life the way nature intended?"

"Derek?" I laugh.

"Yeah, he seemed like a Derek." Wincing at the heat,

Ethan pulls the packages out and tosses one in front of me. I waver. He tears his paper open, revealing pale flakes of steaming fish inside. "A little seasoning . . ." With a flourish, Ethan upends the bag of chips, scattering the last tiny pieces over the top. "And voilà!" He uses a plastic fork and digs in.

"Well . . ." I watch him eat. "I guess if Derek was already a goner. And it was an accident. . . ."

"Fish slaughter," Ethan agrees, blowing on a forkful.

"OK." I give in. Gingerly unwrapping my own paper, I take a forkful. It's delicious: soft, flaky, and unbelievably fresh. "Rest in peace, Derek," I say. And then I take another bite.

CHAPTER SEVENTEEN

Ethan must have cleared things up about our non-romantic relationship, because when I run into Grady in town the next day, he doesn't make a single joke about it. In fact, his noncommittal grunts are about the friendliest I've ever heard from him. And when Susie announces that they've finished another bedroom for me—painted with pretty pale blue paint and far down the hall from Fiona's pit of doom—I feel like things are finally looking up.

But some things never change.

"I don't want lemon yellow! What do you think I am, some kind of freaking moron?" The now-familiar sound of thumping footsteps and slamming doors echoes through the house as Fiona flees another loud argument. As I snuggle deeper in my crisp new linens, I send out silent thanks that I'm no longer prisoner to her moods.

My new room is cool, calm, and utterly peaceful—and free of all scowling emo posters.

When I'm sure the coast is clear, I edge downstairs.

"Morning." I find Susie sitting on the skeletal back porch, surreptitiously smoking a cigarette. She looks up, guilty.

"You didn't see this." She takes another quick drag. "I quit when I met Adam—he hates it."

"These lips, sealed." I mime zipping them shut, taking a seat next to her. The backyard is chaotic, as usual, strewn with tools and haphazard piles of wood. "What is it this time?"

Susie gives me a rueful look. "Does it matter? She finds a way to fight over everything."

I pat her shoulder sympathetically. Susie looks so small and worn out, sitting here in the middle of all this mess, like *she's* the confused teenager, instead of Fiona. "She'll come around eventually," I reassure her, even though I'm not sure it's true. "But . . . I was wondering. What happened with her mom?"

Susie sighs. "She bailed about five years ago. Decided she couldn't make things work with Adam and just took off. She lives down in Houston now, remarried a while ago."

"Why didn't Fiona go with her?"

Susie looks up at me. "I don't think her mom ever asked for her."

"Oh." There's silence, and then Susie speaks.

"I've tried to be supportive, but I just don't know what more I can do." I'm surprised to hear Susie's voice waver. "We're still behind schedule on the construction, and Adam is working all the time, and I'm so busy I barely ever see him." She swallows. "Did you know it's our anniversary today? A year since we met." She lets out a long breath, adding, "I was taking photographs for that travel company I used to work for, and he was in the bar one night . . ."

"That's great." I try to rouse her with a smile. "Have you got anything special planned?"

"We haven't really had time." She sighs. "I think we're going to just wait until things are quieter here, you know, when we're not so stressed."

"Umm, sure. Good plan!" I lie. The whole point of an anniversary is to be celebrated, not delayed, but Susie seems resigned.

"OK, hon." She takes another drag. "I better get back to work." Stubbing out her cigarette, she gives me a bashful grin. "Back to hiding behind gum and air freshener — it's like I'm sixteen again!"

Susie disappears back into the house, but I stay out in the shade a while longer, going over her problems. I can't help thinking that she and Adam need some quality time together. Every time I see them, they're talking about plumbing fixtures or studying blueprints — not exactly the best way to keep the romance alive. No, what they need is a private anniversary celebration, something to help them unwind . . .

Without Fiona.

I sigh. That mountain man manual would say I need to bait and distract my foe, but short of locking her in the basement or kidnapping her, I can't see how she'd leave her father and much-loathed stepmom for a romantic evening alone. Hmmm.

Gathering up my courage, I find the Johnsons' number in the thin town directory again and dial. Ethan answers almost right away.

"Oh, hey," I start, hesitant. Calling someone, (i.e., a boy,) feels weird, like I'm pushing the friendship to another level, but Ethan doesn't sound fazed at all.

"Hi, Jenna. What's up?"

"Nothing much. I actually need some advice." I check the hallway for signs of Fiona and then retreat back onto the porch.

"Go ahead."

"I'm, umm, trying to get Fiona out of the house tonight, and I wondered if you knew anything she'd go for." I keep my voice low. "You've known her for years, right?"

He laughs. "Yeah, that's easy."

"It is?"

I'm still thinking of chloroform and blindfolds when he says, "Sure, we'll just play some Rock Band."

I pause. "Like, the video game?" The thought of Fiona plus social interaction does not compute.

"We do it all the time," he says. "She's pretty vicious when it comes to the drums."

"I can imagine that."

"So I'll set it up?" Ethan offers. "Tonight, our place?"

"Perfect." I grin. "I'll explain everything later."

Susie is sitting in her makeshift office, frowning at a spreadsheet when I poke my head around the door. "Hey, are you going to be around tonight?"

She looks up. "Sure, maybe."

"Well, I was thinking," I begin, crossing my fingers. "If you're not doing anything with Adam, then maybe we could spend the evening together—watch a movie or something."

"That sounds nice." Susie smiles at me weakly. "It's a date."

After that, all it takes is a quick call to Adam, requesting his presence this evening for a "special surprise," and everything is set. Well, almost everything . . .

With my trusty notebook and thin-tipped marker, I get back into planning mode, quickly jotting down a list until I've got every angle covered. Since there are no romantic restaurants in Stillwater—and the greasy burgers at the pub really don't count—I decide a home-cooked meal is the way to go. Unfortunately, event planning in Stillwater is kind of a different challenge compared to planning something back home. To start, there's no handy mall packed full of design props: the hardware store is about all I've got, and it doesn't have much going for it in terms of atmosphere—unless you count camping lamps and mosquito-repellent incense sticks as part of the perfect ambiance.

Thwarted, I move on to groceries. I figure a tried-and-true classic is a better bet than some ambitious haute cuisine project that could leave me with burned pans and empty plates. Then I see the full range of the tiny corner grocery store: frozen food packages and canned goods. Bracing myself, I begin a careful hunt of the dusty shelves. If Jeremiah B. Coombes can conjure a three-course meal out of some tree roots and a stray rabbit, then surely I can make something. . . .

"Let me guess: pasta carbonara."

I bump into Reeve as I'm browsing the aisles in futile search of fresh herbs. He's wearing a black vest that somehow makes his eyes look darker than usual, his faded jeans slung low from a plain nylon belt.

"Umm." I pause, my mind going blank. We haven't really been alone since that weird scene at the lake. I follow his gaze to my basket of bacon, cream, and cheese, and collect myself. "Oh, right! That's the plan, anyway. It's Susie and Adam's anniversary," I explain. "I thought they deserved something special. Only, my cooking skills . . ."

"Are something like your kayaking skills?" He smiles quietly. A smile! I'm so happy he's in a friendly mood, I don't even take offense.

"Something like that," I agree, before adding shyly, "What about you—a taste for pickles?" His basket is full of them, along with gherkins and some pickled beetroot.

Reeve makes a face. "Not me, my mom. She's into her craving phase. Last week she was grossing us out with morning sickness; now she wants vinegar and onions."

"She's pregnant? That's great, congratulations."

"Thanks." He nods, looking around before adding, "She's not due for a while yet, hence the crazy food combos." He pauses. "I heard about the Rock Band night."

"You're coming along? Great!" I hear my own voice come out, way too enthusiastic. I cough. "I mean, it should be fun."

144

"Maybe." He assesses me shrewdly. "This group thing wouldn't have anything to do with those dinner plans . . ."

"You got me," I admit. "I've got food and Fiona covered; there's just the location left. The house is such a mess. I think I'll be spending the afternoon sweeping sawdust shavings."

"Have fun with that." He laughs, almost sarcastic, but still good-natured enough that I don't feel attacked.

"I'll try," I reply, spotting the box of chicken stock behind him. "Could you?" I gesture. He ducks, and I reach past his head to get it.

"Well, I better deliver these, before she starts wanting something else completely. Maybe I'll see you tonight?"

I nod. "I'll drag Fiona there kicking and screaming."

"Now that I will turn up to see." He gives me another grin and then saunters toward the checkout, but something makes me call after him.

"Reeve?"

He turns back, questioning.

"I, umm, I'm sorry. If I . . . offended you or something." The words spill out of my mouth in a rush, and I can feel that heat as my cheeks begin to color. "With all that stuff about the environment? I didn't mean . . . I mean, I didn't . . ." I trail off, lost. I don't know how to put it. I don't even know what I'm trying to say; I just feel like I need to say *something*.

Reeve looks away, awkward. "Uh, don't worry. I shouldn't have . . ."

"But I—"

"You didn't . . ." He shifts uncomfortably, a muscle in his arm twitching as he swings his basket back and forth. "You know, it's not your fault. I kind of overreacted."

"Oh. But still . . ."

We stand there, looking anywhere but at each other for a moment. Then I snap out of it. "I, umm, should probably get back to . . ." I wave my basket as some kind of evidence.

"Me too!" He blinks, backing away. "So, I'll . . ."

"See you later!"

"Right. Uh, you too."

I disappear behind a shelf of canned tomatoes and despair. Right, because that really made things *less* awkward!

CHAPTER EIGHTEEN

Everyone seems to be out, so I have the place to myself for the rest of the afternoon: sweeping, dusting, and cleaning in an effort to get at least one of the downstairs rooms into a habitable state. Soon, the dining room is sawdust-free, with the drapes from my bedroom blocking out the charming view of a cement mixer outside. Success. Before taking up residence in the bathroom for my hundred-year shower, I duck into Susie's makeshift office to print out the pasta recipe, careful not to disturb the piles of paperwork she has laid out in precarious stacks.

Projected repayment schedule.

One of the titles catches my eye. I know it's wrong to snoop, but I can't help taking a quick look, scanning the chart. According to her calculations, they'll have enough money to keep up with mortgage and loan repayments—

as long as they have at least a quarter of the rooms full. Every week.

Frowning, I flip through the other papers. Bills, invoices, and there — the bookings schedule. The *empty* bookings schedule. I stare at it with trepidation. We're weeks away from opening, and Susie doesn't even have a single room booked. No wonder she's running ragged to get this place finished.

I hear a voice calling me from out front. Guilty, I drop the papers and immediately push everything back into place. But when I rush out, breathless, I find Reeve setting a box down on the porch.

"Oh, hi." I'm caught off guard. Quickly, I push my sweaty bangs off my face and adjust my tank straps, wishing I didn't look like such a mess.

"Hey, sorry — did I interrupt? I was going to just leave this . . ." Reeve's changed T-shirts since I saw him last: now he's wearing a red one, emblazoned with CREEK COUNTY FIRE DEPARTMENT. I feel weird for even noticing.

"No, it's fine," I say quickly. "What's up?"

Reeve hands me the box with a lopsided smile. "I found some stuff you might want. I figured these might help with that dinner."

"Wow, thanks!" I rummage through the carton. There are Christmas lights, little lanterns, and even some cute candlesticks. "This is great. Are you sure it's OK — for me to borrow them? I can have them back to you tomorrow," I promise.

"Don't rush." He shrugs. "They were only gathering dust in the attic."

"Well, thanks," I say again, touched by an actual show of friendship. "They'll really help."

He looks embarrassed. Running a hand over the top of his head, he begins to edge away. "Uh, I better go. I guess I'll catch you later?"

"At Ethan's, right."

I watch him stroll back to his truck. Ever since that first night at the lake, I've had him pegged as moody and unpredictable, but now I wonder if I got him all wrong.

"Fiona, hi, and you must be Jenna! I've been dying to meet you!" The door swings open that evening to reveal a middle-aged woman, her hair blond and cut short in that soccer-mom style. She pulls me into a hug before I can even say a word, enveloping me in her huge knit cardigan.

"Umm, hi." I detach myself and take a breath, laced with the scent of lavender and butter. "Mrs. Johnso—"

"Call me Katie!" she exclaims, before I even have a chance to finish. "Come in, both of you. The boys are down in the basement, but how about you come and talk with me in the kitchen? I made some pie, and—"

"Mom, they didn't come to hang out with you." Ethan thunders up the stairs and intercepts us. "Sorry," he mouths in my direction before turning back to her. "You can't just attack every girl who comes through that door."

"It's OK," I pipe up as Fiona disappears quickly toward the basement. "It's nice to meet you, too."

"Come on." Ethan yanks me away. "Before she starts showing you the baby pictures."

"She did that?" I ask, following him down the staircase lined with school portraits of him and Grady.

"For real. Fiona was trapped up there for an hour one time, and she only came over to study."

I laugh. "That explains her quick escape."

The basement room is surprisingly light and cheery, furnished with old brown couches and a big TV that has obviously seen better days. Fiona is already gripping one of the plastic guitars, while Grady and Reeve are sprawled on the floor among cushions, soda cans, and junk-food debris, focused intently on decimating each other in the violent fantasy realm on-screen.

"Hey, guys," I greet them.

"Hi, Jenna."

"Hey."

They're only monosyllables, but I'm impressed. Reeve actually looks up from the game and smiles, while Grady's murmur is almost enthusiastic.

"Ha!" Suddenly, Grady jerks his controller up, and the screen explodes in an impressive firebomb. "Suck it, baby!"

"What? Aw, come on!" Reeve throws his remote down in defeat. "That was totally unfair."

"And so is life, my friend," Grady gloats. "The strong shall rise and the weak shall perish. Mwha-ha-ha."

"I thought it was the meek who inherit the earth." Ethan flops down on one of the couches next to Fiona, so I wander over to the La-Z-Boy, which is spilling its innards from a deep tear in the seat. I move around a couple of loose springs and sit, curling my legs up under me.

"Not in this world." Grady grabs a handful of chips. "Might is right!" He turns to me and Fiona. "Want some?"

"Duh." Fiona takes the whole bag. "So now that you're done destroying this loser, can we get on to the real game?"

"I call drums!" Grady yells, spraying chip fragments everywhere.

"Dude, gross." Ethan sighs.

"I take bass. Which means one of you has to sing." Reeve grins at Ethan, pulling the rest of the instruments out of the corner.

"Don't look at me." Ethan puts his hands up. "Jenna, it's all yours."

"You're going to regret that," I tell them. "Seriously. I'm awful. Think *American Idol* auditions kind of awful."

"That's part of the fun." Ethan laughs, passing me the mic. "And you can't be worse than my brother, I promise."

"Dude, my Bon Jovi was epic," Grady informs us.

"Yeah, epically awful."

"Says the guy who managed to mess up 'Black Hole Sun.' Even Fiona did better than you!"

Fiona looks up and smirks. "Like that's hard."

I laugh, relaxing. For the first time since I arrived in town, it actually feels as though I belong—like I'm really part of the group. I look around happily. "So, since I got stuck singing, does that mean I get to pick the song?"

CHAPTER NINETEEN

If I had any doubts that all my effort would be worth it, the vibe between Susie and Adam in the week after their dinner makes everything clear: from making baby eyes over breakfast to sneaking quick kisses as they pass each other in the hallway, the spark in their relationship is definitely back.

"This is all your fault." Fiona watches them through the kitchen window, her arms folded. Adam is sanding some wooden planks but stops every few minutes to hug and kiss Susie. Fiona makes a face. "What did you do?"

"Nothing," I answer breezily. "You coming on this climbing trip? I'm leaving now."

"Nope." She turns back, starting to pull down items from the cupboard. I watch as she assembles flour, sugar, and eggs on the countertop.

"You're . . . baking?" I stare, confused.

"And?" She glares at me, ripping open a package of butter and dumping it in a bowl with a scoop of sugar. Wielding a wooden spoon like it's an offensive weapon, she begins to beat the mixture into submission.

"Nothing." I blink, watching her. "I didn't know you were into that kind of thing."

"You get to eat cake," she replies, beating harder. "What's not to like?"

I begin to feel sorry for the sugar.

I wonder for a moment if she finds it exhausting—the constant sullen sighs, the petulant disapproval. Surely it would be easier all around if she just gave it a break. I'm tempted for a moment to go look in that mountain man manual for advice on dealing with rabid beasts, but then I remember: I sent it to Olivia in my last package, along with some photos of Stillwater and a *Johnsons' Home & Hardware* T-shirt. I figured my work here was done, but I guess I was too optimistic.

Fiona keeps mixing with a malevolent look, so I decide to leave her to it. It's not like I want her to be the one holding my guide rope, or whatever it is that's going to keep me suspended halfway up a cliff face.

An hour later, I'm not so sure. It turns out that Ethan and Grady had to stay and help out with a delivery back at the store, so it's just me, Reeve, and a looming rock face. Moral support of any type would be kind of great right now. "You want me to climb . . . *that*?" I stare up at it in horror. "With my bare hands?"

"Not bare." Reeve laughs. "You've got gloves, see?" He hands me a small pair of stiff, fingerless gloves. The leather is curling at the edges and stained white with old resin.

"Wow," I say faintly. "These will make all the difference."

We're deep in the woods, at what apparently is the best natural climbing spot for miles around. Chunks of gray rock jut out of the hillside, covered in places with moss and shrubbery. They cast long shadows over the foliage below, bathing us in a cool, green light.

My terror must show, because Reeve pauses, taking pity on me. "It's not so scary, really. Look, there are tons of ledges and pockets to grip. It couldn't be easier if there were a ladder all the way up."

"Uh-huh." I swallow. That teeny-tiny problem I have with heights suddenly doesn't seem so small.

"You'll have fun—I promise."

That I doubt. My plan was to stay safely on the ground today, but for some crazy reason, I didn't call the whole thing off when I heard it would be just the two of us. Reeve has gone to all this trouble to set the trip up. Now that we're alone, I can't bring myself to back out and look pathetic.

Reeve pulls on his own gloves, completely unaware that even proximity to the rock face is making my stomach tangle in knots. "I'll go first." He grins, cocky. "Then you can see how easy it is."

"Wait, aren't you going to put on a harness or—?" Before I can even finish, he strides over and nimbly hops up onto a small ledge, about three feet from the ground. His hands are already skimming across the rock, seeking out a hold, and soon he's crawling ten, fifteen feet up.

"See?" Turning, he calls down to me. "Easy!"

I gulp. He's got no safety rope or net or anything, just slim canvas shoes and bare arms, but still he's scrambling easily up the vertical drop like he weighs nothing at all. It's like he's decided gravity doesn't apply to him.

"Look at my feet," he calls. "You have to use your legs to push higher. Find tiny creases in the rock to stand in." On cue, he lodges his right toe in a thin crack in the rock, using the force to push up and reach for a ledge, I gasp. For a few moments, his whole body is dangling by his fingertips, and then he finds another hold and swings sideways to reach it.

By the time he reaches the top of the rock, my stomach isn't just tangled; it's knotted tight.

"See? Nothing to worry about!" Reeve skids down the dirt path that winds around the side of the rock. Or, as I like to think of it: the sensible way up.

"You're sure you didn't get bitten by a radioactive spider or something?" I try and delay the inevitable that little bit longer. "Hey, wait a second while I get some general nature footage." I busy myself taking pictures for the website while Reeve grabs a coil of rope from his duffel bag. He scrambles back up the dirt path, runs the rope through a bolt at the top of the rock, and lets both ends fall all the way down to me.

Too soon, he's back by my side, holding out the harness for me to step into. "Ready?" He seems genuinely excited, blue eyes lit up and his whole face animated. I nod reluctantly.

I can be brave. I can be adventurous. I can climb stuff.

Pulling the harness around my pelvis, I tighten the straps and then stand awkwardly as Reeve attaches the various pulls and hooks to my body. "This is your safety rope." He shows me, looping it securely through the front of my harness and tying a strange knot. "It goes up through that bolt and then back down to me, so you don't need to worry at all. If you slip, or lose your grip or anything, I've got you." My expression must be less than reassured, because he puts a hand on my arm and says it again: "I've got you."

"OK." I breathe, trying to talk myself into this. Rock. Holds. Momentum. Think of it like a jungle gym, I tell myself, or a flight of stairs. A flight of perilous, invisible stairs. "And how do I get down?"

His face creases in a smile. "I'll talk you through it when the time comes."

I'm thinking that time will come sooner, rather than later.

Reeve takes up his position, feeding his end of the rope through a metal loop, and I slowly edge over to the bottom of the rock.

"You can do this—I promise," Reeve adds when I linger there without moving. "Just break it down: one move, then another."

The rock feels cool and damp against my palms. Taking a deep breath, I step up onto that first easy ledge.

"Great job!" I hear Reeve's voice, but don't dare look

around. "Now reach up with your left hand. There's a ledge right there." I follow his instructions, running my fingers over cracks until I find a crevice large enough to grip. "Then put all your weight on your left foot and find a new hold."

It takes me another moment to actually do as he says, but after scrabbling at the rock with my toe, I find another ledge. Shifting slowly, I ease up onto it and grab at a new nook with my fingertips. Now I'm balanced on the tips of my toes, my whole body flat against the rock.

"You've got it!" Reeve sounds way too enthusiastic. After all, I am still only five feet above the ground: I could jump down without a problem. But something about the certainty in his voice makes me feel stronger. I keep going.

Left foot, left hand; shift weight; right foot, right hand; shift weight. With Reeve yelling out suggestions, I gradually move up the rock, feeling muscles I never knew I had strain under the unexpected weight. But the higher I go, the more my stomach lurches in terror. Don't look down, I tell myself, staring at etchings and moss just inches from my nose. Just don't look down.

I shift sideways along the wall, following a seam of easy footholds until I'm out on the far left. But the seam ends. I'm stuck.

"Reeve!" I call down. "I can't see anything!" There are tiny pockmarks and cracks but nothing I can get a toe or hand into. "Reeve!"

"Hang on. Let me look. Er, I think you're going to have to come back."

"Back where?" Without the momentum of my reach-and-shift routine, I start to feel my weight pull. I have one foot jammed up to the side and the other lodged in only a toehold, gripping tightly with my fingertips in one single crack. I begin to panic. "I don't know what to do!"

"Try sliding along and up," Reeve calls. I hear him pacing closer to the rock. "There's a ledge just out of your reach, on the right."

I tentatively let go with one hand and grab for the ledge. "It's too far!" I quickly cling back to the crack in front of me. My hands are aching, but I don't dare ease my grip. "I can't go anywhere!"

"Shh, it's OK, Jenna. Just breathe."

"But I can't move!" I take a gulp of air. It doesn't make me feel any calmer. "Reeve?"

"Do you want to get down—?"

"Yes!" I cry before he even has time to finish.

Reeve laughs, calm and reassuring. "OK, you're going to need to let go of the wall and lean back. Just hold on to your harness and walk down backward."

Let go? Walk backward? *Just?*

I stay frozen in place, fear washing over my body in a cold shiver. I should never have tried this; I should be safely on the ground. Bad things happen to people who think they can cheat gravity: things involving falling, and pain, and bloody bone-shattering death.

And then I look down.

"Oh, God," I whimper. "I'm going to die."

"No, you're not!" Reeve insists. He would. He's on the ground. All the way down there.

"Maybe not die. Maybe I'll just break my neck."

"You need to move, Jenna. Just take a breath and lean out. I've got your rope; you can't fall."

We both wait.

"OK, how about plan B?" Reeve still sounds relaxed. "Hang tight—I'm coming up."

"But what about my safety rope!"

"I'm securing it—don't worry."

I don't hear anything for a while but scrapes and scrabbling. I'm starting to get a cramp in my calves. I don't want to think about what will happen when my legs give out.

"Hey." I hear Reeve's voice, breathless, just beside me. I force myself to turn my head, resting my cheek against the cool rock. He's climbed a different route and is about five feet away from me, just out of reach. He looks over at me casually, as if we've accidentally run into each other. Because I'm always running into sweaty, shirtless climbers halfway up a rock. "So, what's up?"

I make a garbled noise, equal parts laughter and sheer terror.

"OK then, let's see if we can sort you out." He looks at my position. "Are your feet comfortable?"

I shake my head.

"Well, I can see a ledge right by your foot. It would help stretch you out."

I stay frozen.

"I want to move," I explain miserably. "And I think about moving. But when it comes to actually moving . . ."

"That's OK." Reeve's voice is soft and reassuring. "Take your time." Gathering every last ounce of courage,

I force my foot to move, just an inch. "Nearly!" Reeve promises. "Just a bit more." I grit my teeth and push a tiny bit farther. "There! You feel that? Shift your weight." I do as he says, and right away, the pain in my legs starts to ease.

"Thanks," I say in a small voice. "And, I'm sorry about this." I feel completely useless.

"It's OK," he reassures me. "I'm sorry, too. I mean, I promised this would be fun."

"It was!" I gulp. "Kind of. Before I lost all control over my limbs and had a major panic attack."

He laughs again, and the sound is weirdly soothing. "What do you want to do now?"

"Umm, I have options?" I take another breath. "OK, maybe, if I just stay here a while, I'll un-freeze and be able to move again?"

"Then we're staying put." Reeve shifts to a more comfortable position. I wish I had the luxury. "So, how are things going?"

I can't help but smile—a small pitiful smile, but a smile all the same. "Oh, just great. You know, hanging out."

"Ouch!" Reeve flashes me a grin.

"Yes, well, I'm kind of distracted." Despite my better instincts, I find myself glancing down again to the—

"Hey, hey, Jenna!" Reeve snaps my attention back. "Just keep looking at me, OK? Straight over here at me."

"Uh-huh." I have nothing else to do, so I follow his orders and look straight over at him.

Reeve isn't wearing a shirt.

I must have registered this earlier, but in my terrified haze, I didn't really pay much attention. Now I do.

"Are you feeling any calmer?" he asks, concerned.

"Umm, maybe." I'm still gazing at his chest. Inappropriate, perhaps, but excellent distraction from my impending death. "Talk to me. I think it helps."

"About what?"

"I don't know, anything. How's your mom?"

"OK." He shifts position again, light and easy. "She's not craving pickles anymore."

"No?"

"Nope, now it's hot sauce. With everything. She made lasagna last night; I nearly died."

I manage to smile. "When's she due?"

"December." He pauses, looking back at the rock before adding, "It's kind of why I'm not sure about college this year. She says she'll be fine, but I don't know about leaving her alone. I have two younger sisters. They're kind of a handful already."

"Oh. Is your dad not . . . ?" I trail off, embarrassed.

He gives me a rueful look. "Yeah, no. He's not. He took off a few years back. And this kid's father isn't around, either." Reeve lets out a long breath. "So . . . I'm kind of the only man left standing. Sorry," he says, forcing a laugh. "I didn't mean to lay all of this—"

"No! It's fine." I pause a moment, watching. "I think it's good, what you're doing for your mom," I add shyly.

"Thanks." He looks awkward. "What about your folks? You must miss them, being away all summer."

I flex my aching fingers and sigh. "I do and I don't." He gives me a curious look, but even though he's confided in me, I don't know what to say. I've become so used to pushing back all the cold, scary thoughts of my parents, and the future, and everything else, that I almost can't think about them now when I want to.

"Things, at home, I don't know if they'll be OK." It's all I manage, in a quiet voice. "Dad's working abroad, and they say it's just for the summer, but I don't know. . . ." I stop. I've been trying not to think about it, and the way Dad keeps hinting about having to stay longer. "It's a great opportunity here," he said three times during our last phone call. "You'll love it." Like I don't know what that means. He might not be coming back.

When I look over again, Reeve is watching me. His expression is soft, as if he understands everything I can't say. For a moment, our eyes meet, and I forget I'm hanging precariously from a tiny ledge.

Something other than fear pulls inside me. I never noticed how his lips are —

"Hey, Jenna?"

"Uh-huh," I murmur, the fear gripping me now making way for something else. Something light and warm and —

"You want to move your foot down, to the right?"

"OK." I do as he says, almost without thinking.

"Great, now shift your right arm."

Mid-reach, I wake up. "I'm moving!" I cry.

He laughs. "Yup. You want to keep going?"

"You mean up?" I gulp. "Umm . . ."

"That's OK. You can go down the fun way."

"There's a fun way?"

"Sure. Just let me get back to your rope, and I'll show you."

I wait there, full of relief but at the same time, a little regretful that the moment is over. "Umm, Reeve?"

"Yeah?"

"Thanks."

CHAPTER TWENTY

Sooner than I imagined, life in Stillwater becomes almost routine. My mom calls every few days to check on me, Olivia texts me her latest camp—and Cash—updates, Fiona keeps up her icy demeanor, and I settle into a lazy schedule of sunbathing and helping Susie out with B and B projects. The hours start to drift in that sleepy, summer way, where an afternoon sprawled out reading in the shade of the backyard trees slips past in no time at all. Adam digs me out one of their rusted bicycles, and I start cycling the wide dirt road into town most days, stopping by the gas station for Popsicles and hanging out with Ethan at the hardware store.

But I can't stop thinking about Reeve.

It started that day we went climbing. Something shifted between us up there on the rock, as if we connected for the first time, and suddenly, I'm gone. From zero to crush in twenty minutes, it's crazy, I know—like I've been gripped by some kind of temporary insanity—but I can't help it. I find myself changing shirts three times before leaving the house, trying to get that perfectly casual look, and lingering out by the lake longer than I would just in case he comes for an after-work swim.

It was never like this with my old boyfriend, Mike, even when we were dating, but I can't stop myself. And even though I know I'm building this out of nothing more than a few friendly words, I've become suddenly—painfully—aware of his every move.

"More soda?"

I flinch, startled at Reeve's offer, and send a stack of DVD cases tumbling to the ground.

"Graceful," Fiona informs me. She's lying flat out on the living-room floor at the Johnsons', emptying crumbs from a pack of cookies into her mouth. We're nearing the end of our *Kudos* sci-fi marathon, with Grady sprawled on the cream carpet nearby and Ethan lounging on one of the floral print armchairs.

Reeve is sitting on the couch with me.

"Umm, no thanks," I tell him, scrambling to pick up the mess. "I'm good."

Good is stretching it; *a wreck* might be closer to the truth. All evening, I've been frozen in place, hyper-aware of his body and the tiny section of his jeans touching my leg. Every time he shifts for snacks or the remote, I can't help wondering: Is he leaning closer on purpose? Did that nudge mean anything at all? Does this mean he's comfortable around me or that he couldn't care less? I don't think I've ever focused so much on three square inches in my life.

"I could use another drink," Ethan adds, not lifting his head.

"And if you find any more of those brownies—" Grady burps, the floor around him already littered with junk-food debris.

"Dude, get off your ass." Reeve kicks him as he steps over their bodies.

"Mnueh."

As he disappears toward the kitchen, I look around, checking that nobody has seen my awkwardness. But they're all lolling back, eyes glazed by hours of TV. I try to relax, stretching the muscles that have been set, tense, for hours now. I never realized crushing on a guy could be so exhausting, but the amount of extra effort it takes to act totally casual around Reeve is wiping me out.

"You know, we should probably get going soon," I tell Fiona, noticing the digital display on the TV with some relief. "It's nearly ten thirty."

"So?" She shrugs.

"So, Susie said to be back by then." It's only after I reply that I realize my reason will probably have her camped out here until dawn.

Sure enough, Fiona reaches for the next disc.

"Fiona." I sigh as Reeve wanders back in the room. I pause, distracted. His faded gray shirt hangs close to his torso, and he gives me a half smile, holding up the six-pack of soda.

"Last chance?"

I shake my head. He breaks off cans to toss to the other boys and then collapses back next to me, utterly relaxed. "Where are we up to—episode fifteen, sixteen?"

"The girls might bail." Ethan looks over, questioning.

I pause, torn. I don't want to cause problems with Susie, but if Reeve is staying . . .

"Fine!" Fiona exclaims suddenly, as if I've been nagging her for hours. "We'll go now." She gets to her feet and pulls on a hooded sweater. "You so better not watch any without me," she tells the boys before stalking out of the room, leaving a mess of wrappings and empty cans on the floor.

"Sorry," I apologize tiredly, leaping up. "See you tomorrow?"

"Maybe." Ethan nods. "We might be heading into Kamloops with Dad. I'll call or something."

"Later, Jenna." Reeve nods. Grady makes a noise of agreement as I grab my bag and hurry out.

"Fiona, wait up!"

I catch up with her out on the road. It's dark outside, but she's not using our mandated flashlights; instead, she just kicks at gravel with her hands deep in her front pocket.

"That was kind of rude," I say cautiously, falling into step beside her. The warm glow of the Johnsons' neighbors' light melts away behind us, and I shiver—I'm still wary of wandering around here after dark. "We should have stayed to help clean up."

"So why didn't you? Oh, right, I forgot, you have to

get home to your precious Susie." Her voice sneers on the last word. It's nothing but the same bitchy crap I've been dealing with all month, but for once, something in me snaps.

"What the hell is your problem?" I exclaim. Moving quickly to block her way, I demand, "Seriously, this spoiled brat thing of yours is getting ridiculous."

Fiona rolls her eyes and tries to push past me, but I stand firm in the middle of the dark road. Jeremiah B. Coombes would probably tell me to flee the wild beast and retreat to safety, but I'm sick of tolerating all her crap. No more.

"I mean it," I insist. "What's going on? I get that you're angry and you miss your mom, but don't you want Adam to be happy?"

"I want him to be happy, just not with her." Fiona glares back at me. It's the kind of stare that would wither anyone in their tracks, but I have a jolt of adrenaline running through me now, and I won't quit so easily.

"So what happens if you get your way? Do you really think that will make things better? Your dad will just have another divorce on his hands, and you'll find something else to bitch about."

"Nope." She smiles tightly. "That would pretty much solve everything."

I shake my head in disbelief. "Would you listen to yourself? I'd understand if Susie was the wicked stepmother or something, but she's awesome. Really amazing, and she's falling over herself to give you everything you want!"

"She shouldn't be here," Fiona replies stubbornly.

I throw my hands up. "But she is! And if you don't think the way you act hurts her, you're wrong. And that goes for me too," I add, quieter. I've been tiptoeing around her for too long. "You've been mean since I got here, and I'm sick of it, Fiona."

"And . . . ?" she drawls, extra-sarcastic, like she's just trying to show how insignificant my feelings are.

"And if you keep going like this, you'll end up with nobody!"

Fiona seems unmoved. I wonder if she cares about anyone here. She's got to. Nobody can get by without friends, especially way out here where there's nobody for company for another fifty miles in any direction. "The way you bitch at us all the time—Ethan, Reeve, Grady . . . You know it sucks," I say bluntly, spying my opening. It may not matter what Susie and I think, but the others . . . ? And sure, they tolerate it for now, but one of these days, they'll get sick of it, too, and then you'll be left alone. Is that what you want? Really?"

Fiona is looking at me defiantly, but I think I see something flicker in her expression.

Or maybe that's just sheer rage.

"Think about it." I sigh, backing away. "You just keep acting like the same spoiled, selfish brat you always do, and see who's around to be your friend." Now it's my turn for sarcasm. Crossing my arms, I begin to stride away, but not before I turn back with one last warning. "Either way, for now you're stuck with me!"

· · ·

I soon find that instead of making things better, my fight with Fiona unleashes, well, hell. Her tantrums go from loud to epic, the door-slamming never ends, and over the next three days, Susie is reduced to tears on two different occasions. My headache is most definitely back.

When I head downstairs the morning after a particularly obnoxious fight (in which Fiona screamed that she wished Susie was, and I quote, "mauled by wolves") and find her sitting at the breakfast nook, eating Cocoa Puffs, my heart sinks. I grab some cereal and try to assemble breakfast before she breaks out with another chorus of "I hate you/you're evil/life isn't fair!"

"Morning," Fiona says, not looking up.

I stop dead.

"Umm, hey?" Shooting her a glance, I check for a scowl and sarcasm, but she just looks . . . normal. Almost relaxed.

I edge closer. "How are you?"

"OK." She shrugs, returning to her book, but I can't believe the change. Deciding to push my luck, I actually sit down at the table and pour myself a bowl. Yesterday's paper is folded on the side, so we sit there, reading in companionable silence for a moment, while I try to figure out what's going on. Our fight was days ago, and it's not like she would ever care about my feelings. I pause. Maybe not *mine*, but that stuff I said about the others . . . ?

Perhaps I finally got through to her.

"How's the website going?" Fiona asks out of nowhere.

I blink. Neutral tone, normal expression—now I'm really weirded out.

"Good!" I recover. "Ethan's kind of lost interest, so I was thinking of taking it over. We put up the photos of town, and the video posts, but it's still pretty bare."

She puts her finger in between her pages to keep the place. "You should probably start getting pictures of the house now, right? A couple of rooms are done, and if you look at the outside from way out back, you can get an angle where the plastic doesn't show."

"Oh. Thanks."

Before I try to wrap my head around the miracle of this new, civil Fiona, she adds, "I don't know what good it'll be. I mean, they'll never be done in time."

"Still, it'll help." I decide. Baby steps.

When Susie finds us later, photographing the parts of the house that actually look habitable, her expression is exactly what I expect. After all, there's no screaming, stomping, or sulking going on—unheard of in Fiona-related activities.

"Hi, girls!" She edges over as if the slightest move could unbalance this precious calm.

"Hi, Susie." I look up from the camera. "Everything's coming along great. I like the wallpaper in the living room."

"Thanks." Looking breathlessly between us, she seems at a loss for words. "I was just at the store, and I got some ice cream. Did you girls want some?"

"That sounds great."

"OK," Fiona says reluctantly, and then, quieter, "That would be cool."

Susie's face melts into the biggest grin. "I can dig out sauce, too, and even those cherries you like so much, Fiona. We can make sundaes!" She spins around and heads toward the kitchen, still babbling about the different things we can add and how lovely it is outside.

Fiona turns to me and raises her eyebrows in a familiar show of disdain.

"She means well," I argue, praying her mood-switch holds. And, thank God, it does.

Fiona lets out a weary sigh, but there's no tantrum, just the mutter, "There better be chocolate."

We spend the afternoon lounging around in the sun, even though there are a million other things Susie needs to be doing. (Well, Susie and I lie in the sun; Fiona pulls her blanket into the shade and sits there with a drooping sunhat and sunblock slathered everywhere.) Fiona manages not to make a bitchy comment every ten seconds, and in exchange, I manage to convey to Susie that enthusiastic chatter doesn't exactly help her cause. After fluttering around, making sure we're fully stocked with sundae ingredients, she finally settles down on the grass with one of my cast-off romance novels and a glow of contentment.

"Can you pass the Cool Whip?" Fiona stirs a gloopy concoction that would send even the healthiest person into a diabetic coma. She pauses and then with super-human effort adds, "Please?"

I nearly faint.

"Here you go!" Susie passes her the can. Fiona rolls onto her back and proceeds to squirt artificial cream right into her mouth.

"Eww, gross!" I cry, throwing a jelly bean at her.

"Shut up," she says through the cream.

"Wait, hold that so I can immortalize you." I reach for my camera. Fiona ignores me and flips back onto her stomach, but I start shooting anyway, capturing her lazy pose and the way her hat sends crisscrosses of light over her face. I switch between manual and automatic modes quickly to try different lighting effects, more practiced now.

"Can I see?" Fiona asks.

"Sure." I pass her the camera and watch, a little nervous, as she flicks through the past weeks of images on the digital screen. Too late, I realize there are a few of Reeve—shirtless—in there, but I hope the other stuff disguises my attention to his details. "It's just for fun. I mean, it's not supposed to be like a portfolio or anything."

She lingers on a set of photos I did the other week: a series of the guys with their Rock Band instruments, caught in action during a song. "Those were hard," I say. She's looking at one of Grady flipping his drumsticks. "The light down there was weird, and I had to try and get the movement . . ."

"No, these are . . . actually good." She sounds surprised.

"Thanks." I feel kind of shy. "Like I said, they're just a fun thing." I never really had time for art stuff before, what with all my Green Teen commitments, but out here, I've got nothing but time. My collection of photos is actually a big file by now, and I make a note to upload them to Susie's computer soon.

"Look, Susie, she's got one of you and Dad." Fiona pushes the camera in her direction. It's only a snapshot of them working on the back wall, but Susie can't stop tears from welling up. I have a feeling it's less about my magnificent photography skills than Fiona's civil tone.

"Thank you, Jenna." Her bottom lip is trembling.

"No problem." I exchange a look with Fiona, and we go back to our ice cream and books in silence for the rest of the afternoon.

I think it's the closest thing to domestic harmony this place has ever seen.

CHAPTER TWENTY-ONE

Beep.

"Olivia! Hey, how are you? Just calling to see what's up, but I guess you're out saving the earth or in that yoga cabin again. Umm, nothing much to report here . . . Oh, Fiona's actually acting like a human being now—it's a total mystery, but I'll tell you all that in person. I'm just heading over to Ethan's to hang out with everyone. Anyway, miss you. Call me!"

Beep.

"Hey, Livvy . . . Voice mail again . . . OK. Things are going fine here, good, actually. I spent the day down at the lake today, and Fiona even lent me this old Polaroid camera she hasn't used in ages, so I was able to get these faded old shots. I wish you had e-mail so I could send scans or something; it gets so pretty here, especially in the evening right before the sun sets—the light is just awesome . . . Umm, hope you're having fun. Give me a call back when you can!"

Beep.

"Olivia! Since you're not returning my calls, I figure you've either transcended to a whole new plane of existence or you're shunning modern technology or you've passed out with hunger from that detox of yours. Is everything OK? I miss you. Call me."

Beep.

"Hey, Livvy, I got your text. All twelve words of it. I'm glad you're having a good time out there, and things are going good with Cash. But, ummm, maybe you want to think some more about the whole 'not going to college' thing? I know we've been planning on college together forever, but even if you don't want to do that, there are tons of other options we can think about. Don't do anything rash, OK? Anyway, hopefully we can catch up soon. . . . Miss you!"

Beep.

"Hey Olivia, just checking in. But you're not answering. Again . . . Nothing much to say, just seeing if you're around. Things are good. I'm just heading out to the woods again, so, I guess call me later, OK? Bye."

You can only prepare for so much. All the planning in the world is no match for the real wilderness out there, you've got to learn to deal with the unexpected. Improvise, adapt, get messy. Nothing's fun when you can see it coming a mile away.

—"Outdoor Adventuring,"
The Modern Mountain Man's Survival Guide

CHAPTER TWENTY-TWO

"I've got something for you." Susie pokes her head out onto the back porch to find me and then emerges, dangling a crisp paper bag from one finger. It's late on a Friday afternoon, my favorite time of day. The fierce heat of the day has faded, and now there's a cool breeze slipping through the backyard, the sun sinking lower in the sky.

I push my magazine aside. "Oooh, what?"

She laughs, dropping the bag beside me on the wicker love seat. "Don't get too excited."

I eagerly open it up, pausing when I find a pale, solid package. "Tofu?"

Susie grins, pulling up the rocking chair opposite. "I ordered it in from a health food company. Lentils and beans, too. I know you've been missing that kind of food."

"Aww, that's really sweet of you." I put the bag aside and hug her. To tell the truth, I haven't been missing it that much at all. It turns out Adam picks up most of our fruit and vegetables from local farm stands nearby, which is plenty eco-friendly for me, and as for the rest of it . . . well, chalky tofu is no match for Susie's corn fritters.

"Thank you," I tell her, all the same. "You shouldn't have gone to the trouble."

"I know." Susie's pulled her wet hair back into a braid, and she's actually wearing a crisp shirt instead of her usual paint-splattered T. "But I wanted to say thank you."

"For what?"

She breaks into a proud grin. "We've had our first booking!"

"No way—that's great!" I clap my hands together. "Tell me all the details!"

"It's a family, from Boston. They're driving across the province, and they decided to stay with us for a few nights."

"Ah, I'm so happy for you guys!" I reach over and give her a hug. "It's only the first; there'll be tons more to come."

Susie beams back. "And it's all because of you! They found us through the Stillwater website you guys put up, said it sounded 'rustic and adventurous.' They want to do all those activities you showed, so we'll have to organize the boys to take them out. For a fee, of course."

"They'll be happy to," I promise. "That's really great."

"Isn't it? And the timing's perfect, because I've got a meeting with the bank this afternoon."

"What for?" I remember that stack of paperwork I wasn't supposed to see. "Is everything OK?"

"It will be now," she reassures me, straightening her shirt and smoothing back a stray curl until she looks every inch the respectable business-owner. "And with you and Fiona pitching in, we're even ahead of schedule." She pauses. "I know I shouldn't jinx it, but do you know why . . . ?"

"She's acting human?" I finish. "Nope, no idea. Maybe she finally decided to be mature about it." We pause. "Or maybe she's been taken over by aliens." I offer a more likely scenario.

"Either way, it's wonderful." Susie grins.

I nod. A wonderful mystery.

Inspired by the B and B's first booking, I decide to stop waiting around for Ethan and take charge of the website project myself. He put up the basic Stillwater info and some maps, and we've added video footage of the fun activities available around here, but it could be so much more.

"You could go horseback riding," Fiona suggests through a mouthful of raw brownie mix.

"I don't know. . . ." I hop up on the kitchen cabinet and take a spoonful from the bowl. This time, the baking effort doesn't seem to be a product of sheer rage, so I figure it's safe for me to be around. "The stuff we've done so far has involved all this expensive equipment — the bikes, the kayaks, the fishing gear."

"What, so you want, like, a hike?" Fiona wrinkles her nose. "Thrilling."

"But it would be a way to get loads of photos of how

beautiful it is around here." I ponder, licking brownie mix off my wrist. Now that the idea is in my head, the more I like the plan of going out on another group trip. After all, it's been four days since I last saw Reeve around town. . . . I catch myself, embarrassed, before I can take the thought any further. "Are there any good trails around?" I ask instead.

"There's the path up Mount Jacobs."

"A mountain?"

She rolls her eyes. "It's only like, a big hill. But you get views all over the valley."

"Sounds perfect!" I brighten. "I'll see if the guys want to do it, maybe tomorrow. I think Grady has the day off."

Fiona begins scraping what's left of her mix onto a baking sheet. "I could maybe come too," she says, not looking at me.

I blink, surprised. "Umm, sure, that would be cool!"

"But don't expect me to carry anything."

We meet the next afternoon, equipped with juice, energy bars, a flashlight, and a cardigan—at least, I am. Grady and Fiona look at my bulging backpack with amusement, but I'm taking no chances out there in the forest again. Jeremiah B. Coombes would call me a doggone fool if I went out without proper supplies, and in my serious pair of hiking boots and sturdy shorts, I'm ready for anything.

Almost.

"All set?"

I called to invite him, but Reeve's arrival still catches me off guard. He slams his truck door and walks over, a water bottle still dripping in his hand. I try very hard not to notice the way his soft blue T-shirt brings out his eyes or how he's slung his pack diagonally across his chest so it stretches the fabric taut and—

"Yup!" I exclaim brightly, hoping my sunglasses hide my expression. "I think we're just waiting for Ethan." I glance around. Fiona is dressed in a cute red top for a change, her hair actually brushed, while Grady loiters a few feet from her, spinning his baseball cap on his fingertips. He looks up.

"Didn't he tell you? He has to watch the store today. Our parents are out of town for the weekend."

"Guess you drew the short straw," Fiona says, like it's a question.

Grady shrugs, looking awkward. "I guess."

"OK then!" I say brightly. "Let's get going!"

We set out on foot along road that winds up out of town. Grady assured me it was a half-day hike at most, but I'm not so sure: the peak of Mount Jacobs rises from the valley, blanketed by the same thick forest that stretches all the way down to the lake. It looks pretty far to me.

"Hey." Reeve falls into step beside me, Fiona and Grady lingering behind.

"Hi," I say. Eloquent, I know, but it seems like Reeve is feeling just as talkative. We fall into a companionable silence for a while, walking in the shadows of the forest, with sunlight falling through the tall pine trees. The air is hot and close, and soon I peel off my cardigan, tying it around my waist.

"I hope it doesn't storm later." Reeve looks up at the clear, blue sky. I laugh.

"Seriously? It hasn't rained all week."

"Exactly." He gives me that half smile of his, the one that only curls his lips at the edges. The one that makes me shiver. "They can creep up on you."

"Oh . . ." I fall silent again, unable to think of a single interesting thing to say. I stifle a sigh instead. It didn't used to be like this, I know: I was getting comfortable around him, just hanging out like I do with Ethan. But now? Even mustering a basic sentence seems fraught with peril.

"So, uh, how are things with the B and B? It was looking good today."

"Yes!" I quickly fill him in with the good news about the booking. "That reminds me . . ." I pull out my camera and take a few shots of the surrounding forest. And then I casually snap some of Reeve, too. I need to give Olivia as much visual evidence as possible when I talk about him, I figure. If I ever get her on the phone, that is.

Reeve puts his hands in his pockets and looks away awkwardly, but once I tuck the camera away, he glances at me again. "I wouldn't have thought you'd be into helping out with the tourism project," he says casually, kicking a rock along the road. "I mean, isn't that what you're against?"

"What do you mean?"

"You know, tourists damaging the perfect, natural wilderness," he says. "All those cars, with their bad, bad gas fumes . . ."

"Hey!" I get that he's teasing me.

"What? That's your thing, right—environmentalism?"

I shrug, snatching a leaf from a branch as I pass. I begin to tear it into strips. "Well, yes, but not when you put it like that."

"So how would you put it?" Reeve's tone is still light, but I get the feeling there's more under the question than he's letting on.

I carefully consider my reply. This was a touchy subject with us from the start, and if this is some kind of test, I desperately want to pass it.

"I don't see anything wrong with letting people know how beautiful it is here, and we're doing things to be eco-friendly, like recycling." My big ideas for expensive renovations may have been unrealistic, but there have been plenty of small things to keep the impact low. "I mean, the B and B gets guests, there's more trade in town—everyone wins. Although, I'd prefer it if they didn't drive cross-country in a huge SUV," I can't help from adding.

He chuckles, and I slowly let out a sigh of relief.

Soon, we veer off-road, into the forest at the base of the mountain. The terrain is too steep to just hike straight up, so we follow a broad zigzag of a trail, walking diagonally across the width of the peak before crossing back, a little higher every pass. By the time we stop for a rest about halfway up, my thighs are aching and I'm sweating hard.

"Just a large hill?" I tell Fiona, taking a gulp of juice.

Somehow, she's barely out of breath. "Suck it up."

"Nice." I pause, walking to the edge of the clearing. The valley stretches as far as I can see, Stillwater nothing but a small collection of tiny buildings and the thin thread of Main Street snaking out toward the wider ribbon of highway. I feel very small.

"That's Blue Ridge up there." Reeve points at a collection of faux-log buildings, looming over the top of a far ridge. "They built a whole new road off the highway, just to get construction materials up there."

I carefully lift the video camera from my pack and slowly pan out, away from the ugly resort. Wispy clouds are drifting across the sky, and I swear, the air feels even crisper up here. "Act nice for the camera, Fiona!" I turn to her, but she covers her face with her hands.

"Don't point that thing at me!" She backs away. "I told you: I don't want—argh!" She lets out a sudden cry as she trips and tumbles heavily to the ground.

CHAPTER TWENTY-THREE

"Graceful!" I giggle at her mishap, but she doesn't get up. Instead, Fiona stays folded on the ground, nursing her ankle.

"Thanks a lot, I bet it's broken."

"Oh, no, really?" I lower the camera and start to move toward her, but Grady gets there first.

"Does this hurt?" he asks, crouching down by her and pressing around the edge of her sneaker.

"No, it doesn—OWW!" Fiona cries out. "God, are you all trying to kill me?"

"It's not broken," he reports. "Maybe just bruised, or a sprain?"

"Just? It hurts like hell!"

"Uh, yeah. Sorry."

Reeve looks at her, concerned. "What do you want to do? Wait here a while until it feels better?"

"We can rest as long as you need to." I put a comforting hand on her shoulder. Fiona shakes it off and presses her foot back to the ground, testing the weight for a split second. Then she sighs dramatically.

"No, I don't think I'm up to it."

"You want to go back?" Grady asks, still crouching beside her.

"I think so. Slowly." Taking his arm, Fiona maneuvers herself onto a nearby boulder. "But you guys don't have to quit." She looks over at me and Reeve. "You should keep going."

"No way," I tell her. "We're not letting you off on your own—we have rules, remember?"

"I can go with her," Grady says immediately. "You two finish the hike."

"No, it's OK," I tell him. "We can all—"

"But you wanted the view!" Fiona insists. "You're almost there. It would suck to turn back now."

"I don't mind. It's . . ." Then I pause. She's giving me a particularly meaningful look, but I can't figure out what she wants. Unless . . .

Seriously?

I look from her to Grady and back again. He's waiting, restless, by the boulder, while Fiona doesn't seem to be in pain at all anymore. But she does seem pretty eager to head off down the trail with Grady. Alone.

And just like that, her recent thaw begins to make total sense. I bite my lip to hide my smile as I watch them awkwardly avoid eye contact. I hoped maybe that fight we had made a difference because, deep down, she cared about our feelings, but it turns out there's one person whose feelings she definitely cares about: Grady's. Just how long has this been going on?

"I'll be fine," Fiona says again, taking Grady's arm and pulling herself to a standing position. She leans heavily against him, one of his arms around her shoulder. "Grady can take me home, and you and Reeve make it to the top. Right, Reeve?"

He looks at us all, clearly confused. "Sure, but I mean—"

"Then it's settled," Fiona declares. I swear I see a satisfied smile.

We split the packs and remaining water, and soon she and Grady are heading slowly back down the trail.

"I guess it's down to us."

I turn back to find Reeve waiting for me. "I guess so."

By the time we clear the tree line and make it up the final stretch of trail, I'm dead. No, really. My limbs are practically numb with exhaustion, every breath is a chore, and I figure that the only way I'm still managing to put one heavy foot in front of the other is if I've died and this is my zombified self plodding along.

Man, I need to exercise more.

I'm so busy staring down at the path in front of me that I only realize we've reached the top when Reeve stops walking. I look up to find that we're in a small clearing littered with shrubbery and grasses. Above us, there's nothing but impassable rock all the way to the real summit, but on my left, the cliff falls away.

"There." Reeve grins proudly. "Worth it, don't you think?"

I look out across the valley. He's right. For a moment, I can forget all my aches and pains. It's utterly breathtaking. A dark green blanket of trees, gray mountains under the gray mist of cloud, even . . . "Is that snow?" I squint at the far mountain peaks.

Reeve gulps from his water bottle, then wipes the top with his shirt before passing it to me. He nods. "Some ranges never melt. The Rockies go too high; it doesn't matter if it's baking down in the valleys."

"Wow." I can't believe how far the horizon stretches. I get out the camera and begin filming, shivering slightly.

"You need a sweater?" Reeve asks.

"Hmm? Oh, no, I've got one." As I pull my cardigan on again, a small splatter of rain begins to fall. I turn my face up to the clouds, the water cool relief on my sweaty skin.

He looks around. "We better take cover for a while."

I laugh. "It's just a little rain." At that, a boom of thunder rings over the valley. "Or not."

"Come on." Reeve points across to the far side of the clearing, where a small wooden hut is almost hidden in the trees.

"This is where you say 'I told you so,' right?" I joke, as we dash toward the shelter.

"Yup!" Reeve laughs. He waits for me to get inside before ducking in after me.

"Inside" is kind of an exaggeration, I find. The hut is nothing but a roof and three walls, perched back from the edge of the cliff. The ground is basic concrete, covered in dirt and a couple of food wrappers some other, less careful hikers must have left behind. Reeve kicks them aside and sits down against the back wall as the rain and winds howl away outside the open front.

I join him, gladly sliding off my feet. "Oh, my . . ." I sigh, loosening my boots. It's no warmer in here, but at least the wind isn't whipping around us. "What is this place?"

"Emergency shelter." Reeve shifts to get comfortable on the hard ground. "All the peaks have them around here, for snowstorms mainly."

"People climb these things in the snow?"

He chuckles. "I didn't say it was a good idea."

We sit in silence for a while, the rain thrumming steadily on the roof. The vista outside that had been so clear is now completely opaque. With the world shrouded in clouds outside, it feels like we're the last two people left in the world. I rummage in my pack for an energy bar and wordlessly offer Reeve half. He takes it with a nod, and we sit, watching the rain fall in thick sheets. A flash of lightning streaks through the sky, with another rumble of thunder sounding out right away.

The storm must be on top of us.

"Are we safe in here?" I ask, nervous.

"Safer in here than out there," he reassures me, but it's only after a minute I realize that doesn't quite answer my question. "Are you scared?"

"Of the storm? No." I elbow him lightly. "I'm not that pathetic."

Reeve gives me a brief smile. "Sorry."

"I usually like them—storms, I mean. All the noise and wind . . ." I flinch as another flash of lightning illuminates the valley, and hug my arms tight around my body. "But I'm usually snug inside with four solid walls between me and all that out there." As I talk, Reeve seems more distracted, looking outside at the pouring rain until finally, he cuts me off.

"Wait a sec. I need to check something out." He stands, silhouetted in the open entrance for a moment, and then disappears back the way we came, toward the trail.

"Reeve?" I leap up and call after him, but I soon lose sight of him in the trees. I panic for a moment, wondering if he's left me here, before remembering his patience up on that climbing trip. Reeve isn't the kind of guy to just bail.

I wait, shivering, until he reappears a couple of minutes later, drenched and dripping from the storm.

"We need to get going," he tells me, looking worried. He was only out a short time, but his sweatshirt is already soaked through.

"What, in this?" I protest. "It's still thundering out there."

"I know, but the trail is already way too muddy." He reaches for his pack and reties his boots. "All the water is just streaming down that path, and it's getting darker out. If we wait much longer, we'll be trapped here all night."

For a split second, the idea of being stranded on a

mountaintop with Reeve has a kind of romantic allure. Then I remember that I'm cold and damp and hungry. "OK, let's make a run for it."

"No running," Reeve tells me, his voice low and serious. "You could skid and break your neck. Seriously, Jenna, you've got to be really careful out there."

I nod, chastened, and brace myself to follow him.

The minute I step outside, I'm hit by the noise. Not just the thunder, which still rings out occasionally, but the sound of the rain itself, beating down on every rock and tree branch in a loud drumming that makes it hard to hear a thing. I'm small and insignificant in the huge, gray world. Despite what I told Reeve, I begin to feel scared.

We should have gone back with Fiona and Grady.

"Watch your step!" Reeve yells at me. I start down the trail after him, trying to follow his route exactly as he picks his way through the perilous mud and streams of water gushing down what used to be the plain dirt path. In minutes, my thin cardigan is soaked through, water trickling down my back and the rain freezing my bare legs. I grit my teeth and keep moving.

We manage to keep up a quick enough pace: something less than jogging but faster than a walk. The steep incline that caused my thighs so much grief on the way up now makes just as many problems as I skid and slip down, trying to keep my balance. Five minutes stretches into ten, and then twenty. The ground begins to level out as we descend into the main forest, but my skin is numb from the cold, and even these supposedly-waterproof boots of mine are beginning to squelch around the toes.

I wish I were anywhere but here.

"You OK?" Reeve pauses to glance back at me. I can only imagine what I look like, hair plastered to my cheeks and teeth chattering. I nod, determined not to show how truly miserable I am, and plunge onward past him. Focus on warmth, I tell myself. Long bubble baths. Hot chocolate. Soup. Anything soft and dry and—

Suddenly Reeve yanks me back, his hand gripping my arm hard.

"Oww!"

He clamps his other hand to my mouth and holds me still against him. "Don't move," he murmurs in my ear. "Don't even make a sound."

The urgency in his voice shocks me still; my complaint dies on my lips.

"What?" I whisper back. He jerks his head in the direction we were heading and I turn, following his gaze into the trees ahead of us.

A bear is loping slowly through the forest.

CHAPTER TWENTY-FOUR

I stop breathing.

"Stay calm," Reeve whispers, his mouth against my ear. "It hasn't seen us yet."

The animal is huge, easily bigger than me, and it paces along with a strange rocking gait, black fur dark even in the dim light. My heart races as the rain keeps pouring down on us. I don't know much about bears except that they kill, and maim, and oh, yes, kill. I think of the half-finished energy bar in my pack with a twist of fear.

Oh, God.

I tremble, Reeve's arms locked tight around me. I can feel his heart beating quick against my back through our soaked, thin clothes. We stand frozen, watching the bear sniff and paw at the undergrowth. Every moment stretches into forever as I try not to imagine a dozen grisly ends.

I don't ever think about death. Not really, no more than a flicker of anxiety when I'm trying to merge on the highway or watching a news clip about some unfortunate girl my age. Even then, those are vague, passing ideas—not forty feet away with razor-sharp claws and angry teeth. But standing here, shaking with fear, I suddenly grasp the truth of it: the blood racing in my veins, the sharp tingle of my chilled skin, the intensity of every breath.

This is my life.

I don't know how long it is until the bear lopes out of sight. No more than ten seconds, maybe, but it feels like hours to me.

"Wait a while longer," Reeve whispers, still holding me. "Give it time to get clear."

I nod, adrenaline rushing through my system. Finally, I feel Reeve relax.

"It's gone," he says hoarsely, loosening his grip on my arms and turning me to face him. I still don't move. "Are you OK?"

"I think so. . . ." I waver, and he pulls me back against him, holding me steady. I look up. His eyelashes are wet, water running down his face.

"I'm sorry."

I blink, slowly emerging from my daze. "How . . . I mean, that wasn't your fault."

Reeve shakes his head. "I should have been more careful. I should have made us go back hours ago. I saw the clouds changing."

Maybe it's the endorphins still singing in my blood, or

maybe I'm just plain thankful I'm standing here and not lying in a bloody, mauled heap. Either way, I look straight at him, suddenly reckless. "So why didn't you?"

Our eyes meet for a long moment.

"I didn't . . ." He pauses, moving one hand to brush away the strand of hair sticking to my forehead. I feel a rush that's nothing to do with the near-death experience. There's something in the space between us. I can't be imagining it—this isn't wishful thinking.

Reeve glances away. "I thought, maybe . . ."

And then before he can make another sound, I kiss him.

Our faces are cold from the storm, but I still feel a burst of warmth as I slowly press my lips against his, uncertain at first. I reach my arms around his neck and pull him down to me, kissing him with a bravery I don't think I possessed until just minutes ago.

This is my life.

I don't want to sit around, listening to Olivia's adventures—I want some of my own. All this time, I've kept quiet, stayed in, turned down dates with nice enough guys because I've wanted to really *feel* something. And now that I do, I want it to be mine.

After a heart-stopping moment of panic, he kisses me back.

Pulling me gently against him, Reeve takes my face in his hands. Breathless, I find myself clutching at his shoulders, his neck, overwhelmed with the intensity of his mouth on mine, his teeth grazing at my lips . . .

Oh, God.

I'm not sure how long it is before I break it off. I don't even know why I do it, except . . . it's too much. I pull away, unsteady, tugging at my soaked T-shirt, which has somehow risen up around my bra.

"We better get back," I say, when words finally manage to form in my brain.

"Back. Sure. I mean . . ." He straightens up his own twisted shirt, clearly flustered. I'm gratified to see that he needs to recover, too. At least I'm not alone in feeling overwhelmed by this. After a moment, he picks up his bag.

"The rain's stopped," he says, sounding anything but casual.

"It did?" I look up. The pine trees around us are thick with dewdrops, but there are no more showers or thunder. Instead, there's a heavy silence stretching through the forest. "I didn't notice." I look at him shyly, and to my relief, he grins back—conspiratorial and happy.

"C'mon, before you freeze to death." He holds out his hand, and I take it, feeling completely invincible.

CHAPTER TWENTY-FIVE

He doesn't call.

It's been three days since the hiking trip. Three days since Reeve kissed me like we were the only people in the world, and my giddy elation has faded to anxious insecurity. He still hasn't called me.

"Will you stop that?" Fiona snaps as I reach to check my phone for the thirty-fifth time this afternoon. "Who are you waiting to hear from, anyway?"

"No one," I answer quickly, snapping the display shut. I try not to sigh. "Just . . . Olivia."

"Your little eco-friend?" Fiona expertly stuffs a down pillow into a crisp pillowcase, gives it a swift pummeling, and then tosses it on the pile. Finally, we found a job to suit her. "What's up with her? You don't drone on about her the way you used to."

"Nothing," I say, a little defensive. "She's just . . . busy. I am, too."

"Sure you are." Fiona smirks at me. "Those sheets won't fold themselves."

I keep folding. Despite what I told Fiona, I've been feeling Olivia's absence even more these last few days. She's not answering her cell, and I'm sick of leaving messages only to get a three-word text in reply. Moments like this are when I need my best friend the most, to tell me everything will be OK with Reeve, that this is just a stupid boy thing, and not proof that he regrets it all and never wants to speak to me again. Or, worse still, doesn't even care.

My cell phone starts to ring. I leap for it.

"Hello?" I answer excitedly, but my enthusiasm quickly fades. "Oh, Mom, hey."

"Is this a bad time, sweetie?"

I look around at Fiona and the stacked laundry room. "Nope, it's cool." Leaving the sheets in a warm heap, I wander out into the hallway, barefoot. The screen door is propped open, so I sit down on the step, looking out at the rhododendron bushes in the yard. "What's up?"

"Oh, nothing new really. I just wanted to check and see how you're doing." There's a strain in her tone, as if she's tired, but it's still nice to hear her voice. It's the first time I've been away from her for so long.

"I'm good. Things at the B and B are really coming together, so everyone's working flat out." I pause, picking at the nail polish on my big toe before asking, "How's Dad?"

"Your father's fine. Isn't he e-mailing you?"

"Yes. Well, kind of." I don't want to tell her how much he's raving about Swedish food, Swedish art, and all those freaking fjords. But maybe she already knows, because she suddenly changes the subject.

"Your grandmother sends her love. She's out getting her hair done at the moment, but you should call back later. She'd love to hear your voice."

"OK."

"We went out to dinner last night at that Italian place here. Do you remember it? The one with all those actors' photos on the wall, and . . ."

As she chats, I tell myself I'm being completely para-noid about this whole "summer apart" thing. Her replies are perfectly normal; it doesn't seem like anything's wrong.

"How are the kids, in your classes?" I try to sound cheerful.

She laughs. "A handful to say the least. But I'm enjoy-ing it. I might take up some part-time work when we get back." She pauses. "How would you feel about that?"

"Sure, that sounds cool. What does Dad think?"

There's silence. "Your father is so busy, I haven't men-tioned it yet."

"Oh."

They used to talk about everything.

"Anyway, honey, I wanted to talk to you about some-thing." Her voice drops, suddenly serious. "About next year. We've got to be prepared for some, changes . . ." She trails off, nervous, and there it is again: fear, low in my gut. I can only imagine what kind of changes she means.

"Sorry, Mom—I've got to go!" I say brightly before she can say another word. "Things are . . . busy around here, and I've got plans. Talk soon!"

"OK." She pauses, sighing slightly. "You take care. I love you."

"You too."

I close my phone slowly and then leap up, restless. I don't want to sit around, folding laundry and waiting for a call that's obviously not going to come. Reeve has stayed away so far, so how about I go looking for him?

Or maybe not.

As I cycle slowly down Main Street later that afternoon, the old lady at the gas station shoots me a strange look. I don't blame her. This is my fourth loop around town, and there's still no sign of Reeve. There's barely a sign of anyone at all.

I pull over by the patch of playground and climb off, abandoning my bike and collapsing onto one of the kids' swings. I can't help but feel like an idiot. Reeve must have a good reason for not getting in touch yet: maybe something's happened with his mom, or he's been pulling extra shifts. And here I am, practically stalking him through town in a pair of denim cut-offs and my cutest blue shirt because of one stupid kiss.

OK. One amazing, earth-moving kiss.

I hang on to the swing and lean back, closing my eyes to the looming mountains and green valley stretching up around me.

"Hey, Jenna."

Startled, I nearly fall off the swing. Struggling to keep my balance, I turn to see Ethan sauntering toward me in that awful plaid shirt of his. Grady and Reeve follow, a few paces behind.

Reeve!

"Hi!" I exclaim breathlessly, my pulse picking up right away. "How've you guys been? What's up?" I quickly smooth my hair back and make sure my shirt isn't gaping open. Even as I do, I tell myself to stay relaxed, not make a big deal over this. But I can't help it: even the sight of him with that old red baseball cap jammed low over his eyes is doing strange, fluttery things to my stomach.

And I thought the nervous crush phase was bad.

"Nothing much." Ethan gives me a look, but thankfully he doesn't say anything about my weird behavior. I recover, forcing myself to act casual.

"Cool . . ." My gaze slides over to Reeve. He gives me a quick smile but then turns away, looking down the street. My excitement slips.

I turn back to Ethan, trying to seem unconcerned. "So, did you want to get started on the next DVD marathon, maybe tomorrow?"

"Sure," Grady agrees, kind of quickly.

He elbows Ethan, who says, "Yeah, count me in."

"Reeve?" I ask, letting my eyes drift. Despite my best efforts, there's a whole lot of hope bound up in that one word.

"Nope, can't make it." He finally turns back to me, but his expression is unreadable.

My heart sinks.

"More overtime?" Ethan asks, leaning against the jungle-gym frame. I try to keep a smile fixed on my face.

Reeve nods. "Yup. I figure I should take it while I can."

"Good call."

"Anyway, I've got to go." Reeve jerks his thumb toward the gas station, already edging away. His eyes flicker back to me, just for a moment, and I think I see a private look, but I can't be sure. "Catch you all later."

"Bye . . ." My voice trails uselessly after him.

As I watch him walk away, something clenches in my throat. All this time I've spent replaying that kiss, going over the whole day, and it doesn't mean a thing to him. It was just the moment, the adrenaline—he got caught up. And I was expecting . . . I don't even know what. God, I'm pathetic.

"Want to grab a soda?" I realize Ethan's talking to me. Grady has bailed as well, off down the street on his skateboard, so it's just the two of us left.

"Sure." I nod weakly.

"And you've got to hear the new Devon Darsel tracks; I downloaded them last night." He picks up my bike and begins to wheel it toward the store. I've got nothing better to do than follow him, aching a little inside.

I wallow for the rest of the day, running over every look and conversation until I'm not even sure what's real anymore—and what's a product of my overactive imagination. But no matter how hard I try, I can't figure Reeve out. Are stormy, near-death hook-ups such a regular occurrence for him that this one didn't even register? Or does he think Ethan still likes me and doesn't want to go behind his back? There are too many possibilities, and none of them makes me feel any less insecure.

A text comes through, lighting up my phone. It's from Olivia. *Where the wild things R=awesome movie! Xx.*

I stare at it in disbelief. That's it? I pour my heart out to her voice mail about my parents and Reeve and I get a one-line, nonsense response!

Even though it's got to be at least one a.m. out there, I hit my speed dial. By some miracle, she answers on the second ring.

"Olivia, it's me."

"Wait, who?"

I stop. "It's me, Jenna."

"Hey!" Her voice is high-pitched, and there's laughter and noise in the background. "I was totally just talking about you!"

"Did you get my messages?" I sit, very still on the edge of my bed, hugging my comforter.

"What?" I hear her cover the handset and say something to someone there.

"My messages." I swallow back the lump in my throat and try again. "About Reeve, and everything."

"Uh-huh! See, I told you he liked you, all this time!"

"No, that was Ethan." I grit my teeth. "He's gay, remember? This is Reeve. You know, Reeve."

I must have sent her dozens of texts and e-mails over the past weeks: spelling out in tiny detail every look and touch and smile that's gone between us. The first thing I did when I got back from the hike was call Olivia up and leave a giddy message so she could share in it all. But she doesn't even remember.

"Right, sure, Reeve!" she says quickly, her voice hard to make out over the background noise. "You guys got together—that's so great."

"Sure it is." My voice is flat. "Except we didn't."

"Uh-huh."

I know that tone. It's the one she uses when she couldn't care less about what's being said—not even enough to register what you're talking about "Where are you, anyway?"

"What?"

"I said, where are you?" I speak louder.

"We're in Chicago!" Olivia exclaims. "Setting up camp. We got in this evening to protest the Climate Committee meeting!"

"Wait, what happened to the collective?"

"It didn't work out. They were way too fixed in their rules . . ." Her voice begins to fade out. "So we went . . . Cash says . . . more free-form . . . until . . ."

"Olivia, are you there?"

"With the system, so you . . . overthrowing . . . in the end." I listen closely, but I can't make out more than a few words among the static and laughter. Then Olivia's voice comes back, suddenly clear.

"Here I am! What's up?"

Suddenly, I've had enough.

"You know what? Don't even bother!" I tell her angrily. "If you can't even pay attention to anything I tell you . . ."

"But Jenna—"

"No! I haven't heard from you in forever—and I really needed you this week!" My voice catches on that last part. I sniffle. "It's not like I'm asking much, but with everything going on with Reeve . . . I don't know what to do. I miss you!"

There's nothing but background noise for a moment. I wait, picking at a hangnail, and then I hear her voice again, awkward. "Uh, Jenna, can I call you back tomorrow? It's just, we're about to—"

I hang up on her.

Flopping backward onto my bed, I stare up at the ceiling and despair. I've never hung up on anyone, ever! But God, the way she just brushes me off now . . . I know she's off doing her own thing this summer, and so am I, but that shouldn't mean she can just put our friendship on hold. A slow tear trickles down my cheek, and I wipe it away angrily. Right now, I feel completely alone.

I'm still lying there hours later, clutching the soft throw. The house falls silent, as Fiona turns off her music to sleep, and Adam and Susie lock up and make their way to bed. I should turn in, too, but somehow the effort it would take to find PJs and brush my teeth is beyond me. Maybe I could just fall asleep right here. . . .

Suddenly, there's a rattle at my window. I sit up. There it is again. Crossing the room, I look out, checking that a branch hasn't gotten trapped in the shutters again, or—

"Hey, Jenna!" There's a loud stage whisper from down in the backyard.

"Argh!" I let out a squawk of shock, banging my head

against the frame. "Ethan, is that you?" I squint to make out a shape in the dark. "What are you trying to do, scare me half to death?"

"No, it's me, Reeve."

As I lean out of my window—face red and blotchy from crying, chocolate staining my shirt from where I comfort-ate a half-pint of ice cream—I see him step out from the shadows.

"Can you come down? I, uh, need to talk to you."

CHAPTER TWENTY-SIX

I reel backward in shock. Reeve. Here. Now?

"Jenna?" he calls again.

"Yup?" I edge toward the window, staring like he's some kind of hallucination brought on by too much sugar and wishful thinking.

"Can you come down?"

I can't see his face, just the dark outline of his silhouette. "What for?"

"So we can talk!"

I'm standing, trying to figure out what to do, when I hear footsteps outside my door. I freeze. If someone comes . . . but there's nothing. I exhale, relieved.

"Jenna?" Reeve's voice is louder now. I check the flickering display on my nightstand. It's one a.m.

"Fine! I'll come down," I hiss at him. "But be quiet! Susie will . . . I don't know what she'll do if she finds you here, but it won't be good!"

I close the window and spin around, freaked. What is he even doing here? I'm still dressed in jeans and a T-shirt, so I quickly throw the comforter around my shoulders and pull on a pair of socks. My hair is a tangled mess, and as for my face . . . argh! Skidding silently down the hallway, I lock myself in the bathroom and brush my teeth at record speed. A wipe with my facecloth is all I have time to manage before creeping downstairs and out to the back porch.

Reeve is waiting there for me.

"Hey!" He bounces up from the step, looking anxious. The porch lamp is spilling gold light over him, making his black hair gleam perfectly and his tan appear even darker. I feel a new rush at the sight of him, but force myself to stay cool. I don't want to fall all over myself if he's just here to say it didn't mean anything.

Reeve clears his throat. "I'm really glad you—"

"Shhh!" I hiss, panicked, and quickly check the house for signs of life.

"Sorry!" He lowers his voice.

I wait for a moment, but it seems safe: nothing but the sound of the forest and the low whir of crickets. "So what do you want?" I pull my blanket tight around my shoulders and try to look unconcerned.

Reeve looks down at his battered black sneakers for a moment. "I, uh, wanted to check in. About today . . ."

"What about it?" I manage to sound casual, as if I

haven't spent hours having imaginary versions of this very conversation.

He looks up, meeting my eyes. "I'm . . . sorry. I mean, I was kind of weird before, with the guys."

"Really?" I act nonchalant even as I feel a wave of relief. He's sorry!

"Yeah . . ." Reeve shrugs self-consciously. "I guess, we didn't really talk about . . . You know, how it was going to work. With the others."

"No . . . we didn't," I admit. We didn't do much talking at all.

There's a pause, as I get a very vivid flashback to what we were doing instead of all that mature discussion. By the look I get from Reeve, I'm guessing he's thinking the same thing.

"Umm." I blush. "So . . . maybe we should do that now. The talking?"

He nods immediately. "Right."

Another silence.

"Do you want to go first?" I ask hesitantly. Like ripping off a Band-Aid, I just want to be done with it—good or bad. Bracing myself, I sit down on the porch step and wait.

Reeve sits down as well. He's a safe couple of feet away from me, but I can still feel the presence of his body. Staring straight out at the dark yard, he lets out a long breath. "The thing is . . . I like you, Jenna." His words come tumbling out in a quick rush, and right away, my heart leaps. "But I don't want you to get the wrong idea. About . . . us."

He glances over, cautious. Just as fast, my hopes deflate. This is it? He shows up late at night, throwing pebbles at my window, just to tell me not to get the wrong idea?

Swallowing back the lump in my throat, I play with the frayed edge of the blanket. "So, what is this? I mean . . . what happened, was it a mistake? Because it would be cool if you didn't mean it," I add immediately, not wanting to sound desperate. "I mean, we were both so stressed, and I did kind of throw myself at you and—"

"No!" Reeve exclaims, before remembering to lower his voice. "No, that wasn't just you. It was . . . I wanted it, too."

"Oh." My voice is quiet. I force myself to glance back at him. "Then, what? I don't understand."

Reeve sighs. "Me either. It's just . . ." He looks over at me, the light casting shadows across his face. But I can still see his eyes, and the expression there is almost resigned. "You're only here for the summer, and then you're heading home, right?" I nod slowly. "And I might be going to college, or not, and . . . I don't want to start something I can't follow through." Reeve sits there, leaning forward on his knees, ripping up the dandelion heads that grow up the side of the steps.

I come back down to earth with a bump. I hadn't even thought about the future. I've been so caught up in breathless speculation over if he even likes me or not, that I didn't consider what this could actually be, or for how long.

"And the thing with Ethan . . ." he adds, hesitant.

"Was never ever a thing!" I say quickly.

"Oh. Cool." He looks relieved.

"I don't mind about, you know, the future and stuff."
I cringe. Apparently, awkward moments of intimacy rob
me of all decent vocab. "Just because I'm leaving, it doesn't
mean we can't . . . hang out." Again with the eloquence.

Reeve looks over, his dark eyes inscrutable. "Are
you sure?"

"Absolutely!" I'm breathless now, seeing a way of getting what I want. Of getting Reeve, even for a little while.
"We could just, spend time together. I mean, it's not like I
want to get married!"

He chuckles nervously, and I remember the number-
one rule of teenage boys: Never ever mention the word
marriage. Not even as a joke.

"Like you said, I'm just here for the summer," I add
quickly. "I'm not looking for anything serious."

There's silence, and I begin to wonder if that's made
me sound like some kind of slut, but then Reeve exhales,
his lips curving into a slow grin.

"I feel kind of stupid now," he admits, looking sheep-
ish. "Assuming you wanted . . . I mean . . ."

I manage to laugh. "Full of yourself, huh?"

"I guess so." He stays there for a moment, looking
sideways at me. Then he moves his left hand to overlap
mine on the step. I turn it over, linking my fingers through
his while my heart sings.

He likes me!

"So . . ." Reeve grins at me again, and I grin back,
almost embarrassed.

"So . . ." I echo, amazingly happy and nervous all in
the same moment. Before, in the woods, that was sheer

impulse. I didn't have time to think about impressions or consequences or anything. But now . . . now every second drags out into forever as I sit here, waiting to kiss him again.

And then he leans in, reaching to touch my face as his lips slowly move closer to mine, and I forget everything.

I'm not a total innocent. I've kissed guys before. Guys I liked, guys I didn't, guys who attacked my mouth like their tongue was a whirlpool, and guys who just kind of smushed their lips against mine and stood there, waiting. But none of that comes even close to kissing Reeve.

His breath is warm against my face as I move closer, mirroring him. I swear I'm so tense, I'm almost shaking, but if he notices, he doesn't say. Resting his hand against my cheek for a moment, Reeve pauses, his lips barely touching me. I stop breathing. Then his mouth opens slightly, and his hand slips back toward my hair, and I just . . . fall into him.

Now I understand. Why Olivia sneaks and lies to her parents to spend more time with Cash. Why Ethan is willing to move cross-country to find a boy to date. Why Miriam Park and those other popular girls would trip into class giggly and swooning after making out with their boyfriends against the lockers.

Because this is incredible.

Eventually, we come up for air, Reeve loosening his pull on the back of my neck. I draw away slightly and let out a shaky breath, my whole body flying on some magical mix of hormones and adrenaline and pure Reeve. I fight to form a coherent thought.

"This casual thing . . ." Reeve says, his voice slightly hoarse. He clears his throat and then breaks into a mischievous look. "The person who thought it up deserves a medal."

I laugh, the tension broken. "A Nobel Prize," I agree, grinning.

"C'mere." He reaches over and pulls me against him, one hand around my shoulder and the other twisting around my left hand. He exhales, and I feel it in the rise and fall of his ribs against me. "That's better."

So much better. I rest my head gently on his shoulder, the heat of his body warming me even through my blanket.

"So we're good?" Reeve looks over to check. I nod happily. And then, just because I can, I lean up quickly and kiss his cheek. He grins, tightening his embrace. "Good."

I'm not sure how long I sit there, snug in his arms, but soon I can't help but let out a huge yawn. Reeve starts.

"I'm sorry—I didn't even think."

"It's OK!" I tell him sleepily. "I'm"—yawn—"fine."

Reeve squeezes me. "Sure you are. It's almost . . ." He checks his watch. "After two? Jesus, I've got an early shift."

"Oh, no!" I struggle to my feet. My legs get caught in the blanket and I stumble against him. Reeve catches me.

"Whoa, you don't have to go falling at my feet."

"Very funny." I hit him gently. He grabs my hand and pulls it up to his shoulder. I move closer against him, still thrilled just by having his arms around me, solid and strong.

"About this thing . . ." he starts.

"Mhmmm?" I place a tiny kiss just below his earlobe, and then another just at the curve of his neck. The skin there is soft, and smells faintly of soap and laundry detergent.

"Maybe, we should keep it low-key," Reeve suggests. I look up.

"Like, you mean a secret?"

He nods, dipping his head to kiss my forehead. "This town, it's so small," he explains. "One person finds out, and then they go talk to someone else, and suddenly, everyone knows everything." A weird expression flickers across his face, like a shadow. "It gets so claustrophobic, all that pressure."

"But would that mean you go back to ignoring me again," I say, beginning to feel insecure.

"No way," Reeve promises, shaking his head. "This would just be like, our thing. And when we're out, with everyone, we would be like before. Friends."

"Promise?" I check.

He kisses me lightly on my lips. "I swear. I really am sorry about earlier," he adds, looking anxious.

I relax. "It's OK. I was just, confused. I didn't know how you felt."

"And now you do."

Reeve kisses me again, longer this time. I sigh, reaching up to slide both hands around his neck. Biting down gently on his lower lip, I feel him smile against me.

"I better get back." Reluctantly, he pulls away. "But I'll see you after work, at Ethan's?" I nod. "Maybe I'll give you a ride home. . . ." He gives me this look that melts me from the inside, and I wonder how the hell I'm supposed to act normal around him ever again.

"See you tomorrow," I agree, breathless. He kisses me again, both hands on my cheeks, and then hurries away around the side of the house, swallowed up by the dark.

I sag back against the porch. I'm exhausted, but I know there's no way on earth I'm sleeping tonight, not with this electricity still sparking through my bloodstream.

CHAPTER TWENTY-SEVEN

It seems impossible that things would go on as normal after something so major, but they do. The next week passes much like the ones before: the B and B gradually begins to resemble an actual home (instead of a war zone), another couple of bookings come through, and I finally perfect the guitar solo on that Weezer track for our Rock Band wars. But there is one big difference, the reason I can't check my phone without a tiny grin, and why I'm not getting any sleep even though I turn in for bed before ten.

Reeve.

We've managed two more secret rendezvous since that night on my front porch: down by the lake one evening, and another midnight escape. I nearly woke the whole house tripping on some stray paint cans, but luckily, no one heard. It feels like everyone should be able to tell something's up, the way I'm still buzzing with crazy adrenaline, but nobody notices a thing, not even Ethan.

"I'm bored," he announces at the end of the week. Slumping down until only a mess of brown hair is visible on the countertop, Ethan makes a muffled groaning noise. "I'm so freaking bored!"

"You said that yesterday." I pause from editing a new video, one of Ethan fishing up at the river. I'm practiced now, but it still takes time: cutting the footage on Susie's program and uploading it to the site. I'm going to ace my computer tech classes next semester for sure.

"Yeah, but today is worse." He looks around at the empty aisles, mournful. "We haven't had a single customer all morning."

"That's because everyone sane is indoors." Brushing damp, sweaty hair from my forehead, I pout. "Why didn't you tell me your AC was out?" We've got eight portable fans set up on a side table, all pointed so the cool breeze blows right at us, but it's still not enough to keep this heat wave at bay.

"Because then you wouldn't have come," Ethan replies. He musters an evil grin, still lying with his cheek against the front desk. "And I'd be stuck here, going out of my mind alone."

"You suck." I'm too hot to hit him properly—I just toss an empty packing carton over the register. He doesn't bother to move.

"There's nothing to do."

"We could go to the lake this afternoon," I suggest. And if Reeve stops by . . .

"Boring."

"Or film another one of these videos." Maybe with Reeve along, too . . .

"Mnnaugh."

"You're pathetic," I inform him, even if I am as well—just in a different way. "Tell me that at least your cold water is still running."

Ethan lifts his head slightly. "Yup. I think there might even be some sodas in the fridge."

"Joy." I try to get up, but I'm wearing shorts and my bare thighs are sticking to the seat. I collapse back down. "Maybe later."

"Uh-huh."

We stay lounged in our seats until my phone buzzes. I grab for it expectantly, and then pause when I see the number.

"Hey, Mom." I pull myself out of my seat and head through to the back room.

"Jenna, finally. I've been getting your voice mail for days now."

"I know, sorry." I trap the phone against my shoulder and pull a couple of ice-cold sodas from the fridge. "I've been really busy. Things are hectic, with the B and B, I mean."

"Well, I'm glad I've got you. I still need to talk to you about something." Her voice wavers. I gulp.

"Can it wait?" I interrupt. "I'm just on my way out. I don't want the guys to hang around."

"Oh." Mom sounds disappointed. "I guess. Can you tell me when—?"

"Sure! We'll talk soon. Love you!"

I hang up. I'm still determined not to let my parents' problems creep into my summer, but it's getting harder to pretend nothing's going on. Tucking my phone away, I head back into the front of the store just as the bell over the door chimes. I try not to grin when I see who it is. Finally!

"Oh, it's you." Ethan sighs.

"Gee, thanks." Reeve wanders over, looking back and forth between us. "Wow, you guys look bored."

"See?" Ethan pokes me. I slap his hand away. "Our brains are leaking out," he explains.

"Speak for yourself. What's up?" I ask him ultra-casual. "You need tools, or paint, or something from the basement?"

"Uh, nope." Reeve flashes me a private grin. He's wearing old cut-off jean shorts that fray around his knees and a khaki-colored tank top, the color making his golden tan glow even darker. "I was just wondering if you guys were going to the festival thing later."

"No," Ethan says, at the same time as I ask, "What festival?"

"They have a thing up in Graystone Valley every year," Reeve explains, ignoring Ethan. "With a fair, and rodeo and stuff. It's kind of hokey, but . . ."

"That sounds like fun!" I leap at the chance.

"Cool." Reeve grins back. We share another look.

"I guess if you're all going . . ." Ethan pulls himself up again. "Is Grady coming too?"

"Maybe."

"I could try and drag Fiona along," I suggest. "Make it a group thing." The more people around, the less chance they'll notice if Reeve and I get, umm, separated from the group.

"Awesome." Reeve nods. "I could swing by for you both around five?"

"Sounds good. If I can get her to, you know, be sociable."

He gives me a wry grin. "Good luck with that."

The festival turns out to be something out of central casting. I can't believe it: there's a Ferris wheel, and carnival rides, and even an actual rodeo with cowboy events and calf-wrangling competitions! Everywhere I look, small children are running around with cotton candy, and people are wearing cowboy hats—un-ironically!

"I think you've got enough photos." Reeve laughs, after I've been snapping away for thirty minutes straight. It looks like everyone in a hundred-mile radius has turned out for the event, strolling through the grassy fairgrounds in the evening sun. Above us, the mountains frame the valley with their gray rock, but down here, there's a riot of color and noise.

"You're joking—this is awesome!" I can't believe how quaint it all is, with livestock displays and . . . "No way! Is that a pie-baking contest?!" I bound toward the red-checkered tent with glee. It is. A dozen of Graystone Valley's finest blueberry pies are lined up for judging, next to the pickled chutney stand and a man selling fresh farm cheese. "I can't believe this. My mom is going to be so jealous. She loves stuff like this!"

I feel Reeve's arms slip around my waist. I turn, caught off guard. "Wait, what about . . . ?"

"All clear." He grins, pulling me closer. "Fiona and Grady are off terrorizing small children by the bumper cars, and Ethan said something about ice cream . . ."

I relax back against him, happy. "So what do you want to do?"

"I don't know . . ." He links his hands together, resting them on my stomach so I'm nestled in his arms.

"I've got a couple of ideas." I grin, turning so I'm facing him. We kiss for a long moment, hidden by the folds of the bright tent awning.

"Mmm," I say, pulling away. Then I give him an evil grin. "What was that you said about ice cream?"

"Ouch!" He clutches his chest in mock pain. "I'm not even your number-one priority."

I laugh. "Maybe two, or three—if they have fries!"

They do. They also have veggie burgers, classic slaw, and a dessert table that lasts for days. We pile paper plates high with food and find a spot out by the side of the main stage: a three-foot-high plywood platform where a trio of grizzled men are entertaining the crowd with a banjo and fiddles. It's not my kind of thing, but there's something infectious about their energy.

We laze for a while, chatting quietly in the sun, until I see the others making their way through the crowd. I shift away from Reeve, just in time.

"Dude, you've got to try the corn dogs!" Ethan collapses heavily right next to us. "Fiona ate, like, six."

"Did not!" she protests, wrinkling her nose at the ground before carefully taking a seat. Grady just throws himself down without a second thought, his plate overflowing with three different kinds of pie and a mountain of whipped cream.

"You're really going to eat all of that?" I ask him, trying not to sound flustered. I can feel Reeve's eyes on me, my cheeks hot with our secret.

"Duh. Hey! Get your own!" He bats away my hand as I try to sneak a slice of cherry.

Reeve gives me a quick smile while the others bicker around us. I grin back, happy.

"We saw Kate," Grady adds through a mouthful of food. He gives Reeve this wink. "She's lookin' goooood."

My grin falters. Reeve's face has gone tense. "Who's Kate?" I ask, trying to sound casual.

"The Ex," Ethan announces dramatically. "Except, he still worships and adores her."

"Really?" Forcing a light tone, I pretend to be enthralled by the a capella group onstage, but inside, I'm screaming with questions. What ex? Why haven't I heard about her?

"Guys—" Reeve's complaints are quickly drowned out by Ethan.

"I can't believe you didn't hear." He smears mustard from his chin. "It was like, the big town drama. Epic breakup," he confides before Reeve hurls a can of soda at him. "OUCH! What's your problem, man?"

"No problem." Reeve glares at him, and then catches himself. He shrugs. "Just lay off the gossip. It's ancient history."

"So I didn't have to suffer through your moping like, all of last year?" Ethan snorts. "Come on. Anyway, you might have a chance again. I heard she split with that hockey guy."

I try to ignore the slice of insecurity that runs through me. Of course he's had girlfriends. I mean, look at him!

"She asked about you." Ethan slurps at his slushie. "So if you want to go throw balls at some hoops, now would be a good time, that's all I'm saying."

"And she's put on a couple of pounds," Grady agrees. "In all the right places." Fiona smacks him. "What? It's true!"

Thankfully, the subject changes, and soon the guys are arguing over who ate the most chili fries last year. I pick at my plate, my appetite gone, until Ethan suddenly laughs.

"Ha, told you!" He shades his eyes as he looks over at the crowd. Winding their way toward us are two girls: a petite brunette, and a tall blond girl, casual in jeans and a white T-shirt. "Kate." Ethan grins at me, like this is all a joke. "I said she was asking about Reeve."

I sit there, awkward, while the girls arrive and greet everyone with enthusiasm.

"Hey, Grady." The brunette, Clara, flutters her fingers at him. Fiona's eyes narrow.

"So what's up?" Kate hooks her thumbs through her belt loops and grins at us. It's immature, but I hate her immediately. Her long hair is kind of windswept, her freckled face doesn't have an ounce of makeup, and there's even a reddish sauce stain on the corner of her shirt, but somehow, she makes me feel like a slob.

"Nothing much." Reeve shrugs, getting to his feet and gathering up our trash.

"Where have you been hiding?" she asks. "I haven't seen you all summer." The question is directed at them all, but she lingers on Reeve for much longer.

He looks awkward. "Around."

"We were just heading to check out some of the rides." I leap up, impatient. I get that Reeve and I are a secret, but that doesn't mean I have to sit around watching the hot girls all throw themselves at him.

"Coming, Ethan?"

"I guess. I—" he yelps as I drag him to his feet. "What's the rush?"

"Nothing." I force a grin. "I just want to see everything before it gets too late."

"Great idea!" Kate exclaims, smiling at Reeve. She even has dimples. Great. "Let's do it!"

Foiled.

We wander the festival grounds in a group, pausing for Ethan and Grady to hurl balls/rings/blocks at various stands in a show of macho competition, while I keep one eye on Kate's proximity to Reeve. It's pretty close. Part of me wants to grab his hand, like I'm marking my territory, the way Jeremiah B. Coombes would suggest in that survival book, but it would just look pathetic and desperate. And freak him out. I try not to sigh.

"So you're the new girl I keep hearing about." Kate drags her attention away from him long enough to fall into step beside me. "How have you been finding Stillwater?"

"Good." I manage to smile back.

"I'm guessing the guys gave you a hard time at first, right?" She gives me a sympathetic grin, tucking hair behind her ear. "They're a tough crowd."

"Hey," Ethan protests. "We were total gentleman."

"Uh, no!" I smack him lightly. "Remember that whole 'abandoning me in the woods at night' thing?"

"They didn't!" Kate groans, turning. "Guys, that's just evil."

"See?" I say pointedly. "And they said I was just over-reacting." I glance over at Reeve, but he's got his fists jammed in his pockets, looking uncomfortable.

"You nearly cried," Grady announces.

"You weren't even there!" I protest.

Kate makes a noise of sympathy and links her arm through mine. "Don't mind him," she confides. "He thinks fear is, like, a show of weakness."

"Wait up." Ethan slows as we pass the rodeo ring. "I think some guys from school are riding this year."

They all stop to watch, and I wander closer, glad of the distraction from Kate and Reeve. I've never seen one of these up close. To be honest, I've never really seen one at all. Earlier, I caught a glimpse of cattle being herded, and a bucking-bronco type event, but right now, a boy is racing his horse around a collection of barrels at break-neck speed. He's dressed up for the occasion, in fancy cowboy boots and a big black hat, the metal on his horse's gear gleaming in the sunset light. It's hectic and fast, and I can't help holding my breath as they hurtle around the course.

"They're so cool!" I exclaim to Fiona as the first boy is replaced by another, this time in a bright red shirt and cream cowboy hat.

She looks at me. "I wouldn't have thought it was your kind of thing. Isn't it, like, cruelty to animals or something?" Fiona laughs at her own joke as the others move closer.

"What's up?" Kate beams expectantly. I feel crummy again for wishing she was anywhere but here.

"Jenna's into environmentalism," Fiona explains, grinning. "She wants to protect all the innocent creatures and Mother Earth."

Clara giggles while Kate looks at me again. "Really? That's cool. Have you been converting these guys, too?"

"Nah." Ethan nudges me. "She's given up on us. We're recycling lost causes."

"Never mind." Kate winks at me. "You can probably go back and plant some trees or something, balance them out."

I laugh along, but inside, something twists. It's all still a joke to them. "Well, what can I say?" I answer lightly, as if their teasing means nothing at all. "I know my limits."

I stay with them, watching the next couple of competitors, until I figure I've left it long enough. "I'm just heading to go look . . ." I gesture vaguely in the direction of the food tent and then slip away while they're all laughing over something together.

Wandering idly through the crowd, I try to ignore the knot behind my rib cage. They still laugh about me as the eco-girl, but it's strange to realize that I haven't thought about the Green Teen stuff at all for a while now. It's not just because I've been obsessing over Reeve either: away from all the meetings, and social stuff with Olivia around school, the issues I spent all that time working on have kind of drifted into the background. And being here, away from my usual routines, I haven't felt the urgency, either—that sense I always had that I should be doing *something*, a new project or plan to make my own small difference.

I feel a tremor of guilt. I'm not sure how I should feel about the change.

I'm surprised when Fiona finds me a few minutes later, loitering in line for another scoop of consolation ice cream.

"Hey, are you OK?" She cuts in line beside me, shooting a glare at the family behind us when they make a noise of protest.

"Sure." I shrug. "Want rainbow topping?"

"No, I mean, about all that nature stuff." She looks down, scuffing the dirt with her chunky black boots. "I, umm, I'm sorry about that."

I blink.

"I didn't think," she continues, "if you'd take offense or anything." To my amazement, she seems sincere.

"Oh. Well, thanks." I pause, disconcerted. "Cone?"

"Sure."

We head back toward the others, in time to see Kate

pull Reeve into a car on the Ferris wheel. He spots me, making an awkward shrug as the attendant lowers the safety bar. Kate waves at me, and they swing up into the air. Together.

I turn back to my melting ice cream and console myself with a mouthful of sprinkles. Maybe this secrecy thing isn't as thrilling and sneaky as I thought.

CHAPTER TWENTY-EIGHT

"Hey, Susie." I poke my head around the door to her office on Saturday morning. "I'm just heading out for a walk, take some photos." I brandish my bulging tote bag as evidence.

"OK, sweetie." Susie's sitting in a patch of sunlight by the window, rocking back and forth on an old wooden chair. She looks up from the stack of papers in her lap and gives me a warm smile. "Call and check in later."

"Everything on schedule?" We both turn and look at the day planner pinned to the wall. Next Friday is circled in red, with big stars and arrows scribbled over the page. Opening Day. A week below it, there's another, smaller mark I avoid staring at: the one that reads *Jenna leaves* in neat black print.

"I think so!" Susie nods, a now-familiar look of panic lurking in her eyes.

"OK, let me know if you want me to pick anything up." I realize my slip as soon as I say it, but Susie doesn't notice. She gives me another absent smile and turns back to work. I take off before anyone can stop me, bounding down the front steps and hurrying down the road until I'm out of sight, behind the curve of trees.

If I really were taking pictures all day in the woods, then I wouldn't be able to pick anything up in town. But I'm not. As I wait on the grassy verge, Reeve's truck comes into sight.

"Hop in!" He reaches across to open the passenger side, and I scramble up into the seat. Glancing around, he quickly leans across to kiss me. "Any trouble getting away?"

"Nope." I fasten my seat belt. "All clear."

I wait for a moment, half expecting some kind of explanation for the way things ended up at the festival, but he just puts the truck back in gear and drives away. I want to ask about Kate, but I don't want to seem like it bothers me. After all, if we're keeping things casual, things like exes shouldn't matter.

I look around for the first time. "Someone's been busy," I tease, noting the clean interior and smudge-free windows. Instead of the usual piles of equipment and snack wrappers, I can actually see the upholstery, and outside, the paintwork is gleaming.

"Not me." He laughs. "My sisters were being total pains yesterday, so I gave them some chores."

"Nice!" I pretend to hit him. "Your sibling karma must be ruined."

"Uh, yeah." Reeve gives me a grin. "Kind of late for that now."

We cut around Main Street via a series of densely wooded back roads, heading out of town on a dirt track I've never seen. "OK." Reeve exaggerates looking around at the empty intersection. "Evasive maneuvers complete. We are a go!" I laugh, settling back in my seat as we turn onto the highway and pick up speed. Soon, we're flying out of Stillwater, warm air rushing past us, and a rock song playing loud from the old, duct-taped stereo.

I prop my bare feet up on the hot dashboard and relax, one arm slung out the open window. I can see that my legs show all the evidence of my summer adventures: the scrape on my knee from painting the back porch, that bruise on my shin from tumbling off the dirt bike. I wonder how long they'll take to fade when I'm back home.

"So where are you taking me?" I quickly turn to Reeve. He's wearing Ray-Ban–style shades, looking too cool with one hand lazily on the steering wheel. He glances over at me and grins.

"It's a surprise."

"What kind of surprise?"

"The surprising kind!" He laughs, reaching over and taking my hand. Slipping his fingers through mine, they rest together on the seat beside him. I grin and turn back to watch the green valley speed by outside my window.

After driving for about thirty minutes, Reeve turns off the highway onto a small dirt road. We move slowly under looming trees, the track covered in pine needles and leaves. I love the forest here now—at least in daytime. The canopy above us seems to block out the world, sunlight filtering through and making everything around look extra still and peaceful. At last, Reeve pulls off the track and parks. I glance around, seeing nothing but forest.

"Where now?"

"You'll see." Slamming his door, Reeve grins at me, teasing. He pulls a cooler from the back of the truck and waits for me to gather my things. Then, taking my free hand, he leads me deeper into the trees. I walk happily beside him, loving how we don't have to stay alert for Grady to come crashing through the trees at any moment. Out here, we're completely private.

"How do you know about these places?" I look up, at the pine trees and foliage all around. "I mean, you could live your whole life in the area and not know these spots."

"I guess that's the way we like it." He climbs over a fallen log and waits to guide me over it. "It's all word-of-mouth. Someone finds a cool place, tells someone else . . . or they don't. I bet there are places all over the province that only a few people have ever been."

I remember the view from the mountain, the miles of forest and lakes stretching out below us.

"Anyway, we're here. . . ." I could swear Reeve looks kind of nervous as he leads me out of the trees, to a clearing by a lake. Only this one is nothing like back in Stillwater.

"Oh, wow," I breathe, gazing around. The water is deep and blue, fringed with thick forest, but that's not all:

hundreds of flowers line the lake, their flat leaves resting on the water itself and spreading out into the middle of the pool. I drop my bag and walk all the way to the shore. "Are they water lilies?" I peer at the tiny white buds and dark green leaves, just like in that Monet exhibit my mom dragged me to see in New York one time.

Reeve nods. He's standing by our pile of stuff, his hands bunched in his front pockets, almost as if he's waiting for my reaction. I practically skip back to him.

"This is amazing!" I tell him. Throwing my arms around his neck, I kiss him in glee. "I can't believe it, it's so beautiful!"

"Cool." Reeve's face spreads into a smile. "I figured you'd like it here. You brought your camera, right? So, you can take all kinds of photos if you want."

"I will!" I turn back, amazed at the view. "Is the water OK to swim in?" I start to kick off my sneakers even before he nods.

Stripping down to my bikini, I slowly wade out into the lake. The water is freezing, of course, but I edge out farther, the mud squelching between my toes. I don't care. All around me, the water lilies float gently on the surface of the water, bobbing as my movement sends hundreds of ripples out across the lake. It's incredible, but standing in the middle of it all, I'm overcome with a strange sadness, as if I know this is a moment I'll never get back.

I look around, trying to burn everything into my memory. The hot glare of the sun through the edge of my shade, the gorgeous blanket of flowers lapping gently around me, the way my every step sends clouds of mud billowing in the clear water . . . and Reeve, still watching me from the shore. I exhale a slow, shivering breath.

"Come in!" I yell, forcing aside the sadness, and the thought of that neat print on the calendar back at Susie's, marking the end to all of this. "The water's gorgeous!"

We spend hours just lazing by the water that day. Reeve teaches me to skip rocks off the still water, picking out the perfect flat discs and twisting my wrist just right to send them hopping all the way to the middle of the lake. We eat hastily made sandwiches and his mom's fierce pepper brownies from the cooler, and talk about plans for school and our families until the sun begins to sink lower and the air picks up a low chill.

By the time I make it back to Susie's (Reeve dropping me off around the bend again to make sure nobody sees), it's almost six.

"Jenna, have you seen my red—oh, sorry." Susie walks in without knocking, just as I'm getting changed.

"The red sweater?" I straighten up, in my bikini top and shorts. "I think it was down in the kitchen."

"Thanks." She pauses, looking at me for a moment. "Umm, OK." Backing out quickly, Susie all but trips over herself to get away. I stare after her, puzzled, but it's not until I catch a glimpse of myself in the dresser mirror that I see what made her so flustered.

A hickey.

I lean closer, already cringing with embarrassment. The small mark is just below my collarbone, out of sight—if I weren't still in my bikini top! Tugging on a sweatshirt, I wonder if it's possible to avoid Susie for, oh, the next five years.

It's not. After dinner, there's a cautious knock on my door. "Jenna? You got a sec?"

"Sure." I turn the music down, but she's still waiting. "You can come in now," I call.

She edges in with a weird look on her face. "About earlier . . ."

I gulp. "Uh-huh?" My voice comes out squeaky and high-pitched.

Susie takes a seat on the edge of the bed and fixes me with an understanding mom look. "It's all right, Jenna. You don't need to explain yourself to me. You're practically a grown-up."

Oh, boy.

"Really, Susie—"

"You don't need to tell me anything." She ignores my protests, determined to say her piece. "Fiona mentioned something about Ethan a while back."

Ethan!

I sit, silently mortified, while she continues, giving me this knowing, conspiratorial look. "I know what it's like: having desires, experimenting. I'm glad you're having fun."

At this moment, fun is so not on the agenda, but insisting I've never been beyond second base wouldn't achieve anything right now. I have no choice but to sit, meekly listening to her be understanding about all the sex I'm not really having.

"I just wanted to let you know, I've made a special

drawer in the bathroom, full of, well, things you might want." I'm gratified to see even Susie seem slightly freaked out now, despite her supportive act. "Come and see."

"No, really, it's fine . . ." I try to fend her off, but Susie takes my arm and all but drags me to the green-tiled bathroom.

"I know condoms can get expensive," she chatters, pulling open the pretty wooden vanity to reveal a supply that would keep half the population of Stillwater child-free. For a year. "So I bought plenty. Look, even flavored ones!"

There's a moment of silent horror for both of us as we contemplate the implications of those words.

"And, uh, it's for Fiona, too," she adds hurriedly. "So you girls just go right ahead and, well . . . just know it's there."

"Thanks, Susie," I murmur numbly. If only we were still doing construction up here—maybe then there would actually be a chance for the ground to give way and swallow me up.

"And don't worry about your parents. This is just between us." She squeezes my hand reassuringly as I wander blindly back to my room.

"Umm, OK."

"OK," she echoes with a nod. "I'm glad we had this . . . talk. And you'll come to me—if you need anything? Anything at all?"

I can't imagine what I'd ever need that isn't already stocked in that "special drawer" of hers, but I nod along.

"Great." Susie gives me another supportive-yet-freaked-out smile. "See you for dinner!"

The moment the door closes behind her, I hurl myself facedown on the bed.

"Give me ten good reasons why I shouldn't kill you right now!" Fiona bursts into my room minutes later, the murderous-yet-traumatized look in her eyes meaning only one thing . . .

"She showed you the drawer."

"Yes!" she wails. "I don't need to hear any of that. Especially from her!"

"I'm not arguing with you," I tell her.

Fiona throws herself down on the window seat. "Why do parents have to do this? I mean, couldn't they just give us a copy of *Forever* and leave well enough alone?"

"Just be glad it wasn't your dad," I note darkly.

"Oh, it was." She shudders at the memory. "Like, two years ago. He had a textbook and a banana and everything. It was the most uncomfortable ten minutes of my entire life!"

I'm tempted to ask about Grady, and all the kind-of-crush signals she's been giving off, but I don't want to push my luck. Instead, we sit for a moment, reflecting on parental sex-talk terror in a strange kind of companionship. I may not have Olivia, I realize, but it's not as if I'm alone out here.

"I don't suppose you want to get out of town," I suggest hopefully. "Even just to that ice-cream place in Pedley." I name a small town about half an hour away.

Fiona waits a moment before shrugging. "Sure, OK. I don't think Dad's using the car."

I look at her in surprise. I wasn't expecting her to

actually agree. "Great!" I grab my cardigan before she can change her mind.

"Just let me get some CDs." She heads toward her room, and I decide to follow.

"Can I pick? From your music, I mean. Some of your stuff is, well, kind of depressing."

Fiona looks at me for a second, as if she's deciding whether or not it's worth the fight. "I guess," she says at last. "CDs are on the shelf." She pulls on a pair of flip-flops while I make my choice between angry emo guys and angry emo girls. Then I spy a Paramore label buried under the heavier stuff. Aha!

"Ready!" I beam, brandishing my compromise. My eardrums, and fragile emotional state, are safe for another day. "Now let's get out of here."

CHAPTER TWENTY-NINE

Now that Susie's keeping her eyes on me—and my late-night activities—I find it impossible to sneak away and see Reeve, but part of me is relieved. The more time I spend with him, the more I get caught up in our kisses and strange, whispered intimacy. It's getting harder to keep up the casual act, even with the end of summer looming closer all the time.

Luckily the next few days before the big opening are so hectic, I barely have a moment to do anything except polish silverware, touch up paint-jobs, and launder seven bedrooms' worth of crisp linens. Even so, as I throw myself into the chores, I can't help but wonder if that day at the lake really was as final as it felt to me then: a moment out of place in the rest of my regular life. It was only three days ago, but I haven't heard from him since. Already the breathless intensity is fading, and now it just feels like a dream to me, snapshots in somebody else's photo album.

"Please tell me that was the last of the ironing!" I make a return trip from the laundry room to find Susie perched by the kitchen table. Now that the decorating is finished, there are mismatched china plates propped up on an old cabinet, and faded sepia photographs framed on the wall. It looks homey and cute, just like something from those Anthropologie catalogs Fiona was hurling around.

"For now, anyway." Susie laughs, passing me a glass of cold lemonade.

"Thank God." I throw myself down in a chair and stretch. "Next time, can I just do something easy? Building the roof, maybe, or paving the driveway."

"Ironing does suck," she agrees. "Why do you think I run around in all those wrinkled shirts?"

"But not today." I notice that she's dressed elegantly, in a print wrap-dress and dangling gemstone earrings, and for a change, her curls are pinned back in a neat chignon. "Do you have another meeting at the bank?"

Susie gives me a mysterious smile. "Nope. I have something fun planned, for us girls. A way to say thank you for all your hard work. Ta-da!" With a flourish, she produces a glossy pamphlet.

"'A day of indulgence at Blue Ridge,'" I read. "Wait, this is that fancy resort. We can't go—they're competition!"

"Exactly." Susie nods. "We need to research. Some spa treatments, a mud bath—and if that doesn't ease your aching muscles, we'll bring out the heavy artillery: Sven, the Swedish masseur!"

"That's awesome!" I'm easily convinced. "When do we leave?"

"Whenever Fiona's done on the computer. FIONA!" she bellows with the same breath. "We have a download limit, remember!"

A few seconds later, Fiona appears, slouching in the doorway. Tugging at one oversize sleeve, she rolls her eyes. "No need to yell."

"Isn't it great that Susie organized this spa trip?" I say, giving her a meaningful look.

"Uh-huh." It's only a murmured agreement, but Susie leaps up, delighted

"So we're all set!" She beams at us both. "Just grab your suits for the hot springs, and we can go!"

As Susie rushes off to get things together, I turn to Fiona with a warning look. "Please, she really wants this to be a bonding thing."

Fiona wrinkles her lip. "Like, with gossiping about boys and makeup?"

"Maybe." I keep my gaze fixed on her. "She's been working so hard for this place, she deserves some relaxing time."

"Whatever." Fiona sighs, but she gives me a grudging nod. "As long as she doesn't try and give me a makeover!"

As it turns out, even Fiona can't complain about the Blue Ridge experience. Soaking up to our necks in a tub of mineral salts later that afternoon, all domestic disharmony has been forgotten. Or, at the very least, stored up for later.

"So this is how the mega-rich live." I sigh, inhaling

the deep aroma of rosemary and eucalyptus, or whatever magic potion they smeared on my face to release
my pores, stress, and/or tension. "Maybe I should start
buying lottery tickets." Steam drifts above the water, soft
music plays quietly, and a glass wall affords us a stunning
view of the valley.

"No . . ." Susie breathes, her eyes covered with a blue
gel pack. "Who wants exquisite luxury when you can
have creaky pipes and an old front porch?"

"Right," Fiona drawls, only a little sarcastic. "Endless
perfection is, like, sooo boring."

I lean back, gazing out at the gorgeous vista. It's
strange, to have the sprawling wilderness outside and this
high-tech luxury inside. All around us is gleaming marble
and metal, with a hovering host of uniformed "assistants"
waiting to bring us anything we might possibly require.
But this is probably as close to the great outdoors as some
tourists will get: separated by a polished plate-glass window while a manicurist attends to their toes.

Susie lifts her mask and reaches for her flute of sparkling water. "I think it's time for a toast: To the Bramble
Lane Bed and Breakfast. May she break even sometime in
the next two years!"

"You picked a name? That's great." I congratulate her.

"It was Fiona's idea." She beams.

Fiona rolls her eyes, picking at the mud mask on her
face. "I only said that people would have to fight their
way through the brambles to even find the place."

"But it's perfect." I let my toes float to the surface of

the water, wriggling them. "It makes me think the place is ramshackle yet charming."

"That's the plan," Susie agrees. "I decided we should keep up your 'rugged adventuring' marketing strategy."

"It's hardly a strategy!" I laugh, but she shakes her head.

"Don't sell yourself short, Jenna; it's worked out great. Your environmental tips have been a huge help, and we're fully booked for opening week."

"That's because you did such a great job with the renovations."

Fiona interrupts. "What is this—a mutual appreciation society?"

I grin. "OK, so maybe we're all awesome."

We relax again for a moment, lazily drifting in the water until Susie lets out a wistful sigh. "It's been great having you around, kid. You'll always be welcome here again."

Fiona perks up. "When are you leaving?"

"Ten days," I answer quietly. Noticing her expression, I splash water at her. "And you don't have to look so happy about it."

"Am not." She splashes back. "Well, it'll be cool not having to wait around for the bathroom."

There. Just think, a whole summer of bitching, tantrums, and animosity could all have been avoided if only Susie and Adam had renovated those other bathrooms first!

"I'm sure Fiona will miss you," Susie says soothingly, like a true mom. My eyes meet Fiona's across the tub, and we share an amused look. "I know I will."

"She'll just miss your good influence," Fiona murmurs, as if Susie isn't here. "That's why she had you here in the first place."

Susie splutters, "I did—"

"Sure you didn't." Fiona arches a mud-smeared eyebrow, cracking the mask. "You were hoping all her perky enthusiasm would rub off on me."

Perky? Me?

"Now, I don't know about you, but I'm turning into a prune." Susie wisely changes the subject. She displays her wrinkled fingers. "How about we dry off and find something delicious to eat?"

"Something chocolatey," I decide. All this talk about my imminent departure is making me restless, and in need of a sugar fix. "Illegally chocolatey."

When we've consumed enough gooey brownies to make me faintly ill, I take up residence on an overstuffed leather couch in the main lobby. Fiona is off wandering somewhere, and Susie has spotted a woman she knows working maid duty, so they've retreated to a secluded corner somewhere to discuss all the inside information about Blue Ridge. I'm left to people-watch, tucked away in my corner beside the looming stone fireplace as the other guests bustle by.

I'm not ready to go home.

Fairview, high school, my family — it all seems miles away, and a lifetime ago. The past weeks have been a jumble of sawdust and splattered mud and shady trees and cold lake water splashing on my skin. A kind of freedom. And now I think of going back to our house, with the plush peach carpeting and Mom's careful dinner arrangements, and I feel a swell of sadness. I don't know what's waiting for me there, if there will even be a family when I get back. It's not the divorce itself that scares me so much as everything that would come after. Dad moving out, or not coming back from Europe at all; Mom suddenly working long hours; the holiday visitation schedules. No matter how much I've tried to avoid the reality of my parents—and the future—I can't help but see my departure date like some kind of execution.

"Kids, get back over here. Don't touch those!" A couple of young boys run over to play with the small animal carvings by the fire. The lobby is full of activity: a prim-looking lady ordering the staff around, a pair of intimidated tourists looking at some pamphlets, and an old man giving some kind of talk to a group of guests, slowly touring the room with a cane.

"This here was taken back when there was barely a road up through the mountains." He waves his cane at a black-and-white photo on the wall. Dressed in an impeccable suit with heavy gold cuffs at his wrists, he's got a shock of white hair and deep wrinkles on his face. "We had to hike for days with nothing but a hatchet and a good pair of boots!" The group looks suitably impressed.

I pause, his words triggering some kind of déjà vu. A hatchet . . . ?

"Now, there are plenty of tours if you want to explore," he continues, "with fully loaded Jeeps and an expert guide. Or how about a rafting trip? Best way to see the valley!" There's a murmur of excitement, and several guests start flicking through their pamphlets.

I peer at him from across the room. It can't be. . . . As he finishes up his history of the area, I try to remember the photo on the back of that mountain man guide. The man there was much younger, with a bushy beard and rugged plaid shirt, but if I add about fifty years and a thousand dollars of designer tailoring, it could just about be the guy in expensive leather loafers holding court for the rich spa ladies.

My mountain man wears loafers?

Our unspoiled paradise is coming under threat. Every year, those vultures swoop closer, looking to replace pristine mountain ranges with acres of concrete. They should be lined up and shot!

—"The Devil in Disguise,"
The Modern Mountain Man's Survival Guide

CHAPTER THIRTY

When the group finally disperses, I edge over. "Mr. . . . Coombes?" I ask hesitantly, certain I've made a huge mistake. It's been ages since I sent the book to Olivia, and I'm sure plenty of old guys around here swear by the service of a good hatchet—

"That's me." He swings around. There's a square of crisp handkerchief folded in his breast pocket, and a lively gleam in his eyes. "What can I do you for?"

My mouth drops open. "It is you!" I blink at him, trying to match this distinguished gentleman with Jerry's grouchy, no-nonsense voice that I've been carrying around in my mind. "I read your book! Wow, I can't believe it's actually you!"

Mr. Coombes looks at me, kind but clearly clueless.

"The survival guide?" I venture slowly. "For mountain men? It's been a major help to me this summer!" He probably didn't mean for it to save my *social* life, but without that book, I don't know if I'd ever have made inroads with the Stillwater boys or found a way to deal with Fiona.

"Ha!" Mr. Coombes suddenly lets out a booming laugh. "They still have that ol' thing around?"

"I found a copy at this old bookstore in town," I explain. "I think it was one of the originals!"

Shaking his head with amusement, Mr. Coombes looks at me. "Well, kid, you have my apologies."

I frown. "What do you mean?"

"For having to wade through all that self-righteous bull!" He checks his BlackBerry, still chuckling, while I try and get my head around his dismissive tone.

"I don't, I mean, I didn't think it was bad." I blink, completely thrown. It's not like I thought Jeremiah Coombes would be off living in a cave somewhere. Maybe an old log cabin by a fishing pond . . .

"You liked it, eh? Well, good for you." Mr. Coombes looks surprised. "Now, if you don't mind, kid, I need to get back. This place won't run itself!"

"You mean, you own Blue Ridge?" I gape.

He pauses. "That's right, going on a year now." With an expression of sheer pride, the mountain man himself looks around at the spa schedule, gift shop, and line of newly arrived visitors with their stack of designer suitcases.

"I don't . . ." I stop myself, not wanting to offend him, but then I can't help it. "I don't understand. I mean, you used to want to protect the environment!" I realize how accusing it comes out, but part of me doesn't care.

I've spent all summer thinking he's some kind of wilderness guru, and now I see he's turned into just another real-estate developer, with a fancy suit and fake hunting trophies on the wall. How could he be such a sellout?

Mr. Coombes looks back sharply, and for a moment I wonder if I'm about to get thrown out. Then his expression softens. "Come with me, kid."

I pause, wary, but he nods toward the deck. It's the centerpiece of the whole floor, stretching across the front of the building, and right now it's busy with tourists snapping photos of the uninterrupted views. "Come on, it'll only be a second."

Cautiously, I follow him outside. The air is chillier, mists hanging over the mountains in the distance, telling me it will be raining soon. Ever since that hike with Reeve, I've learned to read the clouds better.

"You see that far ridge?" Mr. Coombes gestures with his cane to a craggy peak on the far side of the valley. We're facing north from Stillwater, and there's nothing but mountain, lakes, and valley from here on out. I nod slowly. "All the land between us and there belongs to me. Been buying it up the last twenty years now, and give me another twenty and I'll own the rest, too."

He surveys his domain, satisfied, but I don't understand. "You mean, you're going to expand the resort?" I can't keep the horror from my voice. All the Green Teen protests come back to me like a script I know by heart: the hours we spent writing fierce letters and leaflets about the perils of destroying the wilderness. "But what about all the trees? The wildlife needs the land for their—"

"You see any buildings there, kid?" Mr. Coombes interrupts me. "Any construction, any highways?"

I pause. "No . . ."

"And it'll stay that way. But how am I supposed to pay for it, eh?" Catching my expression, he chuckles again. "Getting back to nature's all well and good, but I learned a long time ago, the only way you know what's going on in those hills is if you own 'em yourself."

"So . . . you're conserving the valley?" I look at Mr. Coombes with confusion. "But that still doesn't explain why you opened Blue Ridge. I mean, what was it you said in the book: 'Every new building is a blight on the whole landscape!'"

"I thought things were real simple back then, eh? Follies of youth!" As if taking pity on me, he pats my arm. "When you're older, you'll understand." He turns to go but I stop him, still feeling betrayed.

"Why don't you explain it now?" If he even can. I know people sell out their principles for an easy life all the time, but I can't believe someone as passionate as Jeremiah B. Coombes would take the dirty money. What happened to him?

He pauses, looking out at his valley, and when he answers, it's slow and deliberate. "Sometimes, kid, your ideals don't make a damn bit of difference. You realize, there is no right answer; it's all just a bunch of choices."

I blink. Whatever self-righteous defense I was expecting, it isn't this. "But . . . of course you can make a difference! We all can!"

He looks at me kindly. "Sure, kid. You can chant and

wave banners if it makes you feel better, but this is the real world. The people around here, they need the trade, and I need the money, and in the end . . . It's a compromise I'm just fine making."

With a nod, he begins to walk away. "I'll fix you up a gift pack, maybe the bubble-bliss bath sets!" he calls back to me. "My staff tells me they're a dream!"

I think about the reinvention of Jeremiah B. Coombes all the drive back to Stillwater. I know what Olivia and the other Green Teens would say about him, and all his jaded self-justification, but I'm not so sure anymore. . . . For a moment, I wonder if I'd feel so betrayed if I hadn't carried around that book of his—if I didn't feel like I knew him as a person. But of course I would, I remind myself. He's everything our group stands against.

". . . do you? Jenna?"

"Huh?" I blink awake as we pull into the driveway.

"Do you want casserole, or my three-cheese mac 'n' cheese?" Susie asks, looking back at me.

"Either!" I decide brightly, trying to put Jeremiah B. Coombes out of my mind. As I climb out of the car, I catch a glimpse of someone on the porch. "Hey, Fi, did Grady say they were coming over, or—"

"JENNA!" A familiar petite figure waves at me in excitement. I watch, stunned, as Olivia drops an over-stuffed duffel bag and races across the yard. She hurls herself at me in a hug. "Omigod, how ARE you?"

CHAPTER THIRTY-ONE

I stare at her, confused. For a moment, I think I'm hallucinating the whole thing from a chocolate overdose, but the arms gripping around my waist feel real enough to me.

"What? I mean . . . What are you doing here?" I finally manage to detangle myself. Olivia is grinning like it's no big deal to show up, a whole continent away from home with no warning at all. I can't believe this.

"Yes," Susie agrees, folding her arms and glancing back and forth between us both. Her lips are pressed thinly together. "Why don't you tell us what's going on?"

I hear a snigger behind me from Fiona. "This better be good."

Releasing me, Olivia turns to Susie. "Susie, it's so great to see you again!" She hugs her too, and attempts to embrace Fiona as well, but Fiona backs away swiftly. Undeterred, Olivia launches into her big explanation. "So the Chicago protest was shut down, which was totally infringing our First Amendment rights, and my parents freaked, of course, but they're on their super-polluting cruise . . ."

As she talks, I study her, trying to take in all the changes. And there have been a ton. Her dark hair is now in full-on dreadlocks, matted in thick clumps around her scalp. Her face is slightly sunburned and peeling, her eyebrows are roaming wild, and she's wearing a bright red shirt daubed with MEAT IS MURDER! and hefty Doc Martens. This is so not the same Olivia who reminded me to pack three different brands of cleanser to keep my pores healthy.

"So I thought I'd drop by! I caught a ride to Seattle and used their emergency credit card to book a flight out here," she finishes, overflowing with enthusiasm despite the fact she just made a six-hour journey, at least. "I looked up the bus and hitchhiked into town. Jenna, it's so good to see you!"

I don't know what to say.

Susie is looking at me with a hint of disapproval, Fiona is blatantly amused, but I just feel . . . invaded. It's been weeks since I spoke to her, and longer since we've had a real conversation, but suddenly here she is in Stillwater.

"I haven't heard from you in ages," I tell her at last. My voice is quiet, but there's an edge there. I know I'm supposed to be happy, but I didn't invite her, and I sure didn't think she would just show up. I mean, this is Canada — you don't just "drop by," hundreds of miles out in the wilderness!

Olivia blinks. "I know, and I'm sorry! It's been so crazy. That's why I came all this way in person. So we could catch up face-to-face!" Again, she beams at me like nothing's wrong.

I stand there, dumb.

"Well, we'll just have to work this out." Susie whisks into gear. She locks up the car and reaches for Olivia. "Come on, we'd better go call your parents. They'll be worried sick!" She ushers her back into the house, already talking about futon beds and return flights. I watch them go, still thrown.

"That's the famous Olivia, huh?" Fiona twists a lock of hair around her finger, watching me.

"I guess. . . ."

"You don't look so thrilled. I thought you guys were, like, BFFs."

I pause. "So did I. Before . . ."

Before what, I'm not sure, but something about this feels wrong, as if two separate parts of my life have just been flung together. With a sigh, I pick up my bag of bubble-bliss bath foam and follow them all inside.

Olivia's parents are as worried as you'd expect after getting a text from their seventeen-year-old daughter reading, *Going 2 canada! Talk l8er!* After an hour of parental bonding, Susie seems to have smoothed things over — reassuring them that Olivia isn't hitchhiking with dangerous strangers anymore and will be put on a flight back to New Jersey on Saturday, when they get back from their cruise. With the first guests arriving soon, all those shiny new bedrooms are off-limits: I set up the inflatable mattress in my room for her and set about bringing her motley collection of mud-stained bags inside.

"Don't even worry!" Olivia tells me as I cross back through the kitchen to find her some sheets. "I can camp outside if I need to. In fact, I'd be more comfortable out there—we've been sleeping out under the stars all summer."

"Uh-huh," I murmur, deciding to leave her duffel out in the laundry room. There's a weird smell coming from the bag . . .

I wander back into the room. Olivia's holding court from over a plate of that tofu (since apparently she's also sworn off wheat and dairy since I saw her last), gesturing wildly as she describes life out in the great wilderness. Of upstate New York.

"So tell me more about this camp of yours." Fiona swings her legs against a cabinet, regarding her with amusement. I pause, curious myself.

"It's a collective," Olivia corrects her, taking a gulp of water. "Although, all that stuff they promised about equality and input was total crap, because the minute Cash spoke up and suggested some changes, they went totally authoritarian on us. Fascists."

"Where is Cash, anyway?" I ask.

"Oh, he's visiting friends. Lying low after the Chicago thing. Anyway, this one time, we were starting to make dinner, and he noticed that the lentils weren't certified organic, but they didn't even—" She stops, looking past me out the back window. "What's going on with that tree?"

Susie looks over. "Oh, the old spruce? We're taking it down next week."

Olivia looks heartbroken. "Is it sick?"

"Hmm? Oh, no." Susie scoops a handful of chips from the bag Fiona is currently tearing through. "But it blocks out the light from at least three of the guest bedrooms, so we figured it would be best out of the way."

Olivia's mouth drops open, and she gets that indignant look that I know by now means trouble.

"How about I show you around town before it gets dark," I interrupt, before she can launch into a lecture. "We can catch up, like you wanted."

"Sure!" Olivia leaps up, leaving her half-finished plate on the table. "Let's go!"

We cycle toward town, winding along the road on a pair of muddy mountain bikes. The sky is fading to a pale yellow dusk, it's a perfect summer evening, and I have my best friend back beside me. So why do I feel so restless, like something is prickling beneath the surface of my skin?

"I see Little Miss Sunshine is still being a total bitch." Olivia pedals slowly, getting used to the old bike. "I don't know how you put up with her."

"Fiona's been great," I say, defensive. "She's really come around."

"Huh. If you say so."

We pass another few houses, buried in the dense tangle of weeds by the road. I try to think of something to say. I was never at a loss for words around her before, but it's been so long since we were together, I feel weirdly shy.

"What are you doing out here, really?" I ask at last, glancing over. She's changed into a threadbare gray tank and baggy khaki shorts, with a scrap of bandana twisted around her head. "We were going to be back home in a week; you didn't have to come all this way."

"But I did." She stops pedaling, putting one foot on the dusty ground to steady herself. I circle around to face her. "I know I've been a crappy friend lately, I just got so busy with everything. . . ." She trails off, her voice regretful. "Anyway, I wanted to make it up to you in person, so we could spend the last part of our vacation together."

"You mean the four days till you get shipped back home?"

Olivia makes a rueful face. "Yeah, maybe I didn't think this one through. But that's what you do, remember? I'm impulsive; you're the planner. We make the perfect team!"

She waits there, hopeful. I soften.

"You really hitchhiked to Seattle?" I ask.

She grins, a familiar smile I must have seen a thousand times. "Well, kinda. A group from the Chicago protest was driving out, so I caught a ride with them. There were like, eight of us squeezed in a VW camper van. I swear, I lost all feeling in my legs!"

I giggle, despite myself. "How did you even end up there?"

"It was totally serendipitous!" She starts pedaling again. "After the collective leaders made such a big deal about Cash and his uprising—"

"His what?"

"They overreacted," she says quickly. "It was supposed to be a democracy! So anyway, one of the other counselors had friends who were gathering in Chicago to protest the meeting, so we hitched a ride with him. It was awesome. We chained ourselves to the gates and sang protest songs. Like, hundreds of people came, and in the end, the police had to break it up with tear gas and riot gear."

I gape at her, nearly swerving into a ditch. "No way! Weren't you scared?"

Olivia pauses. "Well, actually we weren't there when they sent the police in. Cash said it was better that we didn't get arrested, you know—let the foot soldiers take the fall so we could still be around to lead the second wave. But I watched from down the street and it looked so cool!"

"Did anyone get hurt? Those riots always look crazy on TV." I can't believe this.

"That's only because they orchestrate the whole thing!" Olivia exclaims. "I mean, they've got to paint us all as dangerous criminals so nobody listens to the message, the truth. They plant people in the crowd to stir up trouble and then blame us for everything!"

"Umm, who are 'they'?"

"The establishment," Olivia explains in a "Well, duh!" voice. "Corporations, the police, government. They're all in on it together—protecting their stock prices and consumerist society. Because if for one moment, people actually woke up and started paying attention to what's really happening in the world . . ."

I keep pedaling, my unease growing. This isn't Green Teen talk anymore; this is different. Fiercer. I've heard snatches of it before, from kids on the fringe of the protests: the ones who show up just as an excuse to scream at teachers and the cops. But we always steered clear of those kinds of troublemakers—they were just in it to cause a scene. Right?

". . . and it doesn't matter who's president, because they're all tied to special interests and—"

"Look!" I gladly interrupt. "Here were are, Main Street, Stillwater, in all its glory. So where do you want to start?" I ask brightly, hoping to stem the tide of anti-capitalist ranting. "We've got the thrilling map-center-slash-bookstore here." Waving my hands like a spokesmodel, I hop off my bike and lead her down the sidewalk. "Home to an extensive array of trashy romance novels. And there's a raccoon that likes to nest in the back there, too." I turn. "Or there's the gas station, with two whole different kinds of gas and a slushie machine. I can recommend the raspberry."

Olivia looks around slowly. She seems almost disappointed. "I didn't think it would be so built up."

I snort. "Are you kidding?"

She shrugs, pushing the bike along. "I just mean there's all this concrete. I guess it's inevitable; the capitalist industrial machine crushes everything in its path."

"Yes," I say slowly. We're in the middle of a vast, tree-covered valley, and all she can see are the few buildings that are here?

"I don't know. I guess when you talked about how remote it was, I just pictured . . . log cabins, I guess. And maybe a general store for food deliveries."

I laugh. "It's not the 1900s!"

"I know!" She blushes and shoves me. "Maybe I've been reading too much *Walden*."

"Oh, it was a rude awakening for me, too." I smile as we start walking again. "I was picturing all this serene beauty. I mean, it's here, it's lovely too, but things are . . . kind of a little more dirty than that. People have to make a living; it's not just about sitting around, gazing at the forest." She looks blank, but I keep moving, pausing to cross the street. "I think Ethan is working at the store today."

"The gay one?"

I panic.

"Shhh!" I look around. "Livvy, you can't say that. Nobody's supposed to know! Or about me and Reeve either!"

"Relax." She laughs.

"I mean it!" I hiss, nervous. "I shouldn't have even told you, but I never thought . . ." I shoot another look over at the store. "Swear you won't tell a soul? Not even Ethan?"

Olivia rolls her eyes. "Calm down! I pinky-swear, whatever. Now let's go—I want to meet all these cute boys you've been talking about."

She takes off across the street without looking, and I have no choice but to hurry after her, hoping for the best.

CHAPTER THIRTY-TWO

"And you should really install solar panels, because you might as well just hold a blowtorch to the glaciers with it set up like this."

The next morning, I find Olivia in full eco-flow. She's cornered Susie in her office, loudly decrying every element of the B and B as "wasteful" and "irresponsible." She's even waving some pamphlets around while Susie looks for an escape.

"Hey, there you are, Livvy!" I interrupt quickly. "Do you want to go hang out by the lake today?"

Susie leaps up. "Yes! Go! Both of you," she adds quickly. "In fact, take Fiona, too. The first guests are due this afternoon. Just make sure you're back in time to help set up for the party."

"What do you say?" I ask Olivia. "Sun, cool water, some tanning . . . ?"

"OK," she agrees. Susie takes the chance to slip around her and bolt from the room, but not too fast to give me a decidedly exasperated stare.

I know how she feels.

"Look, I didn't want to say anything, but . . . you might want to tone down all the environmentalism stuff," I tell Olivia carefully as we pack up our towels and some snacks. She spent half of last night's Rock Band wars lecturing Grady and Ethan about their lack of a recycling bin for our soda cans and arguing with Reeve about the fuel efficiency of his truck. I felt embarrassed even listening. Did I really sound so self-righteous and condescending when I first arrived? I hope not, but unlike Olivia, at least I knew when to let it drop.

"Why?" She shrugs, looking defensive. "She needs to hear it. I mean, I don't know how you could stand to watch all this awful construction work all summer."

I sigh, packing up the cooler with drinks and chips. "The B and B is a good thing. It'll bring trade through town, remember?"

"But at what cost?" Olivia looks at me disapprovingly. "I know she's your godmother, but you really should be speaking up about this."

"Not everything's a life-or-death issue, Livvy. Sometimes you've got to compromise."

She glares at me. "Tell that to the birds nesting in the spruce tree."

Olivia keeps up her monologue all the way to the lake, ignoring the pretty scatter of sunlight through the trees to rant about the evils of carbon-based fuel systems and how we're all going to die at the hands of greedy corporations. I stroll along beside her, silent and confused. Now that we've spent some time together again, I don't understand this sudden switch in her, all this new anger at the world. Sure, we've always been against polluting companies, and politicians, and all those usual suspects, but that just made us want to work harder in a positive way — to inspire and educate more people so we could all do something about the problem. But now? Every word that comes out of her lips is so bleak, so extreme, it's like she can only see the bad things. The worst part is, I don't even think she's listening to me anymore. Or anyone. She just seems on some mission to recite her list of the world's wrongs, regardless of timing or, I don't know, tact.

Luckily, Fiona isn't as conflicted as me.

"Will you just shut up?" she finally exclaims as we emerge from the trees and reach the shoreline. Turning to me, she adds, "I've tried to make nice because she's your friend and all, but God! I can't take this!"

"Thanks," I tell her, genuinely touched that she's made the effort. The old Fiona would have shut Olivia down right away, but the new, improved version lasted all of five minutes.

Olivia turns to me with a betrayed look. "Didn't you hear what she —?"

"See, the lake!" I announce brightly, putting both hands on her shoulders and swiveling her around to face the beautiful scene. The wind is up, kicking up peaks and foam on the water, while the fluffy clouds sprint across a blue sky. Olivia looks around, and finally, the dissatisfied expression makes way for a smile.

"This is awesome." There, nature will heal all. Or, not quite, because she adds, "At the collective, we meditated by the water every day. You should try that, you know. It totally bonds you to the earth, gets rid of all the capitalist false impulses."

"Uh-huh," I murmur, stripping off my shorts and T-shirt. My navy bikini is fading from all the use, a thread unraveling in one of the straps. "Why don't you relax and, umm, meditate here? I'm going for a swim."

"Me too," Fiona says, and my mouth drops open with shock. I've never seen her do more than dip a reluctant toe in the water all summer. She pulls off her cargo pants and tank top—showing a surprisingly revealing black bikini underneath—and takes off toward the water. I guess Olivia is a surprising motivator.

I pause by our patch of towels and totes, rummaging in my bag. "Have you seen my sunscreen?"

"I tossed it out." Instead of relaxing, Olivia is pulling her feet into a complicated cross-legged position.

"What? Why?"

She shrugs, tying her mat of dreadlocks back with a stretch of colored ribbon. "Those things will kill you. Have you seen the toxins they put in? Cash says—"

"It's OK." I cut her off before I'm treated to another joyful lesson from the Book of Cash. "Just . . . don't go through my stuff, OK?"

She looks at me, hurt. "I was only trying to help. Do you want to pump chemicals into your body?"

"No, but I kind of don't want to get skin cancer, either." I sigh. "Just forget it."

A couple of hours later, things seem to have reached a calm. The guys show up to mess around with inner tubes, Fiona loans me her sunscreen, and Olivia takes a much-appreciated break from her lecture series to bury herself in a dog-eared copy of *No Logo*. With a cool breeze cutting through the midday heat, and my friends lounged around me, I can almost relax.

Almost.

"Hey, Jenna, can you pass those chips?" Reeve rolls over and reaches his hand out, impatient. He's shirtless on our patchwork array of towels and blankets, hair dripping wet from his swim, and even though I haven't been obsessing over him the way I used to, I'm immediately distracted.

"Hmmm?"

"Hello? The chips?" He snaps his fingers at me. I blink at his tone. A few days ago, we were lazing, intertwined by that water-lily lake while he counted every freckle on my back. Now he can't even be polite in public?

"What's the magic word?" I challenge him.

"Uh, now?"

I throw them at him, hard. Discreet is one thing; rude is quite another.

"Jeez, what's gotten into you?"

Olivia looks up from her book. "Aww, trouble in paradise?" she asks with an innocent look.

I glance around, panicked, but nobody else seems to

have noticed her comment. Except Reeve. When I check, his face is tense.

"Don't stress—it's just PMS!" Grady says, lying out with his baseball cap covering his eyes. "It's always freaking PMS with these chicks—argh!" He cries out as Fiona upends her soda over his bare chest. He scrambles to his feet, soaked with the sticky liquid. "What the hell?"

"Whoops," she answers, deadpan. "Must be that darn time of the month."

While they bicker, I try to catch Olivia's eye. How could she almost give me away like that? But she stares, fixed, at her book, as if she doesn't realize what a close call that just was. And maybe she doesn't.

Finally, I lie back down. But instead of dozing idly in the sun, I feel anxiety begin to take hold. Things were fine when home was home and Stillwater was Stillwater, but now everything's tumbling together, and I can't keep it apart. The old Olivia would never spill my secrets—I could trust her with anything. But this new girl, the one who's rude to her hostess, confiscates my things, and won't stop ranting about the impending end of the world? I don't know about her. I feel like I don't *know* her at all.

After a while, Ethan nudges my leg with his bare foot. "I'm heading up to the river tomorrow. Want to come fishing?"

"With my record?"

"Aw, c'mon. We can find a mate to send along to poor Derek in fish heaven."

I relax, laughing as I remember my unwanted success

with the fishing rod. "Knowing my luck, I'll find him a whole gang of friends."

"Exactly." Ethan grins at me warmly. "You'll be my accidental good-luck charm."

"Derek?" Olivia interrupts, turning to me with a questioning look. She's moved into the shade from one of the looming pines, separating herself out from the group.

"He's the fish Jenna caught," Ethan answers for me. "A big one, too!"

"Was not," I protest.

"Sure he was." Ethan gives me a grin. "Took me ages to kill him, smashing away with that rock."

"Eww!" I thump him playfully, and he shoves me back.

"You weren't complaining when you started eating the poor thing."

Olivia gasps, eyes wide. "You started eating meat?"

I brace myself for a protest about vegetarianism, but instead, it's Reeve who speaks up, drawling in a sarcastic voice. "I wouldn't take her near water, dude. She'll just fall in again."

I pretend not to notice the dig, but it still stings. "Are you ever going to let me forget that?"

"No," comes the immediate response from all three boys. Again, a questioning look from Olivia.

"There was a kayak trip that went wrong," I tell her quickly, even though I'm getting tired of explaining. Especially when I've already told her. "I called you about it, I'm sure."

"Maybe you did." She flicks a page. I stare at her for a moment, puzzled. It feels like she's giving me an attitude, but I can't think why.

"Anyway, I think I'll skip this one." I turn back to Ethan. "There's going to be a ton of cleaning up to do from this party tonight."

"I'll just have to struggle on without you." He grins.

"Why don't you take one of your guy friends, Ethan?" Olivia pipes up. "Isn't it kind of a manly thing, fishing? Guys bonding, together, out in the wild with their tackle, all *Brokeback*—"

"Livvy." I sit up so fast, I get a head rush. "Weren't you going to tell me more about that guru guy?"

"He's not a guru; he's a low-impact lifestyle visionary." She frowns at me, launching into a long description of how this guy recycles everything in his life—including bodily waste. It's gross, but at least she stops with her loaded comments about Ethan. For now.

CHAPTER THIRTY-THREE

I manage to keep Olivia away from the group for the rest of the day, but by the time the party gets under way, I don't know what to do. Instead of having a good time and celebrating our success, I'm acting like a glorified babysitter: running around making sure she's not ranting at the guests about free trade, or spilling every secret I told her, or doing anything else to mess up the calm equilibrium we've managed to reach in Stillwater. It's exhausting, and the worst part is, I don't even understand why she's so antagonistic. Livvy used to be happy, and energetic, and upbeat; now she acts as if she has one big grudge against the whole world, and we're all part of the corporate-industrial conspiracy to destroy the earth.

Isn't early-morning meditation supposed to, I don't know, make you calm and content?

"I love this decor—it's so rustic and quaint."

"Mmm, you've got to taste this potato salad!"

"And if the weather holds, we've booked for a kayak trip tomorrow, just like on the website!"

Despite all my tension, I can't help but feel a warm glow of pride as I drift through the backyard, overhearing snatches of conversation from the party. Everything else in my life may be teetering on the edge of disaster, but the B and B is turning out just great. The first guests arrived on schedule—a mousy-looking couple of accountants and that family from Boston—and oohed and aahed with appropriate enthusiasm as Susie showed them around the house. Now it's getting dark, and what must be half of Stillwater has gathered in the backyard to celebrate. We spent the afternoon setting up, and now the place is transformed, with tiny twinkle lights strung up between the trees, trestle tables covered with red-and-white-checkered cloths, and a mouthwatering array of BBQ goodies. I look around happily. Grady is piling his plate with food; Ethan is talking with some older guys; Reeve is—

With Kate.

They're just chatting, casual, but I feel a twist of insecurity all the same. She's wearing jeans and an embroidered shirt, looking breezy and effortless again. Reeve glances away from her for a moment, and I manage to catch his eye, but he just gives me a vague smile and turns back to her.

"Hi, everyone . . ." Susie taps her fork on the edge of the salad bowl and waits for everyone to quiet down. I grab a paper cup of soda and a plate of veggie hot dogs, settling on one of the folding chairs we've put up around the yard, my back to Reeve.

"Don't worry—I won't be long. You know what I'm like with speeches." Susie laughs, all earlier nerves gone. "I just wanted to welcome you all to Bramble Lane and thank everyone for all their hard work." Her curls shine golden in the fading light, and she slips an arm around Adam's waist affectionately. "You've all pitched in to make this happen, and we're both so grateful for the effort. So, I guess, just have fun!" There's applause, and everyone surges forward to congratulate them.

"Hey." I hear a low voice behind me and turn to find Reeve. He grins at me, mischievous. "Come on."

"What?" I protest, but he's already taken my hand and is leading me into the house while everybody's attention is focused outside.

"Cute dress." Reeve pulls me into the tiny laundry room and closes the door. He moves closer, slipping his hands around my waist. Then he kisses me.

For a moment, I let him. He smells like some kind of aftershave or deodorant, fresh and woodsy, and as he pushes me back against the dryer, my pulse picks up again with a jolt. His lips are soft but insistent, his body solid and familiar around me. I relax into his arms and kiss him back, breathless, until—

"Wait." I remember myself, pushing him away.

He grins, pushing hair out of my eyes. "Don't worry, nobody saw." He leans in to kiss me again, but I plant both hands on his chest and push him back, harder.

"Reeve!"

He looks at me, confused. "What?"

I can't believe him.

"What are you doing?"

"What do you think?" Slowly giving that smile that always melts me, he plants tiny kisses on my cheek, working his way toward my mouth. I duck under his arms and slip sideways, out of reach.

"You're serious?" I look at him, amazed. Snatches of noise and laughter from the party outside drift in through the side window, but at last, I'm not worried about getting caught. "You bitch at me in front of our friends, ignore me all evening, and then you expect to come back, for *this*?"

"I was just teasing!"

"No, you were being a jerk." I fold my arms and glare at him. After days of not telling Olivia how I feel, I've had enough of keeping quiet and smoothing things over.

Finally realizing something's not right, Reeve begins to backtrack. "Hey, I'm sorry—I was just messing around at the lake." He takes my hand. "I didn't think you'd take it like that."

"I took it how you said it," I tell him, standing firm. He's twisting his fingers through mine, but I refuse to let that melting feeling in my stomach win this time. "You can't just act like that. It's not right."

He drops my hand. "Hey, you said you were cool with keeping this a secret."

"And I was." I swallow, realizing for the first time

what I have to do. I've insisted I'm fine with this casual thing so much that he actually believes me. But I'm not

"It's been fun, but I don't want to do this anymore," I tell him firmly. I've only got a few days left, but they're not worth feeling this insecure.

There's a long pause. Reeve looks at me. "What do you mean?"

I take a breath. "I mean, I don't want to keep going like this. Sneaking around. I don't like it when you're so, I don't know, casual, around everyone else." I hate laying my feelings out like this, but I force myself to keep going. Meeting his eyes, I add in a quiet voice, "It hurts me."

"But you said—"

"I know I did," I admit. "And it's been great. Really great." I think of our nights on the back porch, of the first thrill of sneaking away. But all Reeve's kisses can't take away the sting I feel when he barely looks my way with the others. "I didn't think it through, OK? I didn't know it would bother me, but it does."

There. It's said.

I wait, hoping for some kind of agreement. For Reeve to tell me that he doesn't like it either, and all the hassle and sneaking is stupid when we could just *be*. Normal.

Instead, his lips press together in a thin line. "What is this, some kind of ultimatum? I've told you: I don't want everyone knowing my business, not again. I mean, you're leaving next week!"

"Right," I say, disappointed, but still calm. "And I get that you have all this stuff from what happened with

Kate." At this, he flinches slightly. "But I don't want to spend my last days in town feeling crappy and ignored." I exhale, feeling a lightness in me. Relief. "So you do whatever you want."

I leave him there, by the pile of Fiona's dirty laundry. I feel a pang as I walk away, but somehow, I think it's more for what we won't be—the fact that I'm leaving and that this will only ever be a brief summer thing.

Walking through the house, I see some kind of commotion in the front yard, lit up by the bright porch lights. There's a truck in the driveway, printed with some kind of official insignia, and Adam is frowning while Olivia gestures wildly to a middle-aged woman in a uniform.

Olivia? I quickly hurry toward them.

"I'm sure we went through the plans when we talked to the permit office," Adam is saying when I arrive. He looks confused. "I just have to find the papers. . . ."

"What's going on?" I ask, directing my question at Olivia. She turns away, stuffing her hands into the pockets of her cargo pants. "Is everything OK? Should I get Susie?"

"No, it's just a misunderstanding," Adam says quickly. "No need to worry her."

The woman shifts, impatient. "I was told this was an environmental emergency."

"Well, what can I say? You know how dramatic kids get." Adam gives Olivia a look, and begins to guide the woman toward the house. "How about you go on back and join the party, while I find those permits?" She seems reluctant, but Adam urges her. "We've got some killer barbecue left, and I know Mrs. Johnson brought some of those famous brownies of hers . . ."

"Oh, well, maybe just a minute." The woman smiles for the first time and follows him toward those famous brownies.

I turn to Olivia.

"What?" she mumbles, sullen. "They were going to cut that tree down. What was I supposed to do?"

"I don't know. How about nothing?" I stare at her in amazement. She actually called the cops on them — or, according to the truck, the Graystone Valley Environmental Protection Agency. I blink, lost for words for a moment.

"I can't believe you!" I exclaim finally. "They fixed things with your parents, and let you stay, and have been so freaking nice to you! This is really how you repay them? By trying to screw up their big opening day, after so much work?"

But Olivia doesn't seem to care. She shrugs, as if nothing I've said even matters. "They shouldn't be cutting it down. And if you were a good Green Teen, you would have called it in weeks ago."

I sag back against the truck and look at her, numb. It's dark out now, shadows looming, and the distance between us I've been trying so hard to ignore can't be denied. It's different now. No matter how much I want to convince myself that she'll come around, or go back to the way she used to be, Olivia isn't the person I've known all these years.

And maybe I'm not, either.

"These people are like family to me." I try to make her see, one last time. "I don't understand how you can do something like this."

"You can't be on their side!" she protests. "You know that what they're doing is wrong."

"Wrong?" I blink. "Livvy, it's not like they're paving over a couple of acres or—or killing baby seals. It's one tree! And don't you think they've thought it through—checked how much damage it'll do, or if there's anything nesting there? Come on, Livvy, not everyone in the world is part of your freaking capitalist conspiracy!"

"I should have known you'd be like this." Olivia's face becomes tight. "Cash said you weren't committed to—"

"Will you just shut up about Cash?" I finally lose all patience. "Do you have a single original thought left, or has he brainwashed you completely?"

"Brainwashed!" Olivia yells back. "You think this is all because of him? That I don't believe in fighting for what's right?"

"But it's not right, is it?" I shake my head at her, amazed at how completely she's missing the point. I've kept quiet for days—out of confusion, and fear that I've lost her completely. But it's done. Her summer has taken her to the extreme of our environmentalism, just as I've realized the other side to my beliefs: compromise and priorities.

"You think waving a placard around and getting arrested will achieve anything at all, besides screwing up your life? God, Olivia, it would be one thing if any of that stuff works, but it doesn't. It's not the way to get things done!"

"And what is the right way?" She glares at me, her features screwed up in a mean expression that I never thought I'd see. "You've abandoned everything we believe in to fit in here. You should see how pathetic you look, falling over yourself for Reeve. Or maybe you don't care!" She gives a snort. "As long as these hicks like you. God, Jenna and her perfect Stillwater gang, what a fucking joke."

"Don't start on them," I warn her, nails digging deep in my palms.

"Why not?" she cries. "They're the reason you're being such a bitch, isn't it? You think Cash has brainwashed me, but what about you, huh? What about killing innocent creatures with your precious gay best friend, Ethan?"

There's a sudden noise behind her, and we both spin around. Standing on the front porch, staring at us in horror, is Ethan.

And Fiona. And Grady.

CHAPTER THIRTY-FOUR

"What the hell?" Grady reels back. He blinks, turning slowly from us to his brother. "What's she talking about?"

Ethan is frozen, eyes wide.

"Nothing!" I say quickly, trying to cover. "She's just kidding around."

"I'm not," Olivia announces. She stalks up the front steps and sneers at Ethan. "Whoopsie, looks like your secret is out. Ha, *out*. Funny." With a mean little smile, she pushes past them and disappears inside, leaving us alone under the glow of the porch lights.

There's a long silence, filled by the noise and laughter from the backyard. It's late, and they're all getting drunk on punch and ice-box beers. There's nobody to hear us here.

"Dude." Grady tugs Ethan's sleeve. "She's talking trash, right? Right?"

Ethan still hasn't moved.

"Come on, Grady." Fiona tries to lead him away. "We were going to get more pie."

He shakes her off. "I don't want pie. I want you to tell me she's full of crap." He stares at Ethan, imploring.

Ethan doesn't say a word.

"No, man . . ." Grady backs away from him, shaking his head. "No way!"

"Grady—" Ethan tries to reach after him, but Grady angrily shoves him back. "Don't you touch me! Don't you dare touch me!"

Ethan stumbles back, useless. His face is stricken. Grady makes as if to lunge at him, but Fiona physically drags him back as I rush forward, planting myself between the boys. "Grady, stop!"

"Ethan? Ethan, it's going to be OK," I tell him, desperate. He won't look at me.

"You freak!" Grady yells, lunging again. He sends a wicker chair clattering to the ground and knocks me into Ethan. We both fall, hard, against the porch swing before Fiona clutches a handful of Grady's shirt and yanks, choking him.

"Calm down!" she screams at him. He suddenly sags, limp in her arms, and with all her strength, she bundles him into the house. The screen door slams.

I turn to Ethan, gripping his arms. "Are you OK?" I'm shaking, but it's not from the fight or Grady's harsh words. No, right now I'm sick to my stomach with the awful, twisted knowledge that this is all my fault.

All. My. Fault.

Finally, Ethan looks at me. His eyes are watery, but he swipes his tears away with the back of his plaid sleeve. "Don't touch me," he says, quiet and fierce.

"But I—"

"Don't!" he yells, snatching away from me. "It's over. Don't you get that? Everything, it's all over!" His face crumples, distraught. Backing away, he knocks into the fallen chair, but doesn't stop, just takes off, sprinting into the dark.

Into the forest.

"Where's Ethan?" Fiona hurries out about fifteen minutes later. I'm slumped on the front steps, my head in my hands. "Grady's locked himself in my room upstairs; he won't talk to me."

"Oh, God." I sniffle, trying to smear away my tears. "Ethan took off, out there somewhere." I nod at the dark shadows, looming out of range of the pools of light from the house. "I didn't know if I should go after him. Fi, the way he looked at me . . ." I choke back another sob. I can't believe this is happening—that I made this happen. He trusted me, and I've screwed up everything.

"What do we do?" She blinks at me, eyes wide with worry. "I could get Susie. And I think the guys' mom is here . . ."

"No!" I stop her, remembering what Ethan told me. "Not their parents. Not yet. We've got to do this ourselves."

"But do what?"

Think, Jenna!

Trying desperately to pull myself back together, I take a breath. "OK. Nobody's noticed anything yet, thank God. So, you go find Reeve. Tell him what happened, get him to talk to Grady."

"But . . . should we be spreading this around?" Fiona pauses.

"This isn't spreading anything," I say, already getting to my feet. "Grady won't listen to us. He needs someone . . . someone to talk some sense into him. I'll go after Ethan."

"Out there?" Fiona looks past me at the forest. She shivers. "Shouldn't you at least get a flashlight or something?"

"There's no time for that," I argue. "And what if we get grabbed by an adult inside? No, I'll be fine."

She wavers for a moment and then launches herself at me in a hug. I stumble, surprised.

"I'm scared," Fiona admits, clutching me. "You should have seen Grady . . . I've never seen him like this."

"Me either, and Ethan . . ." I swallow. "Come on, we'll make this OK. We have to."

She nods, collecting herself. "Good luck out there."

"You too." I manage a weak grin. And then she's gone again, and I start walking slowly away from the house, toward the dark forest.

It's cooler now, and my thin summer dress and sandals are no match for the scrape of tree branches and tangle of tree roots underfoot. Bracing myself, I find the entrance to the path by the road and plunge into the darkness. The trees loom close around me, and even though I've walked this path dozens of times this summer, I can't help but remember the last time I was here in the dark, alone. That first night in Stillwater, I was paralyzed by fear, but this time, I have no choice but to keep moving, stumbling over the dark path as I clutch my arms tight around me and try not to jump at every noise. The trees rustle around me, and every few seconds there's a new sound—a bird calling, a mysterious clatter or high-pitched animal call. I gulp, forcing myself onward. I need to find Ethan.

CHAPTER THIRTY-FIVE

After what feels like forever, I reach the lake. It's lighter here, the moon reflecting off the black water, but still, the valley rises up in huge dark swathes on every side.

"Ethan?" I call, nervous. Part of me still wonders if something's lurking in the trees, but I clear my throat and call again, louder. "It's me. Jenna."

There's no reply, but as I edge farther into the open, I see a hunched figure, far down the shore. I hurry toward him.

"Ethan?" I call again, panicked. He's sitting in the lake, legs stretched in front of him. Water gently laps around him, soaking his jeans and the bottom of his shirt, but he doesn't seem to notice. "What are you doing?" I kick off my sandals and wade out. It's ice-cold, pebbles sharp against my skin. "Ethan, you're getting soaked."

He stays there, staring out at the dark.

"Ethan, come on back to shore at least." I shiver, placing one hand gently on his shoulder. He turns his head a little, like he's only just noticed me. "Come on," I say, trying to keep my voice calm and comforting. "Let's get out of the water."

He tilts his head forward a moment and then struggles to his feet. He stays there, looking out at the lake, and for a terrible moment, I think he's going to walk right out into deep water. Then, to my relief, he turns and follows me back, splashing the few paces to shore.

We sink down on the grass, and I wait, anxious. "I'm sorry, Ethan. God, I'm so sorry!" The words come tumbling out in a frantic rush. "I told her, but I never thought she'd show up here, or be . . . such a bitch!" I swallow, a sharp pain inside as I think about what I've done to him. "But that's no excuse, I know. I made you a promise."

Ethan is motionless as the minutes slip by. I begin to worry that he's gone into some kind of shock: the real kind, from the trauma of his fight with Grady, and the fact that his whole life is splitting apart. But then, finally, he lets out a long sigh.

"It's OK," he says quietly.

"It's not!" I cry. "Ethan, how can you say that?"

"What else am I going to do?" He turns to me, and for a moment I think he's completely defeated, but then I see something else in his expression. The moonlight is shadowed on his face, but I think there's something . . . almost calm. "It's done. It's out now. I'm out," he adds with a bitter laugh. "It was always going to happen eventually."

"But not like this!" My voice sticks. He pats my shoulder—a faint, small gesture.

"It's done," he says again, resigned.

There's more silence.

"So, what . . . what happens now?" I still feel wretched. "Is there anything I can do? Anything at all?"

He shakes his head slowly. "I guess I just have to hope Grady comes around. Eventually. And doesn't tell my parents." He pauses. "God, my parents."

I reach over and take his hand, squeezing it fiercely. "You're going to be OK. And I hate it, that it's like this for you, but . . . you'll get through it." I hope to God that it's true. If only he were in a larger town, or even back in New Jersey. It would be hard there, sure, but there wouldn't be this same spectacle. He wouldn't be going through this alone.

A cloud drifts over the moon, and for a second, we're in the dark again: a thick blackness all around that I can almost touch. The lake swells against the shore with a low swoosh of sound, rhythmic and calming. It would be beautiful if the ugly fight from before wasn't lingering over us both.

"You want to know the weird thing?" Ethan asks, turning to me. His dark hair falls, messy over his eyes. "Before, when Olivia said what she did, I was standing there, and all I could feel was . . . relief. Like, it was finally out of my hands." He swallows, bringing his legs up against his chest. "All this time, I've been trying so hard to keep it secret. To stop everything from changing."

I sigh. "But you can't."

"Nope."

There's a pause. "Maybe this is good," Ethan says, as if he's trying to convince himself. "Maybe now I can figure out what comes next. How to be *this* guy."

"You're still you," I insist. I wish I could be around to support him through this. "What was it you said to me? That you didn't want this one part defining who you are. You're not just gay."

"I know." He gives me a weak smile. "But people, they don't see it like that."

"They should," I say fiercely, but something suddenly catches in my chest. Here I am, swearing that Ethan is more than his sexuality, when I've been doing the same thing. Or rather, the opposite. My environmentalism, the Green Teens—I threw myself into them to fill this space in me. I wanted to quiet the loneliness, and have some kind of power when life seemed totally out of my control, but without noticing, they became almost everything to me.

That's why Olivia changing has been such a shock, I realize, and why I've been so reluctant to see anyone else's point of view. Because if all I am is a Green Teen, what happens when I start questioning our ideals? What will life be like back in New Jersey without Olivia, or my old group, and all that purpose and direction I felt?

Ethan is quiet beside me, lost in his own troubles as I gaze out at the dark lake, thinking back to the meetings, the protests, all those hours I would spend writing letters and handing out pamphlets . . . It made me feel safer, as if I could make some small difference in this vast, scary planet. But for all that effort and energy, I've discovered that things aren't as simple as I thought. The slogans I chanted and the banners I waved don't even come close to addressing the real problems facing the world. The real answers are shades of gray, layered with compromise and priorities I can't even begin to grasp. I want to understand, but I know now that I'm not going to find any of those hard truths just cheerleading recycling drives or waving signs around at construction sites as if that's all it will take to make things better. It's a start, but there's so much more.

I let out a long breath. Ethan's right; my worries may not be as life-changing as his, but it's a relief to have the truth suddenly laid out in front of you. I've been clinging to my Green Teen identity to give me someplace to fit. But I'm more than that. And so is he.

"It'll be OK," I tell him, and for the first time, I believe it for myself. "You'll figure it out."

He gives a dry laugh. "I guess there's no avoiding it. Avoiding anything."

We watch the water awhile, fingers laced together on the dew-damp ground. Then voices sound, back near the trees. We turn.

"Thank God!" Fiona hurtles toward us, lit up by the thin beam of a pocket flashlight. She's pulled on a light jacket, her hair falling out of its thin ponytail. "We've been looking for you forever!"

We?

Reeve emerges out of the shadows behind her. With

Grady. He's looking down, scuffing his sneakers on the ground, but he's here.

I rise to my feet, anxious.

"It's OK." Fiona shoots a look back at Grady. "He's calmed down. There won't be any . . . any scenes. Right?" She thwacks his stomach. He nods reluctantly.

"Should we . . . ?" I look back at Ethan. He hasn't moved from his spot, but his face is even.

"Let's get back," Fiona decides, shivering. "We can cover for a few people, but they'll notice all of us missing soon."

I nod. This must mean Grady didn't tell. And if he hasn't told . . .

"You'll be OK?" I ask Ethan quietly, bending down.

He gives me a smile. "I'll live."

"No more late-night swims, you hear me?" I try to joke, but my fear must show, because suddenly, he reaches up and hugs me. I grip him tightly, but a second later, he pulls back.

"I'm good." He nods, trying to sound brusque. "You'd better go. Don't want them sending out a search party."

I edge away, leaving him curled up there on the shore, Grady lingering a few awkward paces behind him.

"Grady's really calmed down?" I ask Fiona, glancing back.

"I beat some sense into him. It was just shock, I think. I mean, they're brothers. He didn't even know . . ." She trails off. "But he's good now. He'll make it right."

I exhale, a weight lifting from me.

"You OK?" Reeve falls into step beside me as we make our way back into the forest. I blink. I must have registered his presence before, but this is the first time I notice him, looking at me with clear concern.

I nod. "You need to watch out for him," I tell Reeve. "All of you. He's going to need you guys." Again, I feel a pang that I won't be around. IM and cell phones only count for so much.

"It's cool." Reeve manages a smile, but I can barely make it out in the dark. "We've got this."

The tension in my chest eases a little more.

"But what about you?" Reeve presses. "I heard it got pretty ugly with Olivia."

I shrug, resigned. "I think . . . I think we're done. I mean, I can't ever forgive her, not for this."

"I'm sorry." His voice is low, sincere. A moment later, I feel his hand reach for mine. I pull back, but he takes it, firmly.

I look at Fiona, just a bobbing flash of light ahead of us. "I said I didn't want to sneak around anymore," I whisper. It all seems trivial after the dramas of the night, but I want to stand my ground.

"Does it look like I'm sneaking?" Reeve answers me in a normal voice. "Hey, Fiona," he adds, calling ahead. "Just so you know, I'm holding Jenna's hand back here!"

My mouth drops open.

"Whatever!" she calls back, bored.

"See?" He smiles at me again.

"What changed your mind?" I ask, trying to stay

cool. But the feel of his body next to mine is warm and comforting, and after all this tension, it's a relief to relax against him.

"I was worried about you," he says, self-conscious. "When they said you took off into the forest. I was dumb, before." A pause. "I didn't want it to get messed up, like it did with Kate, so maybe . . . maybe I went too far, with the secret thing. I really thought you were OK with it. I'm sorry."

I meet his eyes, black in the shadows, and manage a smile. It doesn't mean much in the big picture, I know—just a few more days of kisses—but in another way, it's everything. I matter enough to him.

"OK," I say softly.

When we reach the road again, the B and B is lit up, full of warm light. Noise and music drift over to us, and through the windows, I can see people laughing. After the dark chill of the forest, it looks like a haven. A home.

Fiona waits for us to catch up. "So what's our story?"

Reeve looks around. "I figure we can just say we went out for an adventure. You know, a moonlit hike for Jenna, or something."

"And Ethan and Grady stayed behind," I agree, "to . . . I don't know, clean up."

Fiona shakes her head. "You guys are terrible liars."

"And that's a bad thing?" I protest. She smiles.

"Lucky you've got me around."

"Truly blessed." I link my arm through hers.

"So, official version," she begins, as we cross the dirt road. "We're having a sleepover at the Johnsons' tonight, to get out of Susie's hair. Ethan and Grady are back there, setting up, and we're just going to pick up our night things."

"That is a good story," Reeve agrees, on my other side. He's still holding my hand, even as we climb the porch steps and open the door to the packed, raucous party. "We should do it for real. Their parents will probably hang out here for ages. And we should be around, you know, for Ethan."

"What about Olivia?" I venture. "I can't just leave her with Adam and Susie—they don't deserve that."

"It's fine," Fiona says, shooting me a sympathetic look. "She was locked in the bedroom, the last I saw, ranting on the phone to some guy about how destructive and thoughtless we all are. She's good until morning. My plan is still perfect."

"OK, OK!" I agree, smiling for what seems like the first time all night. All around us, people are full of celebration, and even though the past few hours have been tragic, stressful, and scary, it feels as though all of that is finally behind us. "You are the undisputed queen of deception. We bow at your lying, sneaky feet."

"Better believe it." Fiona grins, smug. "Now, where is that ice cream . . . ?"

CHAPTER THIRTY-SIX

We sleep on the floor in the Johnsons' basement, overlapping like puppies in a tangle of blankets and sleeping bags. But as soon as I open my eyes, woken by Fiona's sleeping mumbles, I know what I need to do.

I slip on my sandals and creep up the stairs, careful not to wake anyone. Ethan is lying curled in the corner, worn out from his stress — and the three episodes of that sci-fi series I insisted we watch, with brownies and ice cream, after he and Grady slouched back from the lake. I don't know what happened, but it seems like things are OK between them again, a grudging kind of peace. It can only get better.

The route back to the B and B is pale in the early morning light, with birds singing in the trees and a glow from the sun still hanging low over the mountains. I breathe in the crisp air, trying to savor every step as if it's my last.

Because right now, I think it is. I don't know yet about the internship I'll get here next summer, working with the tourism board to promote eco-friendly travel in British Columbia; I haven't seen the small, cute apartment Mom and me will move to, or Dad's place in Sweden, where I'll spend Christmas, stringing sugar cookies to the tree and eating local smorgasbord. I don't know yet about the new friends I'll make in photography class, or how the Green Teens will fall into anarchy after Olivia handcuffs herself to Principal Turner and swallows the key, ranting about corporate control of the social studies syllabus.

No, all of that is still ahead of me, so I can't help but feel sad as I let myself into the silent house, using the key hidden under the ceramic turtle on the porch. There's debris in every room: cups stacked in haphazard towers, streamers, and partly deflated balloons. I retrieve my cell phone from my room, and, wrapped in that snug blanket of mine, I settle down on the back porch to make the call.

"Hi . . . Mom?" I can't remember the last time I talked to her—really talked. Because I'm scared of what she'll have to say, and of what will come after, when the talking's done. I don't know yet that everything will turn out OK, for all of us, but even so, I curl my legs up under me and brace myself for the future. I've faced down white-water rapids, a wild bear, and even Fiona this summer; I can do this.

"I'm ready for that talk."

ACKNOWLEDGMENTS

Many thanks to my marvelous agent, Rosemary, for all your help on the climb. To Liz, Mara, Kaylan, Tracy, Jennifer, and all at Candlewick and Walker for your commitment and support. Thanks to my family, and the Canadian contingent for the hospitality (especially Uncle Don, for getting me up—and down—that mountain!). Thanks to Dom P. for all your patience and help, Narmada T. for the positivity, and Elisabeth D, as always, for everything.